Gabriel's Retaliation

Dark Patriots Book 2

Ciara St James

Copyright

ISBN: 978-1-955751-50-6

Printed in the United States of America
Editing by Mary Kern @ Ms. K Edits
Book cover by Tracie Douglas @ Dark Waters Covers

Warning

This book is intended for adult readers. It contains foul language, adult situations, discusses events such as stalkers, assault, torture and murder that may trigger some readers. Sexual situations are graphic. There is no cheating, no cliffhangers and it has a HEA.

Dark Patriots Members/ Ladies

Mark O'Rourke (Undertaker) w/ Sloan
Sean Walterson w/ Cassidy
Gabe Pagett w/ Gemma
Griffin Voss w/ TBD
Benedict Madris w/ TBD
Heath Rugger w/ TBD
Justin Becker w/ TBD
Beau Powers w/ TBD

Reading Order

For Dublin Falls Archangel's Warriors MC (DFAW), Hunters Creek Archangel's Warriors MC (HCAW), Iron Punishers MC (IPMC), Dark Patriots (DP), & Pagan Souls of Cherokee MC (PSCMC)

Terror's Temptress DFAW 1
Savage's Princess DFAW 2
Steel & Hammer's Hellcat DFAW 3
Menace's Siren DFAW 4
Ranger's Enchantress DFAW 5
Ghost's Beauty DFAW 6
Viper's Vixen DFAW 7
Devil Dog's Precious DFAW 8
Blaze's Spitfire DFAW 9
Smoke's Tigress DFAW 10
Hawk's Huntress DFAW 11
Bull's Duchess HCAW 1
Storm's Flame DFAW 12
Rebel's Firecracker HCAW 2
Ajax's Nymph HCAW 3
Razor's Wildcat DFAW 13
Capone's Wild Thing DFAW 14
Falcon's She Devil DFAW 15
Demon's Hellion HCAW 4
Torch's Tornado DFAW 16
Voodoo's Sorceress DFAW 17
Reaper's Banshee IPMC 1
Bear's Beloved HCAW 5
Outlaw's Jewel HVAW 6
Undertaker's Resurrection DP 1

Agony's Medicine Woman PSCMC 1
Ink's Whirlwind IP 2
Payne's Goddess HCAW 7
Maverick's Kitten HCAW 8
Tiger & Thorn's Tempest DFAW 18
Dare's Doll PSC 2
Maniac's Imp IP 3
Tank's Treasure HCAW 9
Blade's Boo DFAW 19
Law's Valkyrie DFAW 20
Gabriel's Retaliation DP 2

For Ares Infidels MC

Sin's Enticement AIMC 1
Executioner's Enthrallment AIMC 2
Pitbull's Enslavement AIMC 3
Omen's Entrapment AIMC 4
Cuffs' Enchainment AIMC 5
Rampage's Enchantment AIMC 6
Wrecker's Ensnarement AIMC 7
Trident's Enjoyment AIMC 8
Fang's Enlightenment AIMC 9
Talon's Enamorment AIMC 10
Ares Infidels in NY AIMC 11
Phantom's Emblazonment AIMC 12

For O'Sheerans Mafia

Darragh's Dilemma
Cian's Complication

Please follow Ciara on Facebook, For information on new releases & to catch up with Ciara, go to www.ciara-st-james.com or www.facebook.com/ciara.stjames.1 or www.facebook.com/groups/tenilloguardians or https://www.facebook.com/groups/1112302942958940

Blurb:

Gabriel is a man who has served his country in and out of the military. He has made a life filled with meaningful work and men he can call brothers. The one thing he doesn't have is someone special. His past is too dangerous to let that happen, even if he wants one, which he doesn't. A request for help to clean up a criminal family ends with Gabriel going undercover. He's got to live the life of a Mafia capo.

Once he gets to where he's assigned, he lays eyes on a woman who he can't forget. He watches her from the shadows, even though she doesn't know it. He aches for her. Gabriel isn't the only one who wants her. There's another who thinks he has a prior claim to her, and he's not willing to let her go.

Gemma knows it's time to walk away from everything she knows. This is no life. If she's ever to have one, she's got to leave. She's planning her escape when a man who's been after her for years becomes tired of waiting. She runs and ends up in the arms of Gabriel. She's been fascinated with him since she laid eyes on him. Only he's part of the world she's running from. There's no way they can be together.

By rescuing her, Gabriel must reveal his mission in order to protect her. To protect her, he must claim her. He'll have to use all his considerable savvy resources and lethalness to save and keep her. Will he lose her in the end when she finds out who the real Gabriel is? Or will Gabriel's Retaliation not be an ending but the beginning of a beautiful forever?

Italian Dictionary

Asshole- Stronzo (a)
Babe- Piccola
Baby- Bambino
Beautiful- Bellissima
Bitch- Cagna
Boss- Capo
Boy- Ragazzo
Brother- Fratello
Christ- Cristo
Dad- ***Papà***
Daughter- Figlia
Father- Padre/ papa
Fiancée- Fidanzata
Friend- Amico/ Amica
God- Dio
Goddess- Dea
Good night- Buona Notte
Idiot- Idiota
Jesus Christ- Gesù Cristo
Lieutenant- Tenente
Lovely- Bella
Mafia Family- Famiglia Mafiosa
Mister- Signore
Mom- Mamma
Mother- Madre
My Angel- Mio Angelo

My Love- Amore Mio
Princess- Principessa
Prick, Fool- Bischero
Pussy, weak- Femminella
Soldier- Soldato
Stink- La Puzza
Sweetheart, babe- Piccola
Third in command in Mafia, the Boss's counselor- Consiglieri
Treasure, honey, darling- Tesoro
Uncle-Zio

German for asshole/ assholes- arschloch/ arschlöcher

Gabe: Chapter 1

In the months since Mark, aka Undertaker, had been home, our time should've been nothing but days filled with happiness and celebrations. After all, our brother-in-arms, who the world and even family thought had been dead for five long years, had been resurrected and was back with those who loved him.

Undertaker's sacrifice, in order to take down one of the biggest and baddest motorcycle gangs in the country, had been more than appreciated by many, including our government. Well, maybe not so appreciated by his sister, Cassidy when she found out I, Griffin, and her husband, Sean, had all been lying to her for four of those five years. We'd known Mark was alive and undercover after that first year. Although she'd forgiven us, she hadn't forgotten, and we all could feel the difference in our relationship with her. Every one of us hoped and prayed that her distance would go away one day soon.

I knew it was more than just pain that was causing this. Cassidy felt like she couldn't trust us to tell her everything, which wasn't how we wanted it to be with her. She was as much a part of the Dark Patriots as the four of us. She might not have served in the military with us, but she dedicated herself to the company and the causes we fought, just like Mark's wife, Sloan, did.

Having Mark go almost straight back undercover into another dangerous MC hadn't been the plan after he resurfaced. When the request came in asking for our help with a dirty one-percenter MC, we'd tried to talk him out of doing it. He'd already lost too many years to that kind of life. Mark couldn't be persuaded not to help, especially when our fellow friend and brother-in-arms, Reaper, had been targeted. It was that mission which brought Mark and Sloan, a Dark Patriot operative, together. In the end, not only did they eliminate the Soldiers of Corruption MC, who had infiltrated several good clubs, but they'd ended up in love and having a baby.

It was hard to believe all of that started a year-and-a-half ago. Since then, things had settled down into a somewhat calm routine. Or as calm a routine as it could get when you ran one of the premier private contractor companies in the country. We dealt mainly with government work, with some private companies utilizing us for a variety of security work. We dealt in corporate espionage, hacking, embezzlement, you name it. On the flip side, what we did for the government was usually off-the-books work. The kind where if you got caught, the government would claim not to know anything about it. It was a shitty thing to do, some might think, but my friends and I, and those who worked for us, knew it was something that was needed.

The average American had no clue what was done on a daily basis to keep our country and its citizens safe from terrorism and a host of other evil things. Sometimes we were going after crime lords in other countries or taking out drug or human traffickers. The list went on and on. The diversity of our targets made us hire equally diverse people. Our employees covered a whole gamut of fields of expertise. Many of them had prior military experience, although that wasn't a requirement to work for our company.

One of the main men we worked for, who was in the US government in one of those alphabet agencies as we called them, was a man who people in the government agencies knew as Anderson. Everyone seemed to know of him, but no one really knew him. He remained a mystery, but one who was as patriotic as they came. He did whatever was needed to ensure the safety of the innocent and to protect our great country. Which organization he actually worked for, no one knew. He could be found helping the DEA, ATF, FBI, or a host of others, yet they never claimed he was one of theirs.

It wasn't until two years ago that a select number of us found out he had a great-niece who was a doctor. A niece who ended up marrying a biker named Demon. He was part of the Archangel's Warriors MC in Hunters Creek, Tennessee. The Warriors were one of a few MCs that we were good friends with. It was a truly small world when you thought about the odds of that happening.

All these things, watching year after year as those friends settled down, and now seeing two of my best friends finding happiness, were filling me with a restlessness that was becoming close to being out of control. I wasn't sure why. I didn't ever think of myself as being a family man. The idea that I might settle down and have kids one day wasn't something I ever thought about.

With my history, it wouldn't be the smart thing to do. I was happy living my life for moments when I might take a woman home for the night or hook up with one for a few weeks, but that was as far as it ever went. I didn't have girlfriends or anything resembling a serious relationship. In between, I filled my life with exciting and interesting work.

Mark and Sean had been after me and Griffin, telling us we should look to settle down. Griffin, I think, was willing if he could find the right woman. I told them not to hold their breath for me to do it. Being saddled to me would likely be a death sentence to a woman, even if I was dumb enough to have feelings for one. Cassidy and Sloan didn't understand, but Sean, Mark, and Griffin did. They were the only ones who knew my history. They'd sworn never to reveal it. I trusted them to keep that vow. It was this restlessness and need for action that had me sitting at our conference table on the executive floor an hour early for work.

I was eager to get this meeting started. We'd been contacted by Terror, the president of the Archangel's Warriors in Dublin Falls. He said they needed our brand of help. Things were always exciting and dangerous when they asked us to help them.

Drumming my fingers on the table, I watched the clock, counting the minutes until the others joined us and Terror called in as we'd arranged. I ran through various scenarios in my head about what it might be they needed us to do. We'd worked together before on stopping drug cartels, human traffickers, and others. Was it another one of those? It seemed no matter how many of the bad guys we eliminated, there was always more to take their place. It could be a thankless job and depressing if you allowed it to be.

I thought of it this way. Yeah, new people might step up to take over or to begin anew, but what was to say, if we hadn't taken out the ones we did, that things couldn't be even worse in the world? There'd be even more murderers, rapists, criminals, and traffickers running loose. Personally, I relished taking those types of scum out. Sure, going after corporate spies and such was fine, but this got my blood pumping and filled me with excitement.

Finally, about ten minutes before the scheduled call time, the door opened and in came Griffin, Mark, Sean, Sloan, and Cassidy. Although they weren't owners in the company, the two wives were treated as equal partners. A lesson learned from hiding Mark's undercover work from Cassidy. It wasn't as if the two women couldn't be trusted to keep shit confidential. My brothers-in-arms had chosen well. I hoped when the time came, so would Griffin. They all took their seats and gave me surprised looks.

"How long have you been sitting in here doing nothing?" Mark asked with a smirk on his lips.

"Oh, you know me. I love to live the life of leisure, pretending to work but really doing nothing but sitting on my ass. I'd play Candy Crush all day if I could," I told him. He burst out laughing along with the others. They knew me too well to believe that.

"Yeah, right. I'm surprised you even know what that is. Seriously, I had no idea you were in here. Is everything alright?" Sean asked.

"Everything is fine. I'm just anxious to hear what Terror and the club need from us. You know it should be something good."

"Only your crazy ass would think of it as good. I swear, you get stranger the older you get," Cassidy said with a roll of her eyes.

"It's part of my charm. How's Noah and Caleb? Still growing like weeds? I need to come see them. They probably miss their favorite uncle."

"Like hell you're their favorite. My son has better taste than that," Mark grunted.

"Exactly, he has great taste, hence why I'm his favorite and Noah is smart as a whip. He's the smartest eighteen-month-old in the world, so I'm his favorite too," I said of Sean and Cassidy's son.

Both women groaned as this got my friends going on why they were the better choice for the boys than me as their favorite uncle. It was obvious to anyone that any time their names came up or they were in the room, that Sean and Mark couldn't be prouder of their sons. Hell, I might not want any of my own, but I loved those two little guys, and I knew I'd feel the same about any other nephews or nieces this bunch graced me with.

Our instigation of each other was cut short by the buzzing of the conference room phone. Sean answered it. He didn't say anything other than to thank Margie, one of our two assistants, for connecting the call. Margie had been with us since day one when we opened the business years ago with help from Mark's dad. Sean hung up and tapped on the computer keyboard in front of him. The large screen on the far wall filled with the image of Terror and his VP, Savage. They had grim expressions on their faces. After getting the greetings over with, Terror didn't waste time getting to the reason for the call.

"I know you're probably busy as hell, but I'm hoping you might be able to spare us someone to help. The more the better. We have what looks like a large-scale cleanup job that needs to be done as soon as possible. It's kind of outside of our range of expertise. I thought it would be right up your alley."

"What kind of cleanup? You guys have dealt with a shitload of things. Not that we aren't happy to help," Griffin stated. I found my earlier curiosity coming back even harder.

"Let me fill you in on what's happened here. In a nutshell, you know Jake, Nyssa's old partner?" We all nodded. Of course we knew Jake.

"Well, he joined our club as a prospect several months ago. He met and claimed an old lady recently. You might remember her. Her name is Tonya. She's a friend of Soleil's. She's the one who the club found out her husband was cheating on her a couple of years ago, and they got a divorce. Dan is a superbike racer like Soleil."

I did vaguely recall them talking about the couple. I couldn't remember if I'd met her. Mark and Sloan wouldn't know her. I thought at the time and still did that cheating on your wife was a bastard's move, but doubly so when your wife was pregnant with your kid. We'd all thought she'd be better off without the dickhead.

"Yeah, we remember her. Sounds like if she's now with Jake, she's gotten over her ex-husband," Sean said.

"She has, although we've had a bit of trouble with him at first. The problem we've run into is bigger than Dan. A couple of weeks ago, someone shot Tonya while she was driving back to the compound with the kids."

Cassidy gave an exclamation of alarm. Terror was quick to reassure us that Tonya was alright. "She's on the mend. The wound was to her shoulder and missed everything vital. The only unfortunate part is she lost the baby she was carrying, which she and Law, which is Jake's road name by the way, had no idea she was pregnant with. We'd been trying to figure out who was responsible. Her ex is locked in a drug treatment center and hasn't had any outside contact, so we know it wasn't him. Well, we finally found out who it was. Another attack on her happened while Law and a couple of other guys were with her and Soleil two days ago. Three men were killed, and another man was brought to us to talk to."

"Who the fuck would do something like that? She didn't have enemies, did she?" Mark muttered darkly.

"She didn't, but Law does. If you recall, he lost his

first fiancée when her own father and two brothers had her killed after she discovered the family business was really drug dealing and she planned to turn them in. She was Nyssa's best friend and cousin. Matteo Greco and his sons, Carlo and Anthony, have been behind bars for eight years. They caused a bit of trouble when Nyssa and Hawk got together four years ago, but Bull pulled some inside strings to have them babysat in prison. As long as they kept their noses clean, they could continue to breathe."

"So what changed?" I asked. I was impatient to hear what they needed us to do. The background information was good to bring Sloan and Mark up to speed, but I knew all of this already. Sean shot me a look that I knew was supposed to tell me to be patient.

Terror grunted. "I can see Gabe wants me to get to the point. The point is, the babysitter had died, and we didn't know it. Matteo found out Law was engaged to Tonya and he wanted to punish him for putting him away with Nyssa's help after Frankie was murdered. He set it up to kill her and the kids. After the first attempt failed, he added Nyssa and her daughter to the list, plus Law and Hawk."

"You need us to kill those three in their cells," I stated. I wasn't worried about us talking plainly like this. Both of our IT people had the best encrypted phones and computers you could get. No one would be able to hack us and find out what we said.

"No, we're taking care of those three hopefully in the next week or so. What we need help with is cleaning out the rat's nest they apparently still have operating.

Even being in prison hasn't stopped the Grecos from continuing to run some of their old drug trafficking business and illegal betting. We can't risk any of their people taking over and coming after the club. Plus, they need to be shut down. You know we don't condone that shit. We got a bunch of names and locations from the informant. We need those to be verified and to see if more need to be added. Once it's done, then they can be taken care of however you feel is best. Some I expect should go to prison, while others will need a more permanent solution. We don't have the bandwidth to do this. You guys do."

"True, we do have more people and probably experience with this. From the sounds of it, this isn't going to be a quick in-and-out deal. It could take weeks or more to get the information we need, then we'll need to plan our strategies to take out those involved. We have to make it clean and to tie up all the possible loose ends. Where are the Greco family's businesses located?" Griffin asked. He was busy jotting down notes.

"They lived and located their businesses in New Jersey. They weren't a big mob family, although they're considered to have those ties. They were little fish in a big pond. They have nothing on the families who run New York and most of the Eastern Seaboard for the Italians, Russians, and the Irish. However, they did enough damage in their area and still have an impact. The town is called Toms River. It has one of the biggest percentages of its population having Italian roots in the state. They have an above-average income overall and to the public, the main job industries are healthcare, retail and educational jobs, due to colleges nearby. There's disposable cash in a lot of households and its location puts it relatively close to the beaches," Savage finally added.

"Let me guess, Smoke and Everly have been doing some digging already," I quipped. Savage grinned.

"You know those two. They can't resist even if we're not doing the job ourselves. If you can help us out with this, we'll have them send over what we have. If you can't, we'll figure something else out. We know you have your hands full with a lot of Uncle Sam's dirty work," Terror said.

"Oh, we do, but still, I think we can find at least one person who can do work on the back end to dig into them and find stuff out, and at least another person or two to be feet on the ground to get in there and get them ready to take down. This isn't going to be something we can do remotely. We'll need to get someone who can hopefully infiltrate them or at least won't raise too many suspicions by showing up in town and staying for a while," Sean added. I could see the wheels were already churning in his head. He was trying to go through our roster of people and figure out who might be the best ones for the job. I saved him the trouble.

"I can do it. Send me in and I'll be the boots on the ground. I can come up with a good cover story for why I'm there. I'll investigate the people and businesses you got off your informant and see if I can root out any others. Once it's done, we'll set our plans in motion and take them down."

"Why you? We have people who can do this kind

of work," Cassidy said. I saw fear in her eyes. I reached over to take her hand.

"Cass, sweetheart, it's not going to be anything like what Mark did. This isn't going to be something that takes years to bring down. From the sounds of it, the Greco family lost some of their empire when the boss and his sons went to prison. Believe me, if they're running things from this Toms River, people will know it. It's not going to be as big of a secret as you might think. People like to brag. They like to be seen as being important. Many of these mob families have people working for them who've done it for generations. Those walking around, flashing lots of money, driving flashy cars or owning more than they should, won't be too hard to spot. In some ways, the old days of the mob for these kinds of people haven't gone away," I tried to assure her.

"How do you know so much about those kinds of people and families?" Sloan asked curiously.

I shrugged and sat back in my chair. "I just do. The history of the Mafia in the US and abroad has always been a hobby of mine. Plus, look at me. I can pass for being Italian because I'm half-Italian. I can speak the language if necessary. Maybe I can go in proposing I'm with another family who wants to form an alliance with the Greco family. We can say it's to grow the percentage of the business for both of us."

Ideas flitted through my head a mile a minute. I could do this. I knew the way these people would think and act. Coming up with a way to get myself in there wouldn't be super hard. It would be dangerous, but I was used to that. This was exactly the thing I needed to take care of, this growing restlessness inside of me. I saw Mark, Sean, and Griffin giving me searching looks. They knew why I wanted to do this. They didn't voice their thoughts. Instead, they nodded to Savage and Terror.

"Give us a day to talk. We'll find you someone even if it doesn't end up being Gabe. Leave it to us and we'll make it happen. Have Smoke send over what he has so far and we'll take it from there with our team. If you find out anything else on your end, let us know. It might take a little while to clean it up, but we'll get the job done. We promise. We don't like the thought of people like that running around either," Sean promised them.

I could see the relief on their faces. They finished up with a few pleasantries and thanked us before ending the video conference. As the screen went blank, Cassidy began to protest, just like I knew she would.

"I'm all for helping the Warriors with this. However, why does it have to be Gabe? We have a number of people who can get in and find out what we need to know. Sure, the Italian thing is a small plus, but it's unnecessary. I think being Italian might raise their suspicions, not lower them. You'd be more at risk."

"Cassidy, we can't rule out that Gabe might be ideal for this, just because you're scared," Sean said softly.

She glared at him. "Damn right I'm scared. I lost five years with my brother. I don't want to lose months or more with the rest of you. I won't be able to handle that again."

"Sweetheart, it's not going to be like that. I promise, none of us will allow it to happen. We're not going to have our family torn up like that again. I'm sorry I did what I did and you know it," Mark told her. You could hear the remorse in his tone.

She sighed and hunched in her chair. Sean got up and came around to her. He pulled her to her feet and wrapped her in his arms. He was whispering in her ear and kissing her over and over. It was sweet to see. I knew this was some form of PTSD she had from Mark. I didn't know if it would ever go completely away.

"Let's assume Gabe is the one we're going to send in. We need to get someone assigned to remotely work right away on digging up as much information as they can on the Greco family, their holdings in the past and now, the people who are working for them now, etc. As soon as Smoke sends over that file, we can hand it off. Gabe, if you're going to do this, we have to plan it, so you have the least amount of risk possible. We're not naïve. All of us in this room know there'll always be risk involved in what we do. The key is to reduce it as much as we can. I think you should go in with backup," Griffin stated. He'd been mostly quiet until this point.

"Maybe, maybe not. It depends. If I go in like I've been sent by another family to form an alliance, then a second person might be best. If I'm going to just stay in the background and see what I discover, then adding more than one unfamiliar face to the area and their haunts would raise red flags. I'd be better off going in alone. We'll set up regular check-in times and a method for it. If I need to be extracted, we'll have a signal I can send. I'm not suicidal. I don't have a death wish. I just need to work off some excess energy. I need this, guys." It was as close to pleading as I would get. They knew me. If I was admitting this, then they knew I was in need.

After exchanging worried looks, they all nodded. Cassidy had retaken her seat. Sean was now sitting, pressed up against her, holding her hand. A half hour later, after receiving the file from Smoke and discussing the beginning of our strategy, we broke for the day. We agreed to meet back up in the morning to take a deeper dive into this and to get our plans in motion. We didn't want to waste time, especially if the Warriors were going to soon eliminate the three biggest threats in prison. The best time to approach their people was when they were reeling from that loss.

Gemma: Chapter 2

I swear, one of these days I wouldn't be able to control it and they'd be sorry. This thought raced through my head as I watched them laugh and act like they owned the place. It infuriated me that they were allowed to act like this. My *papà* and cousins did nothing to stop it. They just bowed to them like they were our overlords and we were mere feudal subjects. I hated it.

Even now, as they shouted and disturbed other customers and demanded more food and drink that they wouldn't pay for, my *papà* stayed hidden in the kitchen. My cousins, Elijah and Emmet, were nowhere to be found, as usual. They were part owners of the restaurant because their dad had been my father's twin. When he died five years ago, they inherited his half.

Legally, I didn't own any of it, although my *papà*'s share should be mine upon his death since I was his only living child. He'd desperately wanted a son, but it wasn't meant to be. My mamma kept trying to give him one, but she miscarried every time. The third attempt, which was another boy, resulted in her dying. After that, my father had given up on having a son. He never remarried. I was ten years old at the time. To be alone for the last fifteen years was something I hated to think about.

I loved my *papà* and wanted him to be happy and enjoy the remainder of his life. He'd worked hard to make this place a success. He should enjoy it. My only regret was in order to make it happen, he had to compromise and do things he should never have agreed to do. It made him and us sort of slaves to the Greco family. That's why their men came in here and acted the way they did.

I was seventeen when the head of the family, Matteo, and two of his sons, Anthony and Carlo, were sent to prison for some of their crimes. I thought that would mean our freedom. I was wrong. Somehow, they found ways to still run at least part of their criminal domain from prison. We remained beholden to do whatever they asked.

I might not be able to kick their asses out of here, but I didn't and wouldn't put up with their grasping hands and lewd propositions. I had been dodging those since I was fifteen. For the most part, they laughed and went back to talking or eating. A few would push harder before giving up. However, in the past three years, a new man rose in the ranks. I had no idea where he came from, but he was given status quickly and he functioned as one of Greco's lieutenants. Santo Vitale scared me. I knew that one day, my refusal to take what he said seriously would backfire on me. He was more vocal lately that he wanted me.

I'd refused every single one of his advances. He would always stare hard at me. It made me want to shiver and hide, but I didn't. I stood tall and stared back. I wanted him to know that I wouldn't be taken against my will by him or any man. He'd spoken to my *papà* and told him that he wanted to marry me. I refused him. *Papà* had tried to tell me it would be to my advantage to accept his proposal. That I would live a very comfortable life.

As if I wanted to be with a man I knew would cheat on me, likely beat me, and made his living by being a criminal—a drug dealer and enforcer. There was no way I wanted anything to do with that kind of life. I wanted what I think most women wanted—a safe and loving home with a man who loved me and would never cheat on me or raise a hand to me or our children. I didn't care if he was wealthy or not. I worked and I would continue to do it. My father did pay me to work in the restaurant. If he stopped, I'd go to another one. I had experience doing absolutely every job in this place.

As I thought of this and Santo, another thought invaded my mind. It was the man sitting with the Grecos. He seemed more aloof or something. He'd captured my attention the moment I saw him a month ago. He'd walked in like he was in charge and gone right up to Santo, despite his bodyguards, or goons as I called them, trying to stop him.

I hadn't heard what he said to Santo, but when he was done, they had invited him to join them and they spent a few hours in deep conversation. I tried to eavesdrop when I served them, but they were careful to stop talking when I got near them. Ever since that day, Santo and his men had been noticeably absent from our restaurant. I'd been more than relieved. I hoped it meant they had found a new place to haunt. It looked like I'd only been wishing for something that wasn't going to happen. Tonight, they'd walked in like they owned the place as usual. I wanted to stab them and kick them out, but I couldn't.

If I did, they'd hit us with some kind of retaliation. My father and cousins might even lose their lives. The restaurant would continue to be here, since the Grecos used it to launder some of their dirty money. Santo would likely carry out his threat to make me his. I knew that it wouldn't matter to him if I was willing or not. I'd heard the rumors that he had raped more than one woman around the Greco territory.

It was because of this threat of violence and being forced into a life I would hate that I'd come to a hard decision. As much as I loved my *papà* and cousins, I had to get out of here. I had to find a safe place where I might have a chance at the life I wanted. I'd been secretly working to find such a place, and I had found a few. It would be someplace smaller and less likely to attract people like Santo. I'd leave New Jersey and head south. In addition to finding a place to run to, I'd been squirreling away as much of my money as I could.

I didn't buy a lot of things. I lived simply. My money was more important as a means of escape. I'd have to be able to take care of myself until I could establish myself in an apartment or small house and get a job. My car would get me to where I needed to go. It was several years old, but reliable. I wouldn't be able to take much with me, just some clothes and important photos, so that I wouldn't attract attention. I only had to hold on a few more months, then I'd be free. I needed to add a little more to my nest egg.

A sharp whistle followed by a holler got my attention. One of the men with Santo was looking at me. He had a smirk on his ugly face. How I wished I could slap that look right off him. I clenched my fists for a moment, then relaxed them as I stepped out from behind the front hostess stand. I took my time getting to them. I wasn't going to run. The hell with that. I stopped close to the man who whistled. His name was Marcel. He was one of Santo's personal goon squad members. He leered at me.

"Hey, gorgeous, why don't you bring us a couple more bottles of this wine? It's really good. We want to have one of every dessert too. And after you do, why don't you rest? *Capo* would love to have you sit on his lap."

He gestured to Santo when he said *capo*. Him having the title of boss made bile rise in the back of my throat. I wonder what they'd think if I puked all over them. I had to fight not to grin at the image.

"I'll have to see if we have any more of that particular wine. It was a special order. As for dessert, I'll make sure you get some. Again, I'll have to see what's available. Many people have been ordering dessert tonight, and it isn't limitless."

I tried to keep the contempt I felt out of my tone, but I wasn't sure I was successful. Most of them merely shrugged and stared at me. However, I saw Santo's eyes narrow a bit and the mystery man's gaze had sharpened. He was staring at me as if he could see through me. I straightened even more to my full height. Being five foot four made me shorter than a lot of people, but I didn't let that deter me. I would project an image of strength.

"Gemma, come here," Santo ordered softly. I wanted to refuse, but other people were staring and I didn't want to cause a scene. We couldn't afford to lose customers. Reluctantly, I walked further around the table to stand near Santo. The new guy was beside him.

"I need to talk to you tonight. Once we're done with our dinner, I'll come find you. Don't leave."

Dread filled me. This was the first time he'd ever wanted to be alone with me. Was this it? Would tonight be the night he forced his claim? I couldn't allow it. I had to run. I had to get to my safe place and hide. I tried not to shake and when I answered him with a lie, I worked to keep my voice from quivering.

"I'm not sure what we would have to talk about, but I'll be here until we close."

"You know exactly what we need to talk about. Don't play dumb. It's time. I've waited long enough. Now, go get your *papà* and send him to me. I need to talk to him. Fetch the wine and the desserts."

I bit the tip of my tongue to stop from telling him to go fuck himself. God, how I hated him and these other men. They made life for all of us who lived in this town miserable. I wished there was someone who could challenge their authority. Not as another criminal element to just take over their territory and businesses, but someone who would run them off forever.

Nodding my head, I meekly walked off. I didn't waste time going to the kitchen to find my *papà*. As I expected, he was hidden in his office in the back. He gave me a tired look when I entered. To my surprise, Elijah and Emmet were there too. I hadn't seen them come in. They must've snuck in through the back door.

"Santo said to tell you he needs to talk to you right away. He also insisted that he and I need to talk tonight after dinner. I'm to wait for him here."

"Ah, *mia figlia,* my daughter, it's time. No more running and refusing him. You know that you cannot win. He's a *tenente,* lieutenant, for the Greco family. He must be obeyed. Don't think of the negatives. Think of all you'll gain. A beautiful house and a very comfortable lifestyle will be yours. Santo appears to do very well. I've seen his cars and how he dresses. He has money. You and your children will have everything you want and need and will be protected. He'd never allow anyone to hurt or take what is his." I could hear the pleading in his voice. I looked at my cousins. They were standing there like statues.

"And I suppose you two think I should just submit too. Let this man who I hate, take me, and force me to be with him? To bear his children while hating him and my life. A life with him would be hell. To be trapped in a loveless marriage with a man who cheats, abuses, and kills people to protect his criminal activities. Is that what you want for me?" I was almost screaming. I knew if my *papà* didn't go out soon, Santo would send someone to find him, but I had to say this. It burned to get out.

"Listen, Gemma, you're overreacting. Families back in the old country frequently had arranged marriages. Think of it like that. You're ensuring the protection of your family by marrying Santo. Yeah, you might never love him, but after you have a few children and give him a son, he'll likely leave you alone. He'll give his attention to a mistress or someone else. You can make a life for yourself if you try," Emmet said emphatically.

I wanted to bash him over the head with one of the iron skillets we had in the kitchen. Were all of them insane or just that afraid and willing to do anything to maintain their status and safety?

It was true, they and my *papà* did get paid well to launder the money. They had to pay a portion of the restaurant's earnings to the Grecos, but we did a really good business. Add that to what the Grecos paid them and they weren't hurting for money. I saw the things they bought. They loved their fancy clothes and flashy cars and jewelry. They were as bad as Santo anymore.

"Why don't we arrange a marriage for you, Emmet, or you, Elijah, to gain protection for our family?"

"Because we're men and we don't need to do that. You're a woman. It's your duty to do as the men in your family say. Enough of this rebelling. You'll do as your *papà* tells you. No more telling Santo no. When he talks to you tonight, you'll be sweet and accept his offer of marriage gracefully. As soon as it's official, the wedding will be arranged. It needs to happen immediately,"

Elijah ordered.

The whole time my cousins told me what to do, my *papà* sat there mute. A haze of anger tinged with almost hate filled me. Fuck all of them. I was done trying to protect a family who didn't deserve it. They were so willing to sacrifice me like I was nothing more than a cow or horse they were bartering away. Enough being the dutiful daughter. Apparently, my *papà* didn't see a daughter as something to protect and love. After all, I wasn't a son.

They should know by now, I couldn't be commanded. I might go along with it for a while, but in the end, I would do what I thought was best. Screw this, I was out of here. As soon as they went to see Santo and the wine and desserts were brought to them, I'd sneak out the back. I had money and clothes stashed in my trunk just in case I had to run without notice.

Swallowing the curses I wanted to hurl at them, I turned my back on them and went to find the wine and to tell the staff to prepare one of every dessert we had. It killed me to give them the wine. It had been very expensive, although worth it. Customers loved it. Santo and his men drank it like it was water and wouldn't pay a dime for any of it. If I had poison, I'd dose the bottles. Too bad I didn't really know anything about poison or where to get it.

I delivered the bottles to the table. My *papà* and my cousins were sitting with Santo. They stopped talking as I approached and stared at me intently. I ignored them and presented the wine then told them their desserts would be out shortly. As usual, I had to listen to their crude remarks. A few were bold enough to try and grab my ass until they saw Santo's face. He didn't like them touching me. I guess words were okay.

Grinding my teeth practically to the gums, I put on a fake smile and told them to enjoy themselves. I made up the excuse that the chef needed my help in the back. As I left them, I decided to give it ten minutes, to be sure no one came to check on me, then I would make a run for it. To hell with Toms River and the Greco family. The hell with this life. I was ready to start a new one.

Gabe:

The past month with Santo and the other men who worked for the Greco family was enlightening in some ways and helpful to my job. However, I hated it with a passion. It brought too many memories to mind. Watching how they walked these neighborhoods, acting like they were gods and the people living and working here should bow down to them, made me sick and furious. They took whatever they wanted. They had beaten more than one man who didn't do as they told him or didn't get out of their way fast enough. They were nothing but a gang of rapists, murderers, and thieves. It was going to be a pleasure to bring them down.

Santo wasn't the only *capo* the Grecos had, but he seemed to be the one who most of the others deferred to. They didn't like him but they feared him. I'd learned he'd only been here for a few years and, prior to that, he'd worked for another family in Maine. He didn't mention their name, but I had our team working to find out all they could about him. When this went down, we'd have to eliminate him. His going to prison wouldn't be the answer.

One thing I was surprised about was how there was no talk about Matteo, Anthony, and Carlo Greco being dead. They'd been killed in their cell by Law and

Hawk a month ago. It had coincided with me showing up to talk to them about an alliance. Did they not know or was it being kept secret?

I watched as they treated women horribly. I'd heard the rumors of how some of them forced women to sleep with them. Santo seemed to like doing that. It was all I could do not to kill him for it. Luckily for him, he hadn't done anything like that in front of me.

I knew they were still feeling me out. They didn't totally trust me, but I'd given them enough to make them think I was legit and they were on the brink of making even more money because of me, or so they thought. They were greedy and seemed to only want to conquer and accumulate wealth. Again, that brought the memories to mind.

I told them I was from the Rizzo family who was in South Carolina. The Rizzos wanted to increase their trafficking lines to go through the entire East Coast and they needed a partner in the north to accomplish it. I claimed the reason they didn't go to the bigger families was because we all knew they'd just take control and we'd get nothing. The Rizzos were looking to be equal partners.

Santo had been very interested in the idea. However, before he told me anything, he had me checked out. I knew my backstory would hold up. The Rizzo family *did* exist in South Carolina. They were a larger Mafia family who did illegal activities. The catch was, they owed me their lives, and this was me calling in that debt. They would back up anything and everything I said. They didn't know why I was targeting the Grecos and they didn't care. Their honor demanded they repay their debt to me. That was all that mattered to them.

I hated that I had to do it, but it was the only way I knew to get me inside with Santo and the other *capos*. So far, it was working. They'd been taking me around to see their various operations. They were keen to see if the Rizzos might be interested in other joint ventures. They not only laundered money through various businesses, in which they took a chunk of profits from the owners, they were also involved in illegal gambling.

Gambling was legal in New Jersey, just look at Atlantic City. The catch was the places that did offer gambling had to be issued a state permit to operate. The Grecos didn't do that. They offered gambling and other betting in back rooms and hidden dens.

While visiting them, I found out they had another business. One that hadn't been apparent. They offered prostitutes at these gambling hellholes. From the looks of them, a lot of the women weren't there of their own free will. It sickened me. I promised them in my head that I'd free them from their terrible lives. More than once they'd offered one of them to me. I told them that I liked my women not to be prostitutes. They looked at me like I was crazy.

Thinking of women I'd like, a woman came to mind. She was the one I'd seen my first night approaching Santo and his men in this very restaurant, Mia Bella Rosa. It was a local Italian restaurant that I found served some of the best authentic Italian food I'd ever eaten, outside of a real Italian kitchen filled with women all cooking for their family.

Her name was Gemma Marra. Her father, Tommaso, and her cousins, Elijah and Emmet, owned Mia Bella Rosa, and they worked for the Grecos. I wasn't sure they all did it voluntarily. I saw the fear on the men's faces when they saw Santo and his men. They deferred to them. The only one who didn't, or at least tried to hide the fact she detested it, was Gemma.

She was an Italian beauty. Her skin was a light olive and her dark brown hair with lighter streaks was thick and hung to her mid-back like a waterfall of silk. I longed to touch it to see if it was as soft as it looked. She was on the short side, maybe five foot three or so. That made her petite next to my six-foot-three frame. She had sexy curves which gave her an hourglass shape. She wasn't a model-thin woman which I liked. I hated to be with a woman who I was afraid I might break if I got a little exuberant in bed.

The thing to really grab my attention, as if the other stuff wasn't enough, was her eyes. She had slanted eyes, almost like a cat and they were the lightest green I'd ever seen. They appeared to be crystalline. She'd struck me that night and every night that I'd silently watched from the darkness. Tonight was the first night we'd been back here. I'd been relieved to see her.

She had some kind of hold over me that I didn't understand. She drew me to her. I wanted to see her and know that she was alright. I worried about her and I had reason to worry. The behavior and words of Santo and his men told me they all lusted after her. However, Santo wanted her the most. From what I heard him say and what he told her about talking tonight, he was determined to have her.

I knew from listening to the men talk that she'd been resisting Santo's advances for a long time. He'd run out of patience and he was going to make her his, no matter if it was by force or not. I couldn't allow that to happen. I'd stood back, knowing he was hurting women long enough. He couldn't have her. I had to ensure that she was safe from him and the other men working for the Greco family. I just needed to do it in a way that wouldn't blow my cover.

As her father sat at the table, talking to Santo, and she walked off to the kitchen again, I grew infuriated. Her father was agreeing with Santo that his daughter would marry him and give him children. It seemed Santo saw Gemma as his way to ensure his rise even more with the Grecos. Although, how that could be when the masters were dead, I didn't know. My gut was telling me that Santo might be planning a takeover, since there was now a vacancy at the top. Did he have enough men and power to pull it off? That was the big question.

But tonight that had to wait because I had a woman to save. Something in her expression told me when Santo was ready to talk, she wouldn't be here. She was going to make a run for it. While that thought was a good one and she might be able to hide from him, I didn't want that. I didn't want to lose sight of her and not know where she was and if she was safe and happy. I had to be able to physically see her. I didn't know why. Maybe I was going insane.

Clearing my throat to get his attention, I stood up.

"Santo, thank you for this excellent meal. *Signore* Marra, you have a beautiful place here. The food is excellent. I hate to eat and run, but I have a check-in with the Rizzos tonight and I can't be late. You know how it is. I'll see you tomorrow, say around ten. I can stop by your house or the main house. It's up to you."

The main house was owned by the Grecos and it had been used by their men as a sort of office or meeting place since they had gone to prison. There was staff to keep them comfortable and see to their needs. I could only guess the money came from the main money man for the family, Vito. He had been with them for years from what we discovered. He was trusted to handle their money. We were working on breaking that trust in the background. He had no idea our team of computer hackers were in his computer network watching everything he did.

"Are you sure you can't stay to enjoy more of this wine and the desserts?" Santo asked.

"I wish. Next time, I'll definitely stay and try it. I hope you have a wonderful evening. *Buona notte*." I wished them a good night although I was far from meaning it. These scummy bastards made me feel filthy. I hated being close to this life.

"*Buona notte*. Come by the main house at ten and we'll talk. I think we should start working on this new endeavor you brought us," Santo said, surprising me that he was ready to start. Good. This would only help me to wrap this assignment up even faster than I hoped. I knew which of them we would have arrested for a variety of offenses. We had the proof to back us up.

The others, like Santo, would have to disappear, never to be heard of again. The world would be a better place without them breathing our air.

Nodding and raising my chin to most of them, as they called out their good nights, I walked out. I had to make myself not hurry. It would have attracted their attention. I needed to get to the back and wait. She'd be leaving soon, and I had to intercept her. I hoped she wouldn't fight me. I didn't want to force her to come with me, but I would if I had to. When it came to her safety, I'd do anything. That was another surprise that had me off balance. This assignment should be my only focus, but she was stealing it away.

Gemma: Chapter 3

I waited ten minutes like I planned then grabbed my purse and keys and practically ran out the back door. Behind Mia Bella Rosa was a small alley that only led to our place. We had deliveries brought in that way and the garbage man picked up our garbage once a week. It was big enough we could park a car or two there. Usually, I parked here since I was the one who consistently stayed until closing and I didn't relish the thought of walking in the dark and down the street to my car. The lighting wasn't the best on the street.

However, when I came to work today, *Papà* had been parked there as well as someone else. I didn't recognize the car, so I had to park down the street. Hurrying to it, I kept looking around to see if there was anyone in the darkness ready to jump out at me. There were prickles running up my back and neck. I felt like I was being watched.

I clutched the keys tighter between my fingers. If anyone came at me, I'd go for their eyes or throat with my keys. I often wished I had a gun, but my *papà* was adamant that there should never be a gun in the restaurant. Besides, to get it, I'd have to apply for a New Jersey Permit to Carry a Handgun to make it legal here. I didn't know how hard it was to get approval. Maybe in my new town and state, I'd do that. I'd feel better if I had more ways to protect myself than mace and car keys.

I made it to my car which was a relief. I unlocked it and was just opening the driver's door when the prickling increased. I whipped around in time to see a dark, hulking shadow reach for me. I opened my mouth to scream, and I punched out in front of me with my keys. Unfortunately, he was quicker and stronger than me.

One hand covered my mouth while the other pushed my hand away before taking my keys out of my hand. I fought to hold on to them, but he was too strong. Oh my God, was this how it would end? Me dead or raped on a deserted dark street? I struggled to get loose and kicked the man's shins.

"Goddamn it, stop fighting. I'm here to help you, not hurt you. Jesus, would you settle so I can explain? I'm sorry I scared you, but I had to be sure you weren't followed."

I couldn't see him well in the darkness, but his voice made me pause. I knew that voice even though I'd only heard him speak a few times. It was the mystery man who had been with Santo. Fear crawled through me. I was scared because he was friends with Santo. However, a part of me wanted to believe what he said, which was insane. I couldn't believe I stopped fighting him. I glared at him, giving him my best attitude as he moved his hand away.

"Who are you and what gives you the right to follow me and grab me in the dark? Did Santo send you? If he did, I'm sorry to say, but I'm not going back to him.

You'll have to kill me to get me to do that. He's a cruel, abusive man and I have no intention of marrying him. I'll kill myself first," I snarled at him.

I prepared myself to run or fight at the first sign he was relaxing his guard. Men often underestimated women. They thought we were the weaker sex. Our smaller sizes made them think we couldn't handle ourselves. I had news for this man. He'd better watch out. Me cooperating for the moment meant nothing.

"I have no intention of taking you to Santo. I'm here to protect you. I knew you planned to run. I could see it. I'll explain, but first we have to get out of here. He or one of his guys could come looking for you at any moment. It'd be in our best interest that we aren't seen. My car is just over on the next street. Let's take it. They'll be on the lookout for yours when they realize you're gone. You need to ditch it."

"I can't! If I do, I have no way to get out of here. Plus, I have some of my stuff in the trunk. I can't leave with nothing to my name," I protested.

He sighed then grunted. "You can't take the fucking car. If what you have in the trunk isn't much, let's grab it and get the hell out of here. The longer you argue, the greater chance of him finding us. Come on."

He practically dragged me to the trunk and popped the lid with the key fob. Inside, I had two large duffle bags. He hefted them with one hand like they didn't weigh anything then closed the lid.

"Is this all of it?"

I nodded. He gestured for me to go ahead of him. I wondered if I could run for it. He was carrying my stuff. Maybe it would slow him down.

"Don't even think of running. You can't outrun me. If I intended to hurt you, I would've done it already, Gemma. Just behave until we get to my car and I get you somewhere safe. After that, I'll explain."

"I don't even know your name and I'm supposed to trust you? The fact you hang out with Santo and his goons is enough reason for me not to."

"My name is Gabriel. Most people call me Gabe. I may have been hanging with Santo and them, but I am most certainly not with them. They're serving a purpose right now."

"Yeah, to increase your illegal money businesses. I hear things too, Gabriel. I'm not a fool."

I called him by his full name. There was something about it that I loved as it rolled off my tongue. It suited him, which was stupid but true. Honestly, I could picture him as the Archangel Gabriel, the heralder of visions and messenger of God. I'd gone to Sunday school like a good Catholic girl. I knew my Bible.

"I never said you were nor do I think you're a fool, Gemma. I know things look bad, but I promise you it's not. Let's save the arguing and shit until I have you out of here. Get in."

He pointed to an expensive car. I knew it was a Mercedes by the symbol. That was it. I didn't know much about cars. He unlocked it, threw the bags over the front seat into the back, then gently pushed me to sit in the passenger seat. As soon as I was in, he slammed the door and hurried around to the driver's side. My heart raced. I could get out and run. The car was between us. I'd just reached for the handle when the car beeped and I heard the locks engage. I glared at him through the windshield. He smirked at me, the bastard. He didn't unlock them until he was right at the driver's door. He quickly jumped in and shut it.

I opened my mouth to blast him and insist he let me go one more time, when he took me by surprise. In a flash, his hands shot out and something hard and cold encircled my wrist. I gasped as I looked down to see I had a handcuff on my left wrist. He quickly attached the other end to his right wrist.

"I was hoping not to have to use these, but I can't trust you not to run. Hell, you might even try to jump out of a moving car. I can't let you hurt yourself. So, until we get to where we're going and you calm down enough to listen to me, the cuffs stay on, *Principessa*."

I half-screamed in the back of my throat. The arrogant bastard thought he had me, but I'd show him. His smile and calling me princess wouldn't help me to trust him. Deciding to pretend to be going along with him, I leaned back in the comfortable leather seat and closed my eyes. Maybe he'd think I was asleep and be quiet. In reality, I was watching him through tiny slits in my eyelids.

He didn't waste time starting the car and driving away. He didn't hurry. He stuck to the speed limit like he didn't have a care in the world. The cars that passed us had no idea he had a prisoner with him. The dark tinted windows hid me effectively.

As we made our way out of town, I wondered where he was taking me and what would happen once I got there. Had Santo told him to pick me up because he knew I was going to run? Was I being taken to him right now? I felt sick at the thought of him touching me. My stomach heaved, and I leaned forward to gag.

"What's wrong, Gemma?" He sounded worried. Damn, he was good.

"Nothing," I muttered.

"Like hell it's nothing. You almost puked in my car. What's wrong? Why're you sick?"

"You'd be sick too if someone was kidnapping you and taking you to someone who makes your skin crawl. I know what's in store for me when Santo gets his hands on me. Your little act isn't fooling me. I'll be raped and held prisoner. Well, I have news for you, I'll find a way to kill myself before I let him or anyone else touch me," I hissed. All thoughts of playing along flew out the window.

His expression instantly morphed from concerned to angry. He jerked the car to the edge of the road. We were outside of town now and the road was more rural. We hadn't hit the highway yet. He stopped the car on the grass then turned so he was facing toward me.

"No one, and I mean no one, is going to put their

hands on you or rape you. I swear to God that's not going to happen. I'm not taking you to Santo. The man is a monster. I'm not his fucking friend. I'm risking everything by doing this, Gemma."

"What do you mean, you're risking everything? Your precious deal? Why help me? I don't understand." I was becoming more confused by the second. His words and expression made it seem like he was telling me the truth. However, I couldn't forget he'd been hanging out with Santo and his guys for weeks. He was here to broker a deal with another Mafia family. Those in the organization, even people like my *papà*, knew that much.

"This has nothing to do with the deal. I can't tell you everything, but I need you to believe me. I'm only here to protect you."

"Why me? There are plenty of people, even women, in our town who need protection from Santo and his men. Why am I lucky enough to get this and not them?"

He leaned closer to me. His blue eyes stared into mine. I tried to breathe. He was a devastatingly handsome and sexy man. Everything about him called out to me, which was crazy. Men didn't affect me like this.

When I looked at his tall, buff body, and his gorgeous face, I wanted to drool like an idiot. It was obvious he had some kind of Mediterranean heritage. His olive skin, which was darker than mine, attested to that. His hair was darker than mine too. I loved it was short on the sides and longer on top, which suited him. His face looked like he had a thick five-o'clock shadow going at all times. It wasn't a full beard and mustache, but again, it suited him perfectly. His eyes were a surprise. They were a stunning blue. You'd expect them to be brown. The way he threw in Italian words, he might even be Italian.

"Because the thought of him touching one single hair on your head makes me so crazy, I can't think. I've had to sit back for the last month and watch and listen to the depraved shit he does. His men are bad enough, but he's the worst, *bellissima*."

My breath caught at him calling me beautiful. I fought not to fall under his spell or whatever it was, but it was hard.

"If you know he's evil, why work with him? Is making money so important that you don't give a damn about how it hurts other people? We live under the thumb of Santo and the Greco family. The big bosses might be in prison, but they're still in control. They won't be there forever. The town knows not to go against them, or you'll pay dearly. However, I'm not going to give myself to him no matter what my *papà* or cousins say. Doing that isn't the way to protect our family. I won't be used as a sacrificial lamb."

"Good. Don't. Your family can take care of themselves. Hiding behind you is the coward's way. Believe me when I tell you, the Greco family and their control over Toms River is coming to an end."

"Why? How?"

"I'll tell you, but not until we get you to safety. Be patient."

He turned to face the steering wheel and put the car in gear. We shot back out onto the road. This time I kept my eyes open. The scenery flashed by as I thought about what he said. Was he telling the truth? If he was, who was he? Was the nightmare my *papà* had gotten us into when I was small about to end? *God, please say it's true*. Or was I about to go from the frying pan to the fire as the saying goes? I kept silent as the miles raced by us. I'd hold my tongue until we got to wherever it was he was taking me, then I'd get my answers one way or another and decide what I'd do next. At least this had gotten me out of Toms River, which had been my ultimate goal.

Gabe:

I'd lost my ever-loving mind. Here I was running, with a woman I didn't know, away from the Mafia. The funny part was this wasn't the first time I'd had to face people like this or to make hard decisions. Sure, by taking Gemma, I might have blown my cover and all the work I'd done could be for nothing. I was hoping I was wrong. Maybe Santo wouldn't make the connection between me leaving and her disappearing. I had never spoken directly to her. There was no way he could know that there was some kind of connection between us. A connection I didn't understand.

When I decided to take this assignment, in addition to the hotel I had been staying at in town, I'd set up a safe house a couple of hours outside of it. It was north of Toms River rather than south. I didn't want to lead anyone close to my real life in Virginia. It was a place I could go to if I had to get to safety before being extracted. It was a town called Mahwah. It was about a fourth the size of Toms River. I had a place outside of it in the country.

It was a smaller town that had quaint streets and shops in the town square. The houses ranged from very humble to mansions. There was an old reservation and horse properties. It looked like a really decent place to raise a family, as long as you didn't listen to the supposed local legends about a group of supposed degenerates who lived in the mountains decades ago called the Jackson Whites. There had been a lot written and mentioned about them for decades. Who knows what the real truth was. I preferred to enjoy the beauty of the place and the calmness.

The property wasn't in my name nor rented. It had belonged to my mother. When she died, it passed to me, although I'd never taken it out of her parents' names. I escape here about once a year. No one knew to look for me there, except for the guys. They knew what this place meant to me. Since I'd been here off and on for many years, no one would consider me a new face or mention me to anyone if they came looking or asking if strangers had been in town. Everyone knew me simply as Gee.

I was surprised that Gemma remained quiet for the rest of our drive. Before I knew it, because I was so deep in thought, we were pulling into the driveway of my retreat. It wasn't a fancy house. It was a modest three-bedroom, two-bath home that was about a hundred years old. I paid someone to keep the place up when I wasn't here. That included making repairs, keeping the lawn mowed, and the bushes and flowers trimmed. I made sure it didn't have an air of neglect to it.

It was almost midnight. The drive through town had been quiet. Very few cars were on the road at this time of night. People were tucked in their houses sleeping, I imagined. As for me, I longed for bed. With the drama of taking Gemma, it had turned into an exhausting day, although I knew it would be a while before I got any sleep. There was no way she'd wait until morning for me to explain myself.

I'd debated the whole way here about what to tell her. Did I just tell her I was concerned and didn't want her to be hurt by a deviant like Santo or his men? That's what I should do. However, there was a part of me telling me to tell her the truth, which could get me killed. What if she found a way to contact Santo and told him who I was? If that happened, I was a dead man for sure.

The urge to confess all tied back to this yearning I had for her that had me confused and off balance. Why the need to tell her who I was? Or at least partially who and what I was. I'd been on lots of assignments and had never felt the need to unburden myself on a woman.

I could admit, I was sexually attracted to her. Who wouldn't be? She was beautiful. However, I'd had assignments in the past that involved women. If I found myself attracted and they were too, then I hadn't been shy about sleeping with them. As long as they knew and accepted the deal, that it was all in fun and wouldn't go anywhere. I'd found there were plenty of women who were fine with that.

Part of the issue for me was, something told me Gemma wouldn't be okay with that. She didn't sleep with men to simply satisfy an urge. This should've sent me running. Anytime I'd run into that in the past, I had walked away, never to look back. In this case, I knew that if I did walk away, I might regret it for the rest of my life. Could I live with that? Exactly what would I be regretting? The chance to be with a woman in a serious relationship? That had never been my goal. My life and history made it too dangerous to contemplate. I parked the car in the driveway and shut it off. I turned to look at her. She was staring at me.

"We've arrived. Now, the question is, will you come inside with me so I can explain or will we start all over with you trying to run? I'm warning you. I'm tired and not in the mood to chase you."

"Oh well, then by all means, let's not put you out. I'll do as you ask without a peep, so you can get your beauty sleep sooner rather than later." Her sarcasm made me fight not to smile.

"Glad you see it my way, *Principessa*. Let's go. If you're good, there's a hot bath in your future."

"I'm not a princess and there's no need to call me that. I know you mean it as a slight, but I'm far from a spoiled, rich brat." She huffed.

I undid my handcuff and reached over to undo hers as she spoke. I quickly grasped her chin, so she couldn't look away from me. "I don't call you that to be insulting. It's a complement. Hasn't a man ever given you one of those?"

I didn't wait for her to answer. I got out of the car and hurried around to her side. I didn't trust her not to leap out and try to run for it in the dark. As I opened her door, she gave me a lost look.

"No, they haven't," she mumbled as she accepted my hand and got out. What the fuck was wrong with the men in this state if they didn't tell someone like her how gorgeous and wanted she was? Idiots.

I paused long enough to open the back door and grab her two duffle bags, then I escorted her to the front door. The porch light came on automatically, so there was no fumbling in the dark to get the key in the lock. As the door opened and the alarm went off, I quickly pushed her inside ahead of me, before entering the alarm code. No need to get the cops out here. She'd scream to the heavens if they did.

Closing the door and locking it, I reset the alarm. She wouldn't be able to run without setting it off. I'd made sure she didn't see what I entered as the deactivate code. I turned on the lights as I led her to the living room. I dropped her bags by the stairs as we went. She slowly sat down on the couch and gazed around the room.

It wasn't fancy, but it was clean and nice. I sat down across from her in one of the chairs. She was staring intently at me. Her fists were clenched together.

"There's no need to be so tense, Gemma. I'm not going to hurt you. If I intended that, I could've done it back in Toms River."

"Then explain to me why I'm here, Gabriel. I don't know you. You don't know me. Why get involved with this fight I have with Santo? You have to know, he's not going to let you get away with it when he finds out. He'll probably kill you."

"Let me worry about how to handle Santo. I can manage that bastard."

"Bastard? Why the name calling? Aren't you two allies or something? You're here to form some kind of Mafia alliance, aren't you?"

I narrowed my gaze at her. How did she know that? Had Santo mentioned it or had someone been talking? "What do you know about the reason I came to Toms River? Who told you?"

"Come on, I'm not stupid and people talk. Do you think Santo's men or the other *capos* don't talk? They don't care who knows what. They own Toms River or enough of it not to be challenged. Everyone there is too terrified of the threat of what they and the Greco family will do to them. They've been running my town into the ground for decades."

Her displeasure and might I say it, hate, was apparent by her expression and the tone of her voice. She had no love lost for the Greco Mafia. Hmm, could this be something I could use to my advantage? Not anything that would get her hurt, but maybe she had some information she'd be willing to share, if I convinced her I was here to help and not harm anyone.

Buying time to think, I got up and went to the refrigerator to grab a couple bottles of water. I always kept some here. Usually, if I knew I was coming, I'd arrange for groceries to be delivered, but there hadn't been time. I walked back and handed one to her.

"Tell me about the Greco family and Santo. What do you know about them and what they do?"

"Why? Don't you know the men you're getting in

bed with?" she sneered.

"Stop with the attitude! I'm trying to have a serious conversation with you. If you want me to consider letting you go, tell me what I want to know."

She didn't immediately answer. She took sips of her water as she studied me intently. I don't know what she was looking for. I knew my expression wouldn't give anything away unless I wanted it to. Finally, after five minutes or more of intense staring, she answered me.

"What I know of the Greco family and the men who work for them is that they're like a cancer. They invade everywhere and are killing my home. They've had their hooks in it for years. It used to be in a bigger way several years ago, but there was a setback. However, Santo and the ones like him are intent on regaining that business."

"What was the setback?" I asked her, as if I didn't already know.

"The main bosses—Matteo, Carlo, and Anthony, all got sent to prison. I'm not sure what it was all for, but that was eight years ago. When they got sent there, I hoped that meant their stranglehold on Toms River would go away. It lessened but didn't disappear. Unfortunately for my family, the hold didn't. I've been praying for the last several years for there to be a way my family can get out from underneath them. It's a crazy dream, I know, but still, I have it."

"What does your family have to do with the Grecos?"

"Santo didn't tell you?"

I stared hard back at her, raising my eyebrow. She sighed. "Mia Bella Rosa wasn't always as successful as it is now. In the beginning, my parents and my uncle struggled. They were in jeopardy of losing the business when Matteo came along and offered to give them a loan. One that would have cheaper interest rates than going to a bank, even if they could've gotten a bank to give them one, which they couldn't. My family accepted it, knowing what the rumors were about the Grecos. That was the beginning of their fall.

"The Greco family waited a few months then approached my parents and uncle about getting a portion of the profits. They called it repayment of the loan and protection against unsavory people trying to run them out of business. My family knew what it really was. After all, they're Italian. They knew they couldn't say no. After that, it became more and more. They needed us to launder dirty money for them. Their men started using it as an unofficial meeting place. They come in and eat and drink and never pay a dime. They scare the customers. It just goes on and on."

"What's your relationship with Santo? Why is he always watching you and why did he insist on talking to you tonight? Why was the prospect of that talk enough to make you run?"

I hit her with three big ones. She paused and studied me again as I waited to hear what she said. I doubted I'd be surprised, but I wanted to hear her say it.

Gemma: Chapter 4

Just talking about the Grecos and Santo, in particular, made my skin crawl and my stomach churn. Over the years, their men had made me uncomfortable, but none had made me feel like Santo did. I knew he was a serious threat to me and one that if I didn't watch myself, might get me killed. I'd played the game with him for longer than I'd hoped, but it was obvious from his demand to talk to me that he was at the end of his patience.

The fact my *papà* and cousins were so willing to have me give in hurt. They weren't willing to fight for me or to run with me. I was truly alone in this battle. So, with this in mind, and even knowing Gabriel was likely his partner, I said the hell with it. Death would be preferable to having that man touch me.

"Santo Vitale is a snake. He's a killer and a rapist who has no compunction about doing whatever it takes to satisfy his goals and make money for the Greco family. For the past three years, he and I have been dancing around each other. He means nothing to me. As for his intentions toward me, he claims he wants me as his wife. I don't know if that's true or not. Maybe. However, I do know belonging to him in any way would be hell on earth. When he said he wanted to speak to me tonight, I knew he was done waiting. He won't take no for an answer anymore. He's raped other women, so I know my fate. My family seems to think it's preferable for me to submit to him than to resist and cause trouble. They seem to be more worried about their own skin and livelihoods than they are about me. So, I decided to hell with them and to get out while I could. I've been planning it for a while. I'd hoped to get a few more months of money saved, but that didn't happen."

His face kept getting darker and darker as I explained. I knew he was about to explode. I wondered how quick he'd call Santo to tell him where I was. By the look on his face, not long. I frantically scanned the room, looking for a way out or a weapon. I wouldn't go down without a fight. Seeing there was a fireplace and sitting next to it was one of those stands with a shovel and fire poker in it, I took my chance. I launched myself at it. I was closer to it than he was. I could make it.

The weight that bore me to the ground was huge. The air was knocked out of me as hands wrapped around my wrists to stop me from reaching the poker. I screamed in frustration. Attempting to get loose didn't work. He was too heavy and I could barely breathe. His hot breath washed over my neck and I shivered as his lips brushed against my ear.

"Nice try, *bellissima*, but I'm not that dumb. I see I'm going to have to keep my eyes on you."

"Go ahead. Rape me or beat me, who cares? Call Santo and tell him where I'm at. It's not going to make any difference to me. Although Santo might not like you sampling the goods before he does," I hissed at him.

Suddenly, the weight was removed, and I was flipped onto my back so fast my head swam. I gasped for air. His icy stare drilled into me. He still had control of my arms.

"I should beat your ass for telling me that, but I don't beat women or rape them. I'm not a fucking monster. I have no intention of calling Santo and telling him anything about you. And I have no doubt, if I was so inclined to rape you, that he'd take great exception to it. I noticed he lets his guys say stuff to a point and maybe cop a feel once in a while, but they know how far to push it. He's claimed you, Gemma. He's not going to share you with another man."

"Not yet, but once I give him a couple of children, then I doubt he'd care who used me. If you're not going to tell him where I am and you're not going to use me, then why bring me here? What's going on with you and him? Is this a power play to take over his position?"

Slowly, he rose up then got to his feet. He held out his hand. Reluctantly, I took it so he could help me to my feet. He walked me backward until the couch hit the back of my legs and I sat down. He sat beside me this time.

"Tell me something, Gemma. What would you be willing to do in order to get rid of the threat of Santo and the whole Greco organization?"

"I wouldn't trade one set of mobsters for another. However, anything less than that and I'd have to say, anything. Why?"

He took his time to respond. While he did, he kept staring intently at me. He was making me squirm and not just with unease. He was making my body betray me. My nipples were hardening and my pussy was getting slick. *Jesus, this wasn't the time to be interested in a man, especially this man. What was wrong with me?* I berated myself. When he finally answered me, I was beyond stunned at his answer and the implications.

Gabe:

I knew that I had lost my fucking mind when I made the decision to come clean with her. I was going to tell her everything and see what happened. I wasn't sure why or what it would accomplish, but something powerful was pushing me to do it.

"I'm here to take down the whole Greco family. When I'm done, there won't be anyone left to run things. In order to do that, I had to come in and convince them that I was here to create a partnership between them and the Rizzo family. That's what I've spent the last month doing. I've been learning the ins-and-outs of the illegal gambling, betting and drug businesses as well as the ways they launder the money, like they use your restaurant. They're finally ready to move forward with the deal. I've convinced them I'm for real."

Her mouth dropped open. I saw disbelief and shock on her face. I waited to see what she'd say. I didn't have to wait long. "You're lying. There's no way you're here to get rid of them. If the Rizzo family is backing you, then it's a takeover, pure and simple. We won't be any better off than we were before, probably worse."

"I'm not lying. The Rizzos are helping me with my cover story. I can assure you, it's not because they plan to take over the Greco territory. Let's just say, they owe me and this is their way of repaying me. I'm gathering everything I can on who's involved, what they do for the family, and anything else I can. It's all going to be important when the time comes."

"If you're not lying, then who are you? A cop? A federal agent? Are you undercover?"

"I'm undercover, I guess you could say. I'm not a cop or a federal agent. I work for a company that lends its help to a variety of people and companies. We've been asked to help take down the Greco family. That's all you need to know."

"You can't take them all out, Gabriel. The three main men are in prison, but they'll just restart things. People are greedy and will do their bidding. If they aren't doing it out of greed, then they're doing it because the Grecos found some kind of leverage to use against them."

"You'd be right about the leverage, but not this time. Matteo, Anthony, and Carlo Greco died in their prison cell a month ago. I have no idea why Santo and the others haven't mentioned it or don't know it. The remaining son, Lorenzo, has nothing to do with the family business."

Her gasp was louder than the one before. Her eyes widened, and her hand crept up to clutch her throat. "Died? How?"

"It appears they got into an argument with each other before they shanked each other. They bled out before their guards found them." I decided she didn't need to know they'd been killed.

"Yeah, more like someone was paid to make it look like they killed each other, not that I care. If those three are dead and Lorenzo really isn't going to continue the businesses, then we have a chance." I could hear the tentative excitement in her voice.

"Lorenzo doesn't want anything to do with the businesses. I have it on reliable authority. However, in order to make this work, we have to get everyone we can. We can't risk leaving anyone behind who'll see this as their way to climb the ladder or to restart shit."

"When you say that, do you mean even the people who were forced to participate will have to be arrested?"

"If they were truly coerced, then no, I don't mean them. It's the real criminals we want, not innocents who got caught up in this nightmare. Your father and cousins were used. They knew to say no would be a death sentence not only for them but your whole family. Hell, your cousins were only kids back then, like you."

She sagged in relief and buried her face in her hands. I watched as her shoulders began to shake. I knew then that she was crying. I couldn't stand it. I scooted over until I was pressed against her. I wrapped my arm around her and tugged her until she was lying on my chest with her face buried in my shirt. She didn't resist.

"Shh, it's alright, *Principessa*," I murmured. I rubbed my hand up and down her back. As I held her and tried to comfort her, I tried to ignore the feel of her in my arms. Her sweet body was pressed against mine. I could feel her every curve. Her breasts were plastered to my chest. God, she felt amazing and I couldn't stop myself from getting turned on. My cock got hard despite her tears and I chastised myself not to be a bastard.

As I grew thick and my cock throbbed, I fought not to imagine myself stripping her bare and sinking into her softness. The past month had been hell on me. Ever since my first look at her, I'd dreamed about her nightly. I imagined all the ways I could take her. The pleasure we could give each other. The things I could make her crave and need. I'd been beating off more than daily to those thoughts.

Could I have gone out and found women to relieve my sexual tension? Sure, but the one night I tried to do that, I found I was turned off and couldn't even get hard, although I had more than one woman who had offered. After that, I didn't bother trying again. It was this that was driving me crazy and confusing me the most. Why wouldn't any woman do? They always had in the past.

Somehow, I held myself under control but barely. I was relieved when she stopped crying and realized she was practically on my lap. She moved away quickly. I felt cold without her. I didn't let her get far.

She wiped her eyes to clear away the tears. Even with a red nose and eyes, she was still dazzling. She sniffed then coughed before speaking. "What can I do to help?"

"*Piccola*, there's nothing you need to do. I'm going

to have someone come and get you and take you to an even safer place. They'll keep an eye on you until this is over. Once it is, you and your family, if you choose to contact them, can decide what to do. If you want to go back to Toms River, then you can. You can live the kind of life you've always wanted." Calling her babe was an inadvertent slip of the tongue.

"No, I can't do that, Gabriel. Wait. Is Gabriel even your real name?" She frowned.

"Yes, Gabriel is my real name. Of course, my last name isn't Barbieri. Why can't you do that?"

"Because I can help. I know a lot about who's working for them because they've been given no choice and who works for them because they like what they do and are greedy. You've probably found out a lot in the past month, but I doubt you know everything. What about locations? Are you sure you know every place they use to distribute drugs or where they have the gambling dens? All the guys who do illegal betting for them? I do. And if I don't know it, I can find out. Let me help you, Gabriel."

She was pleading with me now. Instantly, I grew upset. I stood up and began to pace in front of the unlit fireplace. "Gemma, there's no way in hell that I'm going to allow you to help. This is dangerous. If they catch on, they'll kill us. With it just being me, I don't have to worry about how fast I can get out if given the chance. If you helped, I'd have to worry about you every second of the day. And even if I said yes, it's not going to work with you here and me there. No, you can't help."

"I can go back to Toms River and help you. No one will expect me to be doing something like this."

"Are you insane!? Santo is at the end of his patience with you. He was going to claim you tonight. You said it yourself. What's to prevent him from doing it the instant you step back into town? There's no way in hell I'm going to risk that." Again, the thought of him touching her made me see red.

"True, he would. So, what we need to do is come up with something that would deter him. Make him think twice before staking a claim. Something that would scare him enough not to do it," she mused.

I snorted. "Yeah, like a bigger and scarier mobster claiming you first. That would work but I don't think you'd like that outcome."

Slowly, she raised her head. She studied me for a moment then nodded. "You're right. That would do it. He'd have to be afraid making a move on me would hurt him in some way. Like maybe ruin the chances of him making a lucrative deal happen for the family. He wouldn't want to mess that up."

As her meaning sank in, I shook my head. "No! No goddamn way am I taking you back there and claiming you. What makes you think he wouldn't just kill me? And if he didn't, I couldn't let you out of my sight for fear he'd get brave and take you. I won't risk him hurting you, Gemma. Even if you can help with the names and places, it's not worth the risk."

She got up and came over to me. She lifted up her

hands to palm my face. Her touch sent shocks through me and it was all I could do not to moan.

"Gabriel, please, I can do this. Yes, there's a risk and we'd have to plan for it, but I know together we can do this. I can help you take them down sooner. I've tried for so long to fight them and to get others to do it and nothing. This way I can get back some of my family's dignity. I can help free them and others from the tyranny of this group. So, unless you're willing to lock me up somewhere, I'm going back and helping. You can't say no. I'm a free woman. I can decide what I do or don't do."

I jerked her against me after giving her a tiny shake. "Do you think I won't have your ass locked up? Don't tempt me, *tesoro*, treasure. If that's what it takes, I'll do it. No matter how pissed you get at me," I snapped.

"Try it and see what happens. I hope whoever you plan to get to help me doesn't need any rest. Because if they give me a chance, I will escape."

"Over my dead body."

"No, the only dead bodies we want are Santo and his men. You know I can help. Stop being stubborn. Think. We can pull this off. If you take me back and tell Santo you claimed me, there's no way he'll push back. He'll hate it. He'll be pissed, but he won't risk the alliance with the Rizzos. They're a bigger and scarier family, aren't they?"

"Yes, they are. They could swallow the Greco family whole and not even notice if they wanted.

Luckily, their help isn't based on them getting more territory."

"What's to stop them from doing it anyway?"

"If they did, they'd have to deal with me and they don't want that. If they make me their enemy, they know that means certain death for them," I told her honestly.

She remained quiet as she absorbed that news. I wondered if she'd ask me why I was that dangerous to them. If she did, I wouldn't be able to tell her. She was better off not knowing why. My dark past needed to stay in the past.

"I can see that if I ask you why that is, you won't tell me. Maybe one day, you'll feel like you can trust me to tell me the whole story. You're a mystery, Gabriel. I'm banking everything on the hope that you're being honest with me and I'm not offering to help another bigger Mafia family move into my town and take over. However, I have to do this. It may be the only chance to stomp everyone out and gain our freedom. I'm begging you. Let me come back with you and help. If you're worried about my safety so much, we can find a solution."

I'd hoped to get to bed before the wee hours of morning. In the end, it didn't happen. We remained up for hours arguing. She argued for me to take her back with me and all the reasons it made sense to do it, and I argued about all the possible things that could go wrong. Finally, I called a truce so we could get some sleep. I told her we'd continue our debate after getting some rest. Both of us were running on fumes and I couldn't think clearly anymore. I was actually considering taking her up on her offer.

I showed her to one of the bedrooms and left her bags with her. As I showered, I thought over the one possible way I could take her back with me and eliminate almost all the risk to her. Nothing would be foolproof, but she could be protected. The only real question was, could I do it?

I didn't get much sleep. I kept tossing and turning, thinking about her. Not only was it about her helping me, but my incessant thoughts for her. My attraction was growing, and I wasn't sure how much longer I could keep from making her aware of them.

If she wasn't interested, I'd never force myself on her. I wasn't that kind of man. However, if she gave me even a tiny indication she might be willing, I'd do everything I could to convince her to submit to me. My desire to have her in my bed was driving me insane. Last night, I woke up from having a hot dream about us. I was so hard, I had no choice but to beat off not once, but twice, before I could get back to sleep. I prayed she hadn't heard my moans. I tried to be quiet, but it was impossible to stifle them completely.

Seeing the door to her room was still shut, I assumed she was still asleep. I went to the kitchen and started a pot of coffee. Knowing I had nothing in the refrigerator to cook for breakfast, I checked out the pantry and the freezer. No luck. Coffee would have to do until we could go into town and get something to eat.

The coffee was made, and I was pouring a cup when she came stumbling into the kitchen. She was yawning and rubbing her eyes. I ate her up with my eyes. She was dressed in shorts and a tank top—nothing unusual to see in the middle of summer. However, on her, they seemed a hundred times sexier than when other women wore them. Her legs might not be super long, but they were toned and sexy. A flash of them wrapped around my waist as I pounded into her came to mind. I fought that idea back.

Her tank was tight and showcased her more than adequate breasts. I wondered what they looked like. Were her nipples large or small? What color were they? How responsive to touch would they be? Fuck! I had to stop this shit. It was getting ridiculous. Never had I been distracted by a woman or sex when on assignment. I could always separate them. This time, I was afraid I was going to fail.

"Coffee?" I grunted.

"Yes, please."

I got another cup and poured some in it. "Sorry, it'll have to be black. No creamer, although if you want sugar, there should be some in that canister." I pointed out one on the counter.

"No, black is fine. So, what's on the agenda for today? I know we'll continue our debate, but do you think we could get something to eat first? I'm starving," she asked, with a smile.

I couldn't help but laugh. “Sure, we can do that. We'll have to go into town to find something. Are you going to scream that I'm a kidnapper as soon as we get there?”

She smiled then shook her head. “No, I won't do that. I'm too hungry to ruin my chance at a meal. Would anyone believe me if I did?”

“Possibly, although they do know me around here. They might just think you're crazy. I've never had a woman with me to accuse me of kidnapping.”

“So, you come here often? They know you. I find it hard to believe you've never had a woman here with you. Or do you have someone in town you meet with when you're here? If so, will me being with you upset her?”

She avoided my eyes as she asked that last part. I fought not to grin. Ah, maybe the *principessa* wasn't completely unattracted to me after all. That thought was a double-edged sword. On the one hand, it made me happy that she wasn't. On the other hand, it scared me since it lowered my resolve to stay away from her.

“I come here to relax. I don't have anyone I regularly see when I come here, so no worries.”

I left it at that. I hadn't said there weren't any women in town I hadn't hooked up with. That would be a lie. The few I had fun with in the past knew it was all fun. She frowned.

“Finish your coffee then get ready. I'm leaving for town in fifteen minutes. If you're not ready, you'll go as-is."

Other than her hair not being brushed, she looked more than okay to go, but I doubted she'd see it that way. She squealed then ran out of the room with her cup clutched in her hands. I laughed. This might be a fun morning after all. Or until we got back and started our fight again.

Gemma: Chapter 5

Gabriel's fifteen minutes gave me enough time to gulp down my coffee, wash my face, brush my teeth and my hair. I put it up in a quick ponytail. I didn't have time to do much else. I put on my tennis shoes. In the one bag, I'd stashed a few bits of makeup. I put a tinted gloss on my lips and curled my eyelashes before applying some mascara.

I met him in the kitchen after I washed my cup. He nodded at me. "Good. Glad to see you don't take an hour to get ready. Let's go. I know a place in town. It's not fancy. It's more of a diner, but the food is really good. I eat there a lot when I'm here. Does that sound alright to you?"

"As long as they have decent food, I'm good. I could eat a horse right now."

He laughed as we went outside. He turned on the alarm and locked the house before opening the car door for me. I admit, having a younger man open doors for me was new. The older generation still did it, but guys my age or even up in their forties didn't seem to think it was needed anymore.

As he drove into town, I got lost in my memories of my mamma. My *papà* adored her. You could tell that they loved each other very much. He was always opening doors, pulling out chairs, touching and kissing her. She'd laugh and smile at him as she'd touch or kiss him back. I heard them tell each other they loved each other all the time. When she died, my *papà* had been heartbroken.

Their love was what I'd always secretly wished for when I grew up. I wanted a man who would love me like that and who I could love back the same. He'd make me and our children the center of his life. He would never give me reason to think he'd stray. I never saw my *papà* look at another woman. He still didn't pay attention to them, even though women flirted with him all the time. He was handsome and still young enough to remarry, although I doubted he ever would.

The car coming to a stop jarred me out of my memories. I looked around to see we were parked outside of a quaint diner. I waited for Gabriel to open my door then held onto his arm as we went inside. The inside was just as cute and homey as the outside. Rather than an impersonal diner motif, this one had color and warmth to it.

We stopped at a hostess stand. A young woman raced by, throwing a smile at us as she said, "Take a seat anywhere and I'll be with you in just a minute. Just as soon as I deliver this food."

Gabriel nodded his head and led me to a table that was toward the back. He pulled out a chair for me. After I sat down, he surprised me by sitting next to me rather than across from me. There were menus on the table, which he handed one to me.

"Everything I've had here has been delicious. I've tried several things on the menu. If you don't see anything you like, let me know. They'll make stuff for you if you want. They don't advertise it, but they will."

Glancing at the menu, I saw it was rather extensive and off the bat, there was more than one thing that caught my interest.

"Don't worry about me. I'd have to be one picky eater not to find something on this menu. Lord, it looks so good."

He grinned then studied his menu. We'd been at it for a minute or two when the waitress came bustling up to our table. Her smile was still in place and looked genuine. "Hi, I'm Bethie Ann. What can I get you to drink? We have coffee, tea, water, orange juice, milk, and sodas."

"I'll have orange juice and water, please," I told her. Gabriel asked for the same.

"Do you need more time to study the menu or do you know what you want?"

"Bethie Ann, why not give us a few minutes? This is her first time here," he said nicely.

"Sure thing. I'll be back with your drinks in a few," she replied before hurrying off. I think she had only one speed. The place wasn't overly crowded, and no one seemed to be demanding her attention, however, there could be other things happening we knew nothing about. I knew that better than anyone after working at Mia Bella Rosa for so many years.

When she returned with our drinks, I made my hard decision. I ordered the fresh berries French toast platter. I was starving. I thought I ordered a huge amount, but it was nothing like what Gabriel ordered. He ordered a lumberjack's breakfast. I wouldn't be surprised if they came out with half a pig or something. When Bethie Ann left, I gave him a stunned look.

"What?" he asked.

"Are you seriously going to eat everything that was listed on the menu in that lumberjack breakfast? Is that even possible in one sitting, or is someone joining us to help you eat it?"

He grinned as he leaned back and patted his washboard stomach. "Why? Do you think I'm getting fat? I've eaten it before and never worried. I'd hate to think I'm developing the middle-age spread."

I rolled my eyes. He was fishing for compliments, as if he needed any. He knew he was good-looking and women would let him know that everywhere he went. I debated calling him on it, then I decided to have fun with him.

"Well, you can never be too careful. You're what, in your thirties now? That's when it starts. Your metabolism slows down and the normal amount of food doesn't get worked off like it did in your twenties. The fat starts to creep up without you even realizing it until you've got the spare tire forming. You try to work out more, but it doesn't help. Then bam, one morning, you wake up with a dad bod or worse, instead of six-pack abs, you've got a whole keg."

I tried not to laugh at the look of utter horror on his face. My smirk must've peeked through because he started to relax. He gave me a look that told me I might be in trouble.

"That's because they increase the wrong exercise. They think lifting more weight or running more will help. They're wrong."

"Oh, so what are the correct exercises they should be doing?" I knew I would probably regret asking, but I was curious to hear what he would say.

He leaned over to whisper in my ear. "They need to increase the amount, variety, and vigor of the sex they engage in. It should be daily if not more. That way, they keep fit, satisfied, and keep their lady or ladies the same."

I knew I was blushing. No matter what, when it came to talking about sex, I always did. I knew it wasn't because I was a prude. It was due to my own inexperience. Something I wouldn't admit to this man in a million years. I turned my head to glance out the window as I replied. I couldn't let him get away with saying that and have nothing to say back. He'd know he had me.

"I guess that might work. Assuming the man knows what he's doing when it comes to sex. So many thinks they do and don't have a clue. There's a reason so many women in the world say they've never had an orgasm. They find they have to take care of it themselves."

I jumped as a sting to my earlobe startled me. I glanced back at him. His eyes were hooded, and he was staring at me intently.

"I know I can make a woman come and scream my name. Is that a challenge, Gemma?"

"Not from me. I would never be that stupid. I'm not looking for a man. I'm looking for a new life. Which brings us to what we need to discuss today. How you're going to let me help you bring down Santo and the rest of the Greco family empire."

"Nice change of topic. I'll let you get away with it…for now. However, this is going to be a short conversation. I'm not going to endanger you by taking you back into the lion's den."

"Gabriel, you know it makes perfect sense. I know the neighborhoods and people. They won't be suspicious of me like they will of a newbie like you. They'll be afraid of you since they've seen you with Santo and the others. They'll suspect it's a trap to get them to say the wrong thing so he can have them punished or killed. It wouldn't be the first time. He's tricked people like that in the past."

"He has? Does it happen often?"

"Not often, but enough times that people are leery of saying or doing the wrong thing. People just venting about their frustrations about them or their methods has led to people being found severely beaten."

"And you want me to take you back to that? Are you crazy, *Principessa*?" he asked incredulously.

"No, I'm not crazy. I'm tired of people like them hurting people like me and my neighbors. Most of them are hardworking people who got caught in something they had no way to say no to. You said you're here to take them out permanently. You're not a cop or federal agent. Why do you care?"

I saw the pensive look he got on his face. He didn't answer me right away. I waited. Finally, he did, although not the way I wanted.

"Let's just say, there are things in my past and things I've seen all over the world that have made me detest seeing people used, abused, and worse by criminals. I happen to work with a bunch of like-minded individuals and we have the means to do something about it. This was brought to our attention by a friend. We want to help. I can help."

"What about the Rizzo family? They're a real *famiglia mafiosa*, Mafia family. You said they owe you a debt and that's why they're helping you. That has to be a pretty huge debt, especially if they're not expecting to gain territory for their help." I knew there was a note of disbelief in my voice. I couldn't help it. In my experience, that kind of family didn't do something for nothing. There had to be a gain or win for them.

"It is a huge debt. They know it's not going to gain them territory or I wouldn't have let them help. However, if this, in some way, eliminates a small competitor in a similar business and that somehow benefits them, that's extra. I don't think it will, but I can't rule that out."

He paused as Bethie Ann came back with our food. When she left, we set about eating. We didn't talk, but I wasn't finished yet. I had more questions for him.

I let my enjoyment of the food lift the gray cloud hanging over me at the thought of what he'd last said. I guess there would always be someone to benefit, and I couldn't expect it never to be the bad guys.

I was done long before him. Not only because he had twice as much food, but because I couldn't eat everything. I scooted my chair back.

"Where are you going?"

"I need to use the bathroom. I'll be back."

I felt his eyes watching me the whole time I walked to where I saw the restroom sign. Inside, I did my business then checked I didn't have syrup on my face before heading back. As I came out of the restroom, I was looking directly across the diner at our table. I stopped. He was no longer alone. There was a woman standing very close to him, bending down over the table. Her ass was facing me. She was wiggling it.

I couldn't see his face, but her body language told me she wasn't just having a casual chat with a stranger. I marched over to see who she was. As I got closer to our table, I could hear what was being said. Her body was blocking his view of me. Neither of them knew I was there.

"I'm not going to tell you again, Constance, back up. I don't want you in my face," he growled. I could hear displeasure in his tone.

"Oh, come on, Gee, you can't tell me you're not excited and happy to see me. When did you get to town? Why haven't you called me? Surely, you weren't going to come and go without seeing me. We have fun when we're together," she practically purred.

It made me sick to hear that. I shouldn't be. He was a man and not an unattractive one. He came here often. It was silly to think he hadn't slept with the women around here. I bet they fought each other to get his favor, even for a night. Something hot shot through my chest. I didn't know what it was, but I didn't like it.

"I had no thought of calling you. There's no reason to. Now, why don't you move along? I want to finish my breakfast and get out of here."

"I can join you and keep you company while you finish."

God, she just didn't take a hint or a blunt order it seemed. A part of me wanted to leave him to squirm and get rid of her himself. Another part wanted me to piss her off. The latter won. I took the last few steps and bumped into her as I squeezed by her to get to his chair and mine beyond. I leaned over his shoulder and gave him a kiss.

His mouth didn't move for a second or two, then he surprised me by grabbing the back of my head and kissing me. It was the best kiss I'd ever had in my life. It lit my body on fire. His lips eagerly moved over mine then his tongue probed my mouth. I let him in without thinking. His tongue tangled with mine. I could taste the sweet syrup from his pancakes on it. I had no idea how long we kissed before I pulled away. At first, he didn't let me, then slowly, he let go of my head. I straightened up, feeling a touch breathless. That's when I saw her. Damn, I'd forgotten all about her. She was standing there with her hands on her hips and a furious expression on her face.

Seeing her up close, I took her in. I knew from behind she had a nice body and long red hair. Her face wasn't ugly, unfortunately. She wore too much makeup, I thought, but she was very attractive. I'd say she was a few years older than me. Fighting to remember why I'd kissed Gabriel in the first place, I ran my eyes up and down her then gave her a bored look. I rested my hand possessively on his chest, as I stood behind him.

"Who's this? An old friend?" I asked, emphasizing the old part.

She took my meaning immediately. Usually, I don't play catty games. I thought women shouldn't do that to each other, but something about her made me do it. His hand came up to grab mine. He lifted it to his lips and kissed the back of it. I couldn't see his face. I wondered what he was thinking. Would he be pissed that I did this?

"*Dea*, this is just someone I know. Her name is Constance. She's an acquaintance. I was trying to explain to her that I wouldn't be seeing her while I was here, since I'm with you. In fact, you're the only one I plan on seeing for the rest of my life."

Him calling me goddess made me want to melt. He was good. His tone made it sound like he meant every word he said to me and that I was his sole focus. Like I thought, he was deadly to women.

"Who's this woman? What's she doing here with you?" Constance practically shrieked. Heads turned to look at us.

"This is my *amore mio*, my love, Gemma. We came to get some time alone together. We can't seem to get enough back home. I wanted to show her my favorite place to eat. You can't beat the breakfasts here. We were starving after our long night last night." His words were full of innuendos.

"Your love? Are you kidding me? Why her? She's not like me. I can be your love and I know I can satisfy you. All you have to do is give me the chance. I've been waiting for you to come back. I've missed you. We're so good together. Does she know about us?" I heard the bewilderment then the spite in her reply. I'd have to be stupid not to have guessed they had been lovers.

"It's so hard to keep track of the women he's fucked and then discarded. I know he's no angel, despite his name, but he hasn't treated me that way. I guess that makes me special. *Il tesoro*, I'm ready to go. Are you? We have so much to do when we get home." I smiled at her as I called him honey. I had no idea if she knew Italian or not, but it would lend to the illusion we were more than fuck buddies. Why I found it so important to do that with her, I had no clue.

"I am. If you'll excuse us. I need to pay and we have to get going. Have a nice day, Constance. I expect this'll be the last we see of you unless it's just in passing."

I moved back, so he could push back his chair and stand. He wrapped an arm around me and pulled me against him, as he moved toward the register. People were still avidly watching. He smiled and nodded at some. The whole time we paid, Constance remained over by the table, staring daggers at us. Well, more at me than him, I think.

As we exited the diner and he took me to the car, I felt the tension increase in my shoulders. He opened the door and assisted me in, then he went around to get in the driver's seat. I sat in silence. He started the car and pulled out of the parking lot. He remained silent.

It wasn't until we were pulling into the driveway at the house that he spoke. "I'm not an angel, you're right. I've been with a lot of women. I hate that she upset you."

"She didn't upset me. I thought you might appreciate help to get her to go away. Was I wrong? Should I have left the two of you alone to make arrangements for later? If you want to see her after all, go ahead. Don't let me stop you. We're not anything to each other. I'm sorry if I read the situation wrong. I reacted without thinking. It won't happen again. In fact, why don't you drop me off at the house and you go find her? I'm sure she'll forgive you for blowing her off. Tell her it was a joke and I'm your sister or something."

He slammed the brakes, causing me to jerk in the seatbelt. I gaped at him in surprise as he shut off the car, threw open his door and slammed it before marching around the car to open mine. He unlatched my belt, and then I was hoisted out of the car and thrown over his shoulder. I cried out in shock. A hand landing on my ass made me cry out louder. He was stomping to the front door.

"Gabriel, what in the hell are you doing? Put me down," I shouted. I squirmed to get free, but it didn't help.

His arm was like a steel band across my thighs. He unlocked the door and marched inside without saying a word. He slammed the door and locked it before entering his alarm code. I thought he'd set me down then, but no, he didn't. Instead, he kept going. He took me up the stairs to the bedroom I'd slept in last night. He dropped me onto the bed. I bounced as I stared at him stunned. His face was dark.

"Why are you—"

I didn't get to finish asking him why he was so pissed off. Like a flash, he was on the bed, straddling me. He pushed me flat and took my hands in his and pinned them to the bed. He leaned down until we were almost nose to nose.

"I think it's time you and I had a talk," he growled.

"A talk? About what?"

"About you and me."

"What about you and me? I don't understand. Why're you so pissed? I said I was sorry about mucking things up for you with her. You can explain it to her. I doubt she's going to stay mad at you."

"That right there is why I'm mad. That you'd think for a fucking instant I'd leave you here alone to go see her. I told you, she means nothing to me. She's just some woman I had sex with in the past."

"So? You can have sex with her again. I don't need a babysitter. Are you afraid I'll run if you leave me here alone? Will it help if I give you my word that I won't?"

"Say one more word about me going to be with her and I'll spank your ass until you can't sit. I don't want to see her or fuck her. There isn't another woman in this town who I want to touch. The only woman I want to touch and be inside of is the one who is currently driving me crazy and making me want to spank her ass."

I gasped as his implication sank in.

"Yeah, now she's starting to get it. Do you know how much I've thought about you over the past month? How many nights I've lain in a lonely bed, dreaming of you and what I wanted to do to you? How I'd make love to you until we both were more than sated?"

Instantly, my nipples hardened and my pussy grew wet. Images of what I'd dreamed about came to mind. Surely, I was hearing him wrong. Or was this how he seduced so many women into his bed? With talk of how much he thought about them?

The idea he'd been lonely in his bed made me snort. "Yeah. I'll bet you were lying in your lonely bed. Can someone be lonely when someone else is with them? I don't believe you were pining away with lust for me and not getting laid, Gabriel. If this is your seduction technique, keep it for the other women. I'm not stupid."

I was beginning to get angry that he was doing this to me. He might only see me as a conquest, but I saw him as more. It hurt to know we were so different. If I was a different person, I might just be tempted to give in to my own desires and sleep with him. His answer was his mouth landing on mine and him kissing me again. I tried to fight it, but I couldn't.

Gabe: Chapter 6

As I took her mouth, I tried to calm myself. I didn't want to hurt her, but I was pissed. Her talk about me wanting to leave her to go to Constance to have sex and then saying my lines wouldn't work on her made me angry. As well as her saying she didn't believe I hadn't been with any women over the past month. A month that I had burned for her.

I knew I shouldn't cross this line. I was in the middle of an assignment. Things were dangerous as hell. I could get killed. Her insistence that she could help me terrified me. All I could think of was her getting hurt. However, on the flip side, the thought of letting her go somewhere and not being able to see her or make sure she was safe, made me wild too.

As our mouths mated, my cock grew hard as a spike. I'd been fighting it since last night. Having her delicious, sexy body pinned underneath mine and us being on a bed only made it worse. There was nothing I wanted more than to strip her bare, feast on her body then take her over and over. I wanted her to scream my name. To crave me like I craved her. I wanted to feel her pussy snug around my cock as I sank into her again and again. Everything in me told me, if I gave into my desire for her, she'd be the last woman I'd ever want.

How could this be happening? I never saw myself settling down. I didn't see a family in my future. Or I hadn't until I laid eyes on this Italian beauty. Now, that's all I could think about. I pictured her at my side, carrying my children. Us having what Sean and Cassidy, and Mark and Sloan had. What so many of our friends had. Why now? God, why bring her to me now, when it was so damn dangerous?

Getting lost in our kiss, I let all of those thoughts float away. I let myself feel. The taste of her and the feel of her lips under mine was perfect. If we didn't need to rest to catch our breaths, I might never have stopped.

As I rose to gaze down at her, I took in the sight before me. Her face was flushed. Her chest was rising rapidly, pushing her luscious breasts against the fabric of her shirt. She was panting. Her tongue snaked out to wet her lips. I wanted to nibble on it. Her eyes were giving me a confusion mixed with shocked look. I knew that I'd have to explain, which meant talking about feelings. Something a man like me rarely, if ever, did. I'd been raised not to talk about them. Well, actually to try and not have them to be honest.

"Why did you kiss me?" she whispered.

"Why do you think? Because I can't resist not doing it any longer. I've been fighting not to, but that kiss at the diner did it. I had to taste you again, *bellissima.* I wasn't lying when I told you I've been thinking of you for a month. Nor was it a lie that I haven't been with a woman. I may lie as part of an assignment, but not about this."

"Gabriel, this is crazy. We don't know each other. I just found out that what I thought I knew about you is a lie. You're playing a part. How can I trust you're who you say you are and that what you say is the truth?"

"I know. I want you to believe me, but I understand why you can't. All I can do is ask you to give me a chance to prove I'm not lying. This whole situation is the worst time for this, I know, but we don't seem to have a choice."

I eased back then off her, although I really wanted to stay pressed against her. I lay down beside her on the bed. She rolled onto her side so she could continue to see my face.

"God, I want to say yes so badly. If you knew me, you'd know how insane that is. I'm not like this. I'm not some woman who throws herself at a man. Honestly, I don't trust men. I've had too many let me down in my life, starting with my father and cousins. Most men I've met are like Santo and his goons. The rest have never interested me. However, one thing I do know is this. If we are to get to know each other, it can't be sometime down the road after you've taken down the Greco family. It can't. I can help you. Having you by my side will keep me safe. Please, let me do this," she pleaded.

I groaned and closed my eyes. "You're not playing fair, Gemma. It would be dangerous for you to return home. Santo might back off because he's afraid of blowing the deal with the Rizzos, but then again, he might not. I wouldn't be able to be with you every minute of the day. I'd worry and that could get us killed."

"Don't you have anyone helping you? If you sent me elsewhere, would I be there alone, or would someone be with me to protect me?"

"I don't have anyone in town with me. I do have help. If I send you away, I have people who'll protect you and watch over you for me."

"Could one of them come to Toms River instead and be my so-called bodyguard there? Would it be unusual for a man like you to leave the woman he's involved with without some kind of protection?"

What she was saying did make sense. There was no way any of the Mafia men I knew would ever leave their women or children without guards. They weren't allowed out of the house without one. As much as I wanted to say no, the pull to keep her with me, so we could see where a relationship would go, was growing.

Fuck! I now knew how Mark had felt when Sloan had insisted on going undercover with him into the MC. He hadn't wanted to take her, but she was a great help. His reputation as Undertaker had protected her. Could I get the Rizzos to increase mine enough to protect Gemma? They knew the real me and knew I'd torture and kill anyone who took something or someone of mine. I had the feeling if I told her no, she'd find a way to come back to town on her own.

We lay there, not saying anything for a long time as I worked through the arguments in my head. Eventually, I gave up and opened my eyes. I grasped her waist and tugged her against me. "If we do this, you have to swear to me, you will do everything I tell you to do. If I tell you at some point it's gotten too dangerous for you to stay in Toms River, then you'll leave with my people without a fight. If I tell you to stay home, you will. You'll go nowhere without me or the person I bring in as your bodyguard. You'll do whatever your guard says. I don't want to do this, *piccola*, but I can't give up the chance for us to get to know each other. I need that. You need that. We owe it to ourselves to find out if this can be what I think it is."

"And what do you think this is, Gabriel?"

"The beginning of the rest of our lives together. I've watched two of my best friends and many other friends go down this road. I'm acting like them, which I never thought I'd do."

"Really, you think we're going to be together forever? Wow, I thought I was the only one wishing for that. I'm scared, I'll admit. Scared of being hurt and left to pick up the pieces if this doesn't work or you're lying. I need you to know, if things don't work out because of natural causes, that's one thing, but if this is a lie to get me into bed, I'll cut your balls off when I leave."

I heard the steel and determination in her voice, and the expression on her face told me she wasn't kidding. She'd do her damndest to cut my balls off. I chuckled. "I believe you and I like my balls too much to ever risk them like that. Okay, if we're going to do this, we need to get a move on. We can't stay away from Toms River for long, or Santo will get suspicious. We'll have to come up with a story as to why you left and didn't stay to talk to him. I need to contact my people, so I can get a bodyguard for you."

"Okay, let's do it. Can you tell me more about the group you work with? I'd like to know more about the real you."

"I'll tell you what I can about the group, but I don't want you to know too much. It's for your protection. As for me, yes, we'll talk. I don't want to hit you with everything at once. It takes people months, if not years, to learn about each other. We have time."

As I told her that, I prayed it would be enough. There were things I would have to tell her if she was really my forever woman. Things only a few people knew. It might change how she felt about me. I wanted to make sure before we had that conversation, that I had her tied to me so securely, she'd never think of leaving me. I might tell her I thought she was my forever, but deep down, I already knew she was. God help us if I lost her. I'd tear the world to pieces if I did.

"Then let's get started," she said, as she went to sit up.

I held her down. "One more kiss to hold me over."

She moved closer and this time, she kissed me. It was just as amazing as the other times. I had to fight myself to let her move away. It was going to be hell keeping my desire for her under wraps, but I would. She had to be ready to come to me fully before we took that final step.

I was hard and aching as we parted. I let her get up off the bed first. When I got up, her gaze settled on my erection that was tenting my pants. She blushed and looked away. I chuckled. It seemed my woman was rather innocent. I wondered how innocent. How much would I be able to corrupt her? I couldn't wait to find out.

First thing to do was give her some background on the Dark Patriots. I wouldn't name them by name, but I'd explain who we were and what kind of work we did. I led her downstairs. It was too tempting to stay in the bedroom. After getting us something to drink, we sat down.

"Let me start by telling you more about my organization. It was started several years ago by myself and three other guys who I served with in the military and became best friends with. When we got out, we decided to form a company. One that would not only work with private companies but who would work as a government contractor if the need was there. It has grown bigger than we ever imagined since we started."

"Is government work your main work? Why would the government choose to use you rather than do it themselves? They have resources most people can only imagine, I would think. What did you do in the military?"

"At times, the government is our biggest employer, but that fluctuates. We help companies with things like their cybersecurity, physical security, and investigate things such as espionage or embezzlement. There's a whole host of things we do. We have a lot of employees with diverse backgrounds. Some of them have served in the military as well. As for why the government would use us, sometimes it's better to have someone else who's neutral to investigate things. Other times, it may be sensitive and they don't want it to be known they were involved. I can't really give you more details than that. I served in the Navy. I was a Navy SEAL."

"Wow, okay, that had to be intense. Your three friends, can I ask their names? Will I meet them?"

"It was intense. I had good and bad experiences while I was in the Navy. It did help me to know what kind of work I wanted to do when I got out. My three friends are Mark, Sean, and Griffin. And yes, you'll meet them, but probably not until after this assignment is over. Sean and Mark are married and each have a kid. Griffin is single. We're not based in New Jersey, but we are on the East Coast."

"I understand why you can't give me too much. You're protecting them. I hope as you feel better about me not betraying you or them, you'll tell me more. The same goes for more personal stuff about you. Can I ask, do you have any siblings?"

"*Piccola*, it's not because I don't trust you. I don't want to give you too much information because the more you know the more at risk you'll be. I want you to know everything and you will, I promise. As for siblings, I have a younger sister, but we don't speak. I have numerous cousins, but again, we don't see or talk to each other. There's a reason that I'll tell you one day." I knew I wasn't giving her much. I hoped she wouldn't get offended and want to stop before we even began.

"Well, you know as much about me as I do you. We'll take our time learning more. Maybe we should move on to doing something else," she finally said.

She was right. I needed to get someone here to be her bodyguard. That was a must. No way could I risk taking her back to Toms River without someone. Santo would be livid when he realized I'd claimed her right under his nose. My hope was that he'd be so focused on getting back at me for it, he'd leave her alone.

"We should do that. The priority is getting someone to come be your bodyguard. I need to speak to my team first and explain what's going on. I don't want to put them on the spot. Would you mind if I spoke to them alone first, then I'll have you come in to speak to them?"

I could tell my request upset her, but she didn't voice an objection. She stood up. "Why don't I go upstairs and read? Or would you prefer I leave the house?"

"No, stay in the house. That's perfect. I'm sorry, this seems like overkill, but it's for a reason." I grasped her hand and squeezed it. She gave me a tiny smile. I let go and watched her leave the room. As soon as I heard her bedroom door close, I got out my phone.

It was one that was scrambled and couldn't be eavesdropped on. Everything said was encrypted, including the texts. After they were sent, they were erased. Checking the time, I knew the guys would still be at the office. I rang Margie. When she answered, I told her what I needed.

"Hello, Margie. I hope you're surviving without me. I need to talk to the three stooges. Can you round them up and get them online with me? It's rather urgent." We all loved to tease Margie, especially if we could get a rise out of her husband, Chuck. He had been our main armorer since right after we began the company. They had been a major find for us.

"I'm trying my hardest, but you know how it is. I'll get them right away. Give me a few minutes then I'll call you back, Mr. Pagett."

"Thank you, Margie, and for the millionth time, it's Gabe."

"Yes, sir, Mr. Pagett. I'll call you right back," she responded primly before hanging up. I couldn't help but laugh. No matter how many times we told her to call us by our first names, she refused to do it. Chuck called us by our first names, but she insisted it was disrespectful to do so. Maybe if we were lucky, by the time she was with us thirty years, she'd give in. If she did, I'd probably have a heart attack.

While I waited, I paced and tried to think of the logistics of bringing Gemma back with me. It was a no-brainer that she wouldn't be able to stay by herself. I'd done enough snooping to know she lived by herself in a tiny studio not far from the restaurant. Her father lived in the house she grew up in. His two nephews lived with him. It wasn't unusual in many Italian families for grown children to remain at home until they married. Gemma living on her own was unusual. Girls were much more sheltered than guys.

It meant that I either move in with her or we find someplace together. Staying at her place wouldn't solve the issue of where her guard would sleep. I didn't want him lodged in a separate hotel room or location, so I guessed that solved it. I needed a place for the three of us.

I was online, searching for nearby rentals when my phone rang. I saw it was work. I answered it immediately. Instead of hearing Margie's sweet voice, I heard Sean's, then in the background I could hear Mark and Griffin.

"What the hell is going on? Your tracker shows you're in Mahwah. Do you need an extraction? Why the hell didn't you call us sooner or push the emergency alert?" he barked.

"Well, good afternoon to you too. No, I don't need an extraction. I had to come up here for a day or two. I do need help with something."

"With what?" Mark asked.

I bet they were in one of their offices crowded around the desk. Sometimes we did this kind of call on video conference, but I wasn't suggesting it this time. I expect they'd insist once I told them what I needed.

"I need you to send me someone who can be a bodyguard. I need them ASAP, as in by tomorrow."

"What the fuck is going on, Gabe? You said you don't need to be extracted, but you need a bodyguard? It doesn't make sense. What's wrong?" Griffin asked gruffly.

"I've gained a partner here. Someone who knows the ins-and-outs of the Greco holdings and everyone who's involved. I want someone to be with her at all times when I can't. She's going to be in danger."

"Son of a bitch. Don't tell us, you picked up a bed partner, and she's telling you shit during pillow talk," Sean grumbled.

I wouldn't lie. In the past, if it helped, I'd been with women who supplied intel. It wasn't unusual for me to find a bed partner while I was on a longer assignment. Their assumption was sound, but it pissed me off.

"No, I'm not banging some chick for information. She's not sharing my bed at all, yet. It's not like that. Goddamn it, I can't do this if she's not protected."

"Whoa, calm down. Start at the beginning. Who's this woman and why her? Surely, you can get the information in other ways. You've never asked for us to protect someone helping you out," Griffin said diplomatically. He was the one most likely to try and keep the peace out of the four of us.

"Her name is Gemma Marra. Her family is one of many who launders money for the Grecos. She knows all the players well. Most of them hang out in her family's restaurant, Mia Bella Rosa. She wants to see them gone as much as we do."

"How can you trust her, Gabe? You don't know her. She could be working for them," Sean protested.

"She's not. I need protection for her. Things are

going to get really hot around here."

"You don't know that she's trustworthy. Why would you be so worried about her? If she's not advertising she's working with you, then how would they know?" Mark asked.

"She's going to be a target because Santo Vitale wants her and has come to the end of his patience in taking no for an answer. When I take her back to Toms River and he finds out she's living with me, he's going to lose his shit. I want her to be safe. The man is a killer and rapist. I can't be worried about her when I'm not with her."

"Why the hell would she need to move in with you?" Sean asked.

"That's what usually happens when you find the woman you want to claim, isn't it? You move her in. I know Sean was slow as hell, but Mark didn't waste any time with Sloan." I dropped the bomb on them.

There was absolute silence for several seconds, then they all began to yell and speak at the same time. I held the phone away from my ear. Finally, they started to quiet down. Griffin was the one to pose the question I knew they all had.

"She's the woman you want to claim? Like in a girlfriend way or the more serious old lady way of our biker friends and our brother, Mark?"

"As in the biker way."

"Jesus Christ, I never saw this coming. Gabe, you always told us you never intended to have a woman or a family. Has the second thing changed too?" Mark asked incredulously.

"Yes, I've pictured what it would be like to have a baby with her. It's a long way off right now. She's cautious of me. She wants to believe I'm telling her the truth about bringing down the Grecos, but she's wary. Her family has been under their thumb since she was a small child."

"What did you tell her about us and this assignment? What does she know about you?" Sean asked gruffly.

"She knows I co-own a company with my three best friends and that we were in the SEALs together. She knows I'm working undercover and the Rizzo family is helping us due to a debt they owe me. She doesn't know about my background yet. I'm saving that. Other than your first names, she doesn't know your last names, our company's name or where we're located. It's not that I don't trust her. I don't want to make her a bigger target and she's leery of committing to me. We're taking this in steps."

"Which means you haven't gotten her into bed. You must be losing your touch," Mark teased.

"No, I've tried to stay away. I'm not going to ruin this by rushing her. Can you find me someone?"

"I don't see why not. Let us work on it. We'll do our best to have them there tomorrow. Do you want them to come to Mahwah or Toms River? Can we meet her?" Sean almost pleaded the last. I knew they'd be curious to see and talk to her as soon as I told them the real deal.

"They can meet us in Toms River. Which reminds me, I'll need a place to rent. A hotel won't do. Her place isn't big enough for all three of us. As for meeting her, if you promise not to scare her off, I can call you back in a couple minutes and we can do a video chat."

"Give us ten minutes, so we can get Sloan or Cassidy working on the bodyguard situation. Hopefully, we might even know who we can send by the time we get done interrogating, I mean talking to your woman," Mark said with laughter in his voice. If he could've seen me, I'd have flipped him off.

"Bastards. I mean it, be nice. Okay, ten minutes, then I'll call back. Talk more then. Bye."

I heard them say bye before I hung up. Not wasting time, I went to find her. She was curled up on the bed with a book in her hand. I had no idea where that came from. She was staring off into space. When she noticed I had opened the door, she came bounding to her feet. "How did it go?"

"They're getting to work on it. They want to meet you and chat. I told them we'd call back in ten minutes, so we can video conference."

I walked over and hugged her close. Inhaling her scent made my body start to come alive. I ignored it.

"Gabriel, why would they want to meet and talk to me?"

I heard the nervousness in her tone. "Because I've never told them I was serious about a woman and planned to claim her before. They want to know the woman who brought me to my knees."

She laughed. "As if a woman could bring you to your knees. What silliness have you been telling them?"

"Only the truth. *Bellissima,* you can very easily bring me to my knees and destroy me. My life and happiness are in your hands. Be gentle with me."

As she gaped at me, I couldn't resist kissing her. A blaze was soon burning within me. I had to fight to back away. I distracted her by telling her we should go get set up. For the video call, I'd use my laptop. It had a much larger screen. As we prepared, I watched to see if her anxiety got worse. This would be a memorable call for the both of us.

Gemma: Chapter 7

Twenty-four hours later and I still couldn't believe the call I had yesterday with Gabriel's friends. I'd been so nervous, I felt nauseous. Seeing those hulking men appear on the screen hadn't soothed those nerves much. All of them had intimidating manners. They were like Gabriel. They could crush me with one hand. They had somber looks on their faces when the call started. In addition to them, there were two women with them. They were giving me more of a curious vibe. I felt a tiny bit better knowing I wasn't the only woman on the video call. None of them wasted time getting to the point after Gabriel introduced me to them and they each told me their names.

"Gabe tells us your family works for the Grecos. Why the hell should he or any of us trust you? What proof do you have that you're not just working for the enemy to get him killed? Let us warn you, if that's your game, anything happens to Gabe and we'll burn you and your whole fucking town to the ground to get revenge," Mark growled. He was the scariest. His hair was long and he looked rougher than the others. In his short sleeves, I could see his arms were covered in tattoos. Gabriel had some on his arms like the other men, but Mark was covered in them.

"Goddamn it, I'm not going to continue this call if all you guys want to do is intimidate her. I told you, she's

not the enemy. She's not going to betray me. Enough of your Undertaker persona," Gabriel shouted back. I could tell he was angry.

Undertaker? This man's nickname was Undertaker! Oh hell no, I wasn't going to do this. I bet they already had a hit out on me. I stood up.

"I'm sorry, but I'm not a threat to any of you. I can't prove it, only time can, however, I'm not going to sit here and be given the third degree either. I don't know any of you either. How do I know this isn't a trick to take over the Grecos' territory? Santo and his men are horrible, but there are worse people too. I'll leave you to talk to Gabriel." I turned away from the table. He tried to grab my arm, but I eluded him.

"Il tesoro, please, don't go. They'll stop or else I'll end this fucking call," he snapped, as he gave me a pleading look then glared at the screen. I hesitated.

"Gemma, please sit back down. Ignore Mark. He's rough around the edges, but it's only because he loves Gabe like we do. None of us want to see him get hurt. He's never been serious about a woman. Did he tell you that?" Cassidy asked sweetly. She, I felt, was approachable. Sloan appeared a bit more hardened, although she was smiling too.

"Alright, I'll dial it back, but she needs to tell us more about herself. Why is she so willing to help? Her family profits from the Greco family," Mark, or Undertaker as he'd forever be to me, asked a tad less gruffly.

Against my better judgment, I retook my seat. Gabriel pulled my chair to be right against his and hugged me close to him.

"Sure, I'll tell you what you want to know. As for me, there's not much to tell. I'm twenty-five. My family owns the Mia Bella Rosa restaurant in Toms River. It's true, I'm ashamed to say, that my family has been laundering money and paying protection to the Greco family for years. When I was little, the restaurant struggled and my parents along with my papà's twin brother were at risk of losing it. They couldn't get a bank loan, so they went to the Greco family. The family gave them the loan and then started to make them pay them a cut of the profits as well as launder their money. My family had no way out. I've been praying for years to find a way to get rid of them. I'd hoped when Matteo and his two sons went to prison that would be it, but it wasn't."

"Other than your dad, is there more of your immediate family involved with them?" Sean asked, as he leaned back in his chair and steepled his fingers together.

"I have two cousins, Emmet and Elijah. They're my uncle Salvatore's sons. When he died, they inherited half of the restaurant. My mother and theirs died when we were younger."

"Gabe mentioned that Santo Vitale has a thing for you. What's up with that? Tell us what you know about him," Griffin asked.

"I don't know a lot. He's kind of a mystery. He showed up out of nowhere three years ago. He didn't come in as a low-ranking goon either. He stepped right into the role of a capo, a boss, which was strange. No one knew if he had some other relationship with the Greco family

which made them place him at that level or what. From the start, he made it clear, anyone standing in his way would be dealt with harshly. There have been lots of beatings. A few people have gone missing. People found murdered. They walk around like they own the town and everyone in it. They use my family's restaurant as their private meeting place. They don't pay for anything. More than one person has whispered that Santo and some of his men have raped women in the area. No one will bring charges against them."

"And he wants you. How long has that been his intent and how have you held him off?" Undertaker asked with a frown.

"From the start, he flirted and was always asking when I'd go out with him. I always laughed it off like it was a joke or I ignored him. Most of his men are the same. They like to say stuff and sometimes touch women. It's been a long dance of cat and mouse. I knew one day he'd get tired of it and I'd be in trouble. I'd made up my mind to leave and never come back. I was just getting a little more money stashed away. However, last night, he informed me that he wanted to talk to me alone after the restaurant closed. I knew what that meant. I ran while they weren't paying attention. Somehow, Gabriel figured out what I was going to do, and he was waiting for me. He kidnapped me and brought me to this safe house."

"He kidnapped you!" Cassidy stated in surprise.

"Yes, he did. That's when he explained he was here to bring down the whole Greco network, not build an alliance like Santo and the other capos believe. I know just about everyone who works for them, pays them money or is being

used by them. I can help you get them all, but I need to be in Toms River to do it. Gabriel is afraid that Santo will target me if I go back."

"So, he's only pretending to be your man to protect you from Santo," Sloan added with a nod of her head.

"I am not. I'm a hundred percent serious about making Gemma mine. I don't want to use her, but she does have valuable insight. Taking her back as my woman will give her a layer of protection. I doubt he's dumb enough to potentially blow the deal with the Rizzos over her, but in case he is, I want someone with her twenty-four seven, hence the need for a bodyguard," Gabriel told them sternly.

"Do you realize that by doing this, you could get killed, Gemma? This isn't a game," Griffin informed me like I was stupid.

"I know it's not a game. My life has been in danger for years. That's not new. This is the only chance I see of getting people free of them. I know many of them might end up serving time. That can't be avoided, but it's better than being dead or a slave to them for the rest of their lives."

"Do you expect us to protect your family from prosecution when the time comes?" Undertaker asked.

"No! I'd never expect that. If that means I have to serve time too, since I knew about it, then so be it, just save my town. Overall, they're mostly really good people who're scared."

They didn't have anything to say to that remark. We stayed on for a few more minutes before they ended the call, promising to find a guard. Gabriel and I spent the rest of the night going over what to do when we got back home. I didn't sleep well. I kept reliving the call.

Here it was, late afternoon the next day, and we were on our way back. I was still dwelling on it, wondering if I was making a mistake. I didn't think his friends liked me very much. That would make things awkward if we did end up permanently together. I wouldn't interfere with his relationship with them. If they wanted to get together, I'd find someplace to go. I wouldn't make them tolerate my unwanted presence.

I was pleasantly surprised when we pulled into the driveway of a small house that his friends had found. I had no idea how they could rent it so fast, but they did. It was a small house which sat on a small cul-de-sac with seven other houses. It was at the end and backed up to an open area. I took in the neat lawn and the light blue paint and black shutters as we parked. There was a car already in the driveway. Gabriel helped me out of his car and led me to the front door. It opened as we got to it and there stood another handsome though intimidating man.

He was a couple of inches shorter than Gabriel. His arms were huge. They were so big, I didn't know how his sleeves kept from ripping at the seams. He was tanned and had short dark brown hair with reddish streaks in it. His eyes were green. Looking at him, I had no problem picturing him as a bodyguard. He shook hands with Gabriel and nodded at me as we entered the house. He shut and locked the door behind us.

"Looks like you two made good time. Come this way. I'll show you the living room and kitchen. Are there bags in the car for me to carry?" he asked as he led us into the room off to the left of the foyer. Gabriel gestured for me to sit on the couch then he sat beside me. The man sat across from us in a chair.

"Hold on a sec. First, let's get introductions out of the way. This is Gemma. She's the one you'll be guarding. I believe Sean and the others filled you in on what the situation here is."

The man nodded his head yes. "They did. Sorry, I get in the zone and forget sometimes I have to actually have manners. Don't tell my sister I was rude, or she'll kick my ass," he said with a grin. "I'm Beau. It's great to meet you, Gemma." He held out his hand. I leaned forward and took it. His grip was firm, but he didn't try to crush my hand. Thank goodness, or he would've broken all my fingers.

"Nice to meet you too, Beau. Who's your sister? So I know if I ever meet her. Is she a bodyguard like you?"

He laughed for a long minute while Gabriel chuckled until the other man got himself under control. "Well, Bryony is a dynamite badass, but she's not a bodyguard. She's an accountant. Actually, I have two people to worry about. If she wants, she'll *sic* her old man, Storm, on me. He's always looking for a reason to try and beat me down."

"Old man? Storm? Does he work with you guys?" I asked, wondering if Storm was like Undertaker, some kind of nickname or had his parents actually named him that.

Beau looked at Gabriel. Something passed

between them, some kind of communication. It was Gabriel who answered me. “Sean, Grif, Mark and I have a variety of friends. Some of them happen to be in motorcycle clubs. Storm is in one of those. That's his road name. Old man is the term used by the woman whose man is a member of the club. He calls her his old lady.”

“Is she his wife?”

“An old lady doesn't have to be, no, but in her case, yes, they're married. They have a two-and-a-half-year-old son, Tristan. He keeps us all on our toes,” Gabriel said with a smile.

“Oh, I see I have a lot to learn. Well, I promise not to tell Bryony of your faux pas as long as it doesn't happen again. Can I ask how you became part of Gabriel's company? Is that allowed? Were you in the military with him?”

“I did serve several years as a Marine. I got out just over two years ago. I wasn't fortunate to serve with Gabe and the others, although I did serve with Sloan, Mark's wife. It was because of Storm I found this job.”

“This assignment is probably going to bore you to death. I mean, besides working at the restaurant, I don't do much else. I take some meals to the elderly who can't get out and run some errands for them. Good news is I don't shop, so I won't be dragging you to a bunch of stores for hours. I tend to cook even when at home.”

“So you don't shop, you cook, help people, work your ass off, are beautiful and I bet you're smart too. Do you have a sister or can I steal you away from Gabe?” he asked with a smirk on his face. I could tell he had a sense of humor when he wasn't serious about his work.

"That's a one-way ticket to unemployment and a hospital stay that would last months, Beau. Remember that before you pour the charm on her. She's mine and no one is going to steal her away. And no, she has no sisters. She does have two male cousins, if you swing that way, although they're nothing like her," Gabriel told him with a smirk.

Beau burst out laughing and shook his head. "Sorry, I don't bat for that team. No offense to any who do, but I'm purely all into the ladies. Oh well, I guess I'll have to keep looking. Sean and the others filled me in at headquarters on what I'm to do. I think you'll find this place should suit us. We have a clear line of sight all around the perimeter. There's a decent security system. The open area next to us leads to a wooded one. I've stashed another car there in case we need it. I have trackers for her phone and car as well as anything else you want to apply one to. There are three bedrooms and two bathrooms. I've gone ahead and laid out some weapons. I'll show you where they are and I expect you'll want to add more."

His abrupt switch to work mode made my head whirl. I remained quiet and observed for the next hour as we were given the tour and shown where Beau had stashed weapons. We learned how to set the alarm system and they placed trackers in my purse, shoes, and car. The last they did when they went to bring in the few bags we had. I didn't know which room was mine, so I just dropped my bag in one. I could move it later if one of them wanted it. Back in the living room, they continued to talk.

"I wish we'd had time to ask Smoke for one of his trackers. They're way better than this. You and the guys should think about them, at least for the women. You never know," Beau said, as he relaxed and drank a beer with Gabriel. I stuck to soda.

"What kind of tracker?" I asked curiously.

"They have access to state-of-the-art stuff. Ones that can be injected under your skin. It can't be lost or taken off you. It's helped them numerous times when they've had trouble," Beau explained.

"That sounds like science fiction," I told him.

"It does. Smoke does crazy computer stuff, and he has access to things you can't believe. More than one club uses them. Not exactly what they were made for, but hey, if it helps protect women and children, who cares?"

"I'll mention that to the others. It's a good idea and we should have no trouble getting them too," Gabriel said.

Deciding they might need to talk about stuff they couldn't say in front of me, I stood up. "I think I'll go unpack and then take a bath if you don't mind. It's been a long day. When I get done, I'll check out the kitchen to see what we have to make for dinner."

"*Principessa,* take all the time you need. Relax. We can bring something in tonight, then tomorrow you give me the list of what you want and I'll get it for us. Also, we'll go by your place tomorrow to get more of your things. Did you check me out of the hotel?" he asked Beau.

"I did. I put your stuff in the first bedroom."

Nodding my head, I went to leave. Gabriel pulled me back and tugged on my hand until I bent down. He gave me a kiss. It wasn't one of his most passionate ones, but it still made my body tingle. "Have fun. Yell if you need anything," he told me with a smile after he let go.

"I will," I dazedly mumbled. He gave me a wink.

Going to the bedroom I chose, I got out a set of clean clothes and my bath stuff. The bathroom was in the hall, but it was nice and had a tub. Just what I needed. I closed the door and started the water as I stripped. I had so much to process. The hot water would help.

Gabe:

I was happy as hell that they were able to get Beau. Not that our other operatives weren't competent to act as a bodyguard, they were. But he was different. Maybe it's because he was the oldest of five brothers and a sister and he was always in protective mode. He was ultra protective of Bryony and his nephew. After what she went through—being taken by human traffickers almost four years ago—who could blame him. It was how she met Storm and his club, the Archangel's Warriors. Beau knew how truly dangerous the world could be for a woman. I knew he'd give his life if he had to, to protect Gemma.

"She seems really sweet and nice. How in the hell did you catch her, man? I never thought I'd see you settling for one woman. Or is this just for this assignment? Is she a cover?"

"No, she's not a damn cover. I'm dead serious about her. I plan on us being together long after this assignment is over. I have no idea how I got so lucky to have her return my interest, but I thank God she does. I don't need to tell you how damn vulnerable she is. Santo Vitale is the main *capo*. He's worse than the others and he has the tightest hold here. He wants Gemma. When he finds out I took her out from under his nose, he's going to be furious. My hope is he aims that fury at me and not her. However, in case I'm wrong and he's dumb enough to target her despite the alliance, I want her protected."

"Gabe, you have nothing to worry about. I'll protect her with my life. If I think things are going south and you're not available, I'll get her somewhere safe then come back and back you up. I know how important this is. Storm and Bryony had already told me what went down with the Grecos, Law, and Hawk."

"Excellent. Tomorrow, I plan to make a reappearance with her on my arm. You can hang in the background. I'll introduce you as a *soldato*, a soldier from the Rizzo family. I'll make sure to inform them they sent you to me. Expect them to bluster and try to intimidate you. You know, the usual hazing bullshit. Nothing you haven't experienced before. I expect I'll be working most of the day."

"Shouldn't you have your own bodyguard now too? If he's going to come after you for taking Gemma, it would be a good idea."

"Maybe, but we'll play it by ear. I don't want to tie up our resources if I don't have to."

"I have a suggestion if you're open to going outside the Dark Patriots for men to help. Why not use Sniper or Gunner from Dublin Falls? They both have military experience. They know how to keep their mouths shut and if the club isn't in need of them, it won't tie up Patriots' resources. I'll be honest, I'd feel better if you had someone on you too."

I mulled over what he suggested. Although I

wanted to say I could take care of myself, this had just gotten way more dangerous.

"Tell you what. I'll see how tomorrow goes and if it looks like he's going to come after me, I'll call Terror and see if he has someone, as well as asking Sean. If they don't, maybe Bull does over in Hunters Creek."

"Or you could ask Reaper. His club is closer still."

That was true. Our old SEAL comrade was the president of his own MC and he'd have guys too. Some served like he did. I'd keep it in mind. With this dealt with for the moment, we chatted and caught up on other stuff until Gemma rejoined us. From there, we spent a quiet evening at the house. Gemma cooked for us which was a treat. When it was time to retire, it killed me to leave her at the door of her room, but I wouldn't push her to share a bed with me, even if it was only to sleep.

As I drifted into an uneasy sleep after my shower, I wondered what tomorrow was going to be like. A part of me was going to enjoy seeing Santo's face when he realized Gemma was mine. There was a deep male satisfaction in that.

Gabe: Chapter 8

I could tell Gemma was extremely nervous about facing Santo today. I didn't blame her. I wasn't nervous, rather anticipating it. A part of me was hoping for a fight. Nothing would make me feel better, other than to kill the bastard, than to beat his ass.

We'd gone over the cover story of where she'd been for the last couple of days several times, which was close to the truth. I told her to let me tell him. I didn't need her to be making excuses to him. From now on, if he wanted to know anything about her, he had to ask me.

I thought it was telling that for those two days, I hadn't gotten a single text or call from Santo. I knew it was because he'd been running around trying to find Gemma. Otherwise, he would've been bombarding me with them like he'd done for the month I'd been here. He'd constantly wanted to meet up, talk, or hang out. I'd accommodated most of his requests, but not all. I had news for him, those days were well in the past. It was time for me to step up to be the leader in this game. I'd given him enough rope to hang himself with and to get him feeling like he was running the show. Time to reveal the real boss in this alliance.

Earlier, I'd sent him a text telling him to meet me

at Mia Bella Rosa. He'd replied saying he couldn't. I let him know it wasn't an option. I knew that had to piss him off. After sending it, Beau and I had driven Gemma to the restaurant. I thought about taking her to her studio apartment to get more of her stuff, but I figured they were watching it. We could do that later.

At the restaurant, I'd parked right at the back door and smuggled her inside. If he had his guys watching, I didn't want to give away the surprise that was awaiting him when he came. I was going to drop the news she was back and mine in one big swoop. Her father and cousins were there when we got inside. No surprise her father was, but the cousins were rarely around. The look of astonishment on their faces was comical. Her father practically ran over to her.

"Gemma Rosa Marra, where have you been? We've been calling and texting you for two days. Why didn't you answer? Better yet, why did you leave and not talk to Santo the other night? He's furious. He's been stalking us, our house and here. He doesn't believe we don't know where you are. I was afraid he was going to kill one of us."

"Yeah, way to be selfish, Gemma. Leaving us to clean up your mess. I see he got his friend, Gabe, to track your ass down and to put a man on you," Emmet said, as he nodded first at me then at Beau. I didn't give her a chance to respond.

"Gemma doesn't answer to any of you. She doesn't need to tell you where she's been. If you have questions, ask me," I ordered them.

All three of them took a step back at my tone and the look I gave them. It was clear that I wasn't going to take any shit off them.

"W-what right do you have to talk to us this way? Just because you work for Santo doesn't mean you can tell us what to do. We have a right to know where she's been. We're her family," Elijah stuttered.

"Your right as her family is over with. She's my responsibility now. If you were a real family, you wouldn't have let things get to the point they have."

"We didn't know she was going to take off and hide from Santo. I don't know what's wrong with her. She could have it so easy and so could we, if she'd stop playing games with him," Emmet added indignantly.

"She hasn't been playing a game, you *idiota*. She wants nothing to do with Santo or any of his men. I might be the minority around here, but no woman should be forced to be with a man she doesn't want to be with."

All I got was shocked looks and sputtering. After almost a minute of that, her father finally said something. "What does that mean exactly? You're Santo's partner. Does he know she's with you? Didn't you bring her here for him?"

"No, I didn't bring her here to give to him. I'll explain once he gets here. Until then, no one is to text or call him or any of his men to tell them she's back. If I find out you did, you won't like the consequences. Have I made myself clear?"

I casually pushed back the side of my jacket, so they could catch a glimpse of my gun. Beau did the same. I knew she probably was hating this, but I'd warned her it might get uncomfortable with her family and that we couldn't risk any of them knowing the truth. I didn't trust them to keep their mouths shut, especially her cousins. Something about them rubbed me the wrong way. She agreed to let me take the lead.

Leaving them to do whatever, I set up in the back so Beau and I could keep an eye on her. The restaurant was open and serving people, but we'd planned this so we'd arrive after the lunchtime rush and before the dinner rush. The fewer people in the line of fire when Santo went off the better. I had debated waiting until after it closed, but that was too late. We had other things to do.

I knew when we left, we'd be followed and they'd discover where we were staying. I hadn't planned to hide it. If I did, it would make it seem like I was afraid of him. I wasn't. Plus, as his partner, he should know where to find me, just like I knew where he lived.

Gemma tried to stay busy in the back and out of sight. The staff gave her curious looks, but none of them asked where she'd been. I couldn't be sure none of them wouldn't tell Santo she was here, but that was a chance I'd take. If he arrived early, so be it.

Ten minutes before two, I got an alert that told me they were here. Sean and our tech crew had tapped into the area cameras and had been monitoring them for this reason. I whispered to Beau and her,

"Showtime."

Her tension doubled. I rubbed her back and gave her a kiss. Once I felt her relax, I told her, "Everything is going to be alright. Just do what we planned. Let me do the talking. Stay close to me and Beau. Don't let them get between us and you. We'll keep you safe, *piccola*, I swear."

"I know. I'll try," she told me softly.

I gave Santo and his men time to enter and take a seat at their usual table. As soon as they were seated and demanding the waitstaff to bring them wine and bread, I came sauntering out of the back like I didn't have a care in the world and owned the place. Behind me came Beau and bringing up the rear was Gemma. Due to our height, they couldn't see her at first. Santo gave me a slightly interested look when he saw me coming from the kitchen, but nothing too surprised. His eyes flickered a bit when he spotted Beau. It was when we moved and he caught sight of her that he reacted.

He came bounding to his feet. His chair fell over on the floor, making a loud crashing noise. The other customers gasped, and I saw a few start to inch their way toward the counter. They were trying to get out of here before all hell broke loose. Smart people.

"Gemma, where the fuck have you been? I've been looking all over for you. Since when don't you answer your texts or calls? I told you the other night that I wanted to talk to you after work. Why did you leave? Come here, right now." He barked at her like he was talking to a dog he was trying to bring to heel. I took a deep breath to keep from planting my fist in his face.

I held up my hand. He gave me a puzzled look but went silent. Gemma stayed where she was and didn't answer him, like we rehearsed.

"If you have questions for Gemma, you can direct those to me. Oh and by the way, going forward, she'll answer texts and calls with people I say it's okay for her to communicate with," I growled, as I gave him my best narrow-eyed look. I watched him stiffen and an expression of disbelief moved across his face.

"What the fuck? Who're you to talk to me like this, Gabe? You're here as an ally, not as my boss. This has nothing to do with you. This is between me and my woman."

As he ranted, I was careful to keep his men in my peripheral vision. I didn't trust them. Beau had been given instructions that they were his priority. I would keep my eyes on Santo. Although, it didn't hurt to be aware of everything going on around you. That kept you alive. For example, more customers were quietly getting up to leave after paying. Her father and cousins had come from the back and were huddled over in a corner, watching us. Her father was wringing his hands and her cousins appeared to be apprehensive.

"No, you're the one who's mistaken, Santo. Yes, I came to form an alliance between the Grecos and the Rizzos, however, we have never been equals. My family is the larger and more powerful family. Any agreement will have you reporting to us, not the other way around. If you've gotten the impression it's otherwise, that's your mistake. Now that we've ironed out most of the preliminary negotiating, it's time to get serious. As for Gemma being your business and woman, you're wrong again."

I took a step closer to him. I pulled out a chair and sat down at a table near his. I gave a chin lift to Beau. He took up position behind me. I waved Gemma over and pulled out a chair for her. One that was right up against mine. As she sat down, I put my left arm around her shoulder and teased her neck with my thumb. Santo's mouth dropped open.

"Gemma is totally my business. You demanded to know where she's been, why she hasn't answered you and why she left. I usually don't bother to explain myself to underlings, but this one time, I'll make an exception. She's been with me. I whisked her away the other night as a surprise. I wanted us to have some time alone, just the two of us. A lovers' retreat if you will. She didn't know about it, so she couldn't tell you she wasn't going to make the meeting you insisted on. In order to give us quality time together, I told her not to answer anyone's calls or texts." I gave her a heated look. She smiled at me. Her hand was resting on my thigh. Something Santo didn't fail to notice.

"A lovers' retreat! Since when are the two of you lovers? You can't be. She's mine. I claimed her first," he shouted.

"No, you didn't. You didn't ask her to be yours and she didn't say yes. That means she wasn't. I'm not sure how things are around here, but where I come from, we ask our women to be with us. We don't dictate.

It makes for a much more pleasurable and long-term relationship when your woman is willing. I've asked her to be mine and she's agreed, end of story. There'll be no more remarks, touches, or anything else I deem inappropriate toward her from you or anyone else. If there are, the person or persons involved won't like what happens. She's mine and I take very good care of what's mine." I let him see the killer in me.

Up until this point, I'd been affable and hadn't flexed my muscles. I wanted to lull him into thinking he was the bigger and badder wolf. He wasn't. He had no idea how bad I could get. If I didn't have plans for this asshole, I would've already killed him.

His face was almost purple. He was so mad and trying not to say anything. I waited for him to blow. It didn't take long. See, that right there was why he'd never make a good *capo*. He couldn't contain his emotions. There were many times you needed to do that, even if you were furious.

"This isn't fucking happening! You can't come in here and take over my territory. I don't care if your family is bigger than mine. I've been here for three years and everyone knows, I claimed Gemma as mine right after I got here," he yelled.

I came up out of my chair like a shot. He didn't expect it and neither did his goons. In a flash, I had his throat in my hand. I squeezed tightly, causing him to gasp for air. I shook him.

"Listen, you little upstart fucker. I don't take orders from the likes of you. You may think you're a big deal but you're not. In three years, Gemma hasn't been out on a date with you, shared your bed, home or anything else. That makes her a free woman. She's in my house and my bed now. That makes her mine. I won't say it again. She's mine and you better stay the fuck away from her or else."

I let him gasp for several long moments before letting go. He collapsed into a different chair at his table. His guys were glancing around as if they had no idea what to do. A few had come to their feet, but they quickly sat back down. Acting as if we hadn't almost come to blows, I got down to business.

"I've brought in an associate of mine. He'll be around for the remainder of this deal. His name is Beau. If you have questions and I'm not around, ask him. He'll either tell you what to do or contact me. No more texts and calls at all hours of the day and night. I'll be busy," I said, as I glanced at Gemma and smiled. The fury rolling off Santo was palpable.

"Also, there's a possibility I might be bringing in another associate. The Rizzos want to ensure nothing interferes with us bringing this new business relationship to fruition. They don't take kindly to failure or people not doing their jobs. They're anxious to get this started. They've given me a deadline. I need to know all your people, distribution lines and points for the businesses and the schedules. They expect everything to be up and fully running to both our benefits within the month."

"A month! That's not going to be possible. We still have to talk more about cuts and other stuff," Santo objected.

“We've already talked about those. Your request for a bigger cut has been denied. With the increase in business they're bringing, your cut of that is more than adequate compensation. Besides, they're the ones using the most resources. You have some people and suppliers. They have three to four times as many. If you continue to argue, the deal is off and they'll take it elsewhere.”

I was playing hardball with them now. They'd hate it. However, this was exactly what they should expect when dealing with a *mafiosa*, especially a bigger one. They were the underdog and would be kept in their place.

“What do the Rizzos think of your…woman? Has she met any of them yet?” Santo asked sharply.

“They haven't had the chance to meet her yet, but they're happy that I found someone. I've been encouraged for years to settle down and produce children. It'll only strengthen the family. Gemma is the perfect woman for that.”

When I came here, I had been introduced as a cousin to the Rizzos. I wasn't just a *capo* or *soldato*. I'd told them that I wasn't one of the main cousins which everyone knew, but a distant favored one. I would be expected to marry and add to the strength of the family.

“Settle down? So, you're planning to marry her?” Emmet asked out of nowhere.

“I do. Her ring is being sized otherwise she could

show it to you. It should be ready in a couple of days. The wedding will be soon. I'm anxious to start our family."

I'd warned her earlier that I might say things that would surprise her and that she needed not to react like it was news. She was doing a great job of looking serene and into me. She was leaning into my touch and giving me loving glances.

"Shouldn't an important man like you in the Rizzo family marry someone who brings more to the family? Gemma has no new alliances, property, or money to bring," Santo said. I could hear the snideness in his voice.

"She brings Italian blood, impeccable breeding, and a tie to the Grecos, even if it's tiny. She doesn't need to bring anything else. I have more than enough of the rest to satisfy me and the family."

There was a long pause before he said anything else. "Where do you want to begin?" Santo asked. I could tell that asking that question stuck in his throat and made him want to puke. I gave him a condescending smile.

I was pouring it on a little thick, but not enough to overplay my hand. I knew a lot of *mafiosa* who acted like this. I wanted to cement his attention and animosity on me, not Gemma.

"I'll contact you tomorrow for us to meet and go over where I want to start. As for today, I have plans with my *fidanzata*. We have to get her moved the rest of the way into the house with me." I knew calling her my fiancée only made him madder.

As he sat there fuming and plotting against me, I watched his men. They were exchanging worried glances. They weren't their usual confident, cocky selves. They'd seen that Santo wasn't the big dog they all had thought he was. From what we had found out, he'd been throwing his weight around since the moment he showed up here. We were still trying to find out how he'd walked into such an elevated position when he had been unknown. He had to have some kind of tie to the Grecos.

Standing up, I helped Gemma to her feet. "Come on, *amore mio*, let's go get you settled in our temporary home. I can't wait for you to see our real home. Just think, within a month, you'll be there. I'll see you later," I offhandedly told Santo.

"I can't wait either, *il tesoro*. I already have so many ideas for the house based on the pictures you showed me," she said sweetly.

I laughed. "Ah, I see it's going to cost me money. Oh well, change whatever you want. As long as you're comfortable and happy, so will I."

She raised up on her toes and gave me a kiss. It was more than a peck on the mouth. I gave it my all. I made sure it was passionate, and we left them in no doubt we were into each other and our attraction was very real. When I reluctantly broke it off, I covertly looked at Santo. The fury on his face would've intimidated a lesser man. Too bad for him, I'd known a lot scarier men than him during my lifetime.

Without saying another word, I walked toward the back again. Beau brought up the rear. When we arrived earlier, he'd left my car in the back, right underneath a camera. The Patriots' tech guys had been monitoring it to make sure it wasn't tampered with. It was unlikely this soon, but you could never be too careful. From now on, we'd park it in the garage at the house and try to have eyes on it at all times when not there. It would be checked thoroughly before we would re-enter it. After seeing his reaction to my news, I was going to ask for an extra person. It wouldn't do any of us any good if I got killed.

Gemma's family followed us out to the car. "Gemma, this is crazy. You can't do this. Santo isn't a man to mess with," her father whined.

I swung around to get in his face. He shrank away from me. I knew he was her father, but I had zero respect for the man after the way he hadn't tried to protect his daughter.

"I'm the man you should be worrying about, not Santo. It's done. She's mine and that's the end of it. If you'd like to remain a part of her life even a little, I suggest you get that through your head. We have things to do, so we'll see you when we see you."

"Goodbye, *Papà*," she told him wistfully.

I opened her door and helped her inside while Beau went to open mine. His eyes were constantly scanning the surrounding area, just as mine were. Once we were safely in the car, I saw Gemma's body relax. Beau was in the front driving, acting as our chauffeur.

She laid her head on my shoulder.

"Are you okay, *Principessa*? I know that was hard," I said, as I rubbed up and down her arm and kissed the top of her head.

She nodded. "Yes, it was. I hated to treat my family like that, but they've done nothing to deserve my respect. I detest that. My mamma must be looking down from heaven and crying at what we've become. I shouldn't be surprised at Emmet and Elijah. We've never been really close, but my *papà* and I were. I was his little girl growing up."

"I'm sorry. I hate that for you too. But just think, you're gaining a whole family with my friends."

She groaned. "Yeah, that's what everyone needs. A guy called Undertaker, who looks like he wants to kill you with one hand, as your family. I'm waiting for him to take a hit out on me."

"He'd never do that. Mark is scary, I agree. He spent a long time undercover and it changed him. He became more hardened, however, underneath those tats and his scowl is a very loving guy."

"What did he do undercover? Or should I not ask?"

"He spent five years pretending to be dead so he could infiltrate and take down one of the biggest motorcycle clubs in the nation."

She gasped and sat up. "Really? Wow, no wonder he looks like that. I don't think I'd survive a day in one of those let alone five years."

"They weren't your average club. They were into so much ugly stuff it was insane. Taking them off the streets made the world a much better place. He's still getting used to not having to be a badass twenty-four seven. Just know, he'll defend you with his life. Family and friends mean everything to him and the others."

"I'll try to get to know him, I promise. Are we going to my place now?"

"Yes. We need to get you packed and over to the house. I'm going to call in another guard. I don't want to take any chances. Santo will kill me if he can get away with it without anyone knowing it was him. He's furious that you're with me."

"I could tell. I thought at one point his head was going to explode, he turned so red," she said.

I shrugged. In no time, we were at her place. Beau set himself up so he could guard outside the apartment while still keeping an eye on the car. It took us well over an hour to figure out what she wanted to take and what could wait. I helped her to pack it in suitcases and bags. As soon as they were loaded into the car, we headed back to the rental. I had calls to make. I needed to get our second guard here ASAP.

Gemma: Chapter 9

The past two days had passed with me feeling like I was walking on glass. It wasn't because of anything Gabriel or Beau were doing or saying. It was because of my worry about what Santo was plotting. I knew the man didn't like to lose. He would want revenge.

After our meeting with Santo at the restaurant and moving my stuff to the rental house, Gabriel had made calls to his people. He asked them to get him a second guard. He rambled off the names of several groups that meant nothing to me. They were weird names. Sean, Undertaker, and Griffin had assured him they'd have someone here today to help. We were waiting for that person to arrive.

I'd tried to keep busy at the restaurant when I could. Emmet, Elijah, and *Papà* were still giving me crazy looks. They didn't say anything because either Gabriel or Beau was always with me. They didn't want to upset them.

Gabriel had been having meetings with Santo and the other men. He didn't give me a lot of details. The only thing he did say was that they were now telling him more about the running of the Greco territory. At the house, at night, I was making lists for him of the people I knew were involved as well as any places or information I'd heard about their business. He was checking out what was true versus rumors.

We were all still mystified why no one appeared to know that the Grecos had been killed in prison. Did they really not know? Or was someone, likely Santo, hiding it for a reason? Gabriel and his contacts were somehow keeping the news out of the media. I knew the murder of three Mafia bosses would usually make the news. Or maybe the world had forgotten about them after this long.

At the moment, we were at Mia Bella Rosa. I was helping out since our hostess had called off. No matter what was happening in my life, I still felt I had a duty to help the family business. It was more to help our employees than anything. My *papà* couldn't serve or play hostess. He got distracted with other things or dropped plates. We'd ruled that out a long time ago. My cousins didn't think it was their job, so they refused to do it. They always expected me to pick up the slack. I could tell it pissed Gabriel off. He had held his tongue so far, but I didn't know how much longer it would last.

I was coming back to the front, after seating a couple at their table, when the door opened and in came Santo and his entourage. I glanced around and felt relief when I saw both Gabriel and Beau had seen them. Gabriel was on his phone talking to someone. He nodded his head at me to let me know he saw them. I had no idea who he was talking to or about what. Beau shifted so he was closer to me, but still far enough back, not to seem to be hovering.

"Afternoon, your usual table?" I asked calmly as

I grabbed a handful of menus and started walking toward their spot.

Santo fell into step beside me. "Gemma, I need to talk to you. Tell me where we can meet in private," Santo hissed softly. He was being careful not to touch me or crowd me. I knew he was worried about what Gabriel would do.

"I'm sorry, but that's not possible. Besides, we have nothing to talk about. I'll have someone come take your drink orders in a minute. Enjoy," I said as I laid down the menus. I was turning away to walk back to the hostess stand when Santo reached out and grabbed my elbow. It stopped me in my tracks.

"Don't walk away from me," he hissed.

Before I could respond, Beau and Gabriel were there. The expression on Gabriel's face was scary. He glowered at Santo. "I suggest if you want to keep your fucking hand, you let go of Gemma. She's not to be touched. Whatever you need, tell me."

"I just didn't want her to walk off. I didn't mean anything by it. Sorry. I was going to see how this month's profits are looking," he lied, as he dropped his hand like my arm was on fire.

"You have business questions, ask Tommaso or one of her cousins. She's no longer the one responsible for keeping things running around here. They have to learn to do that for themselves. After all, she'll be moving away with me in a month, remember?"

It was a taunt, pure and simple. He wanted Santo

to get in his face or do something to warrant punishing him. I knew he hated him and was looking for any excuse to make an example of him in front of his goons.

"Honey, I'm fine," I tried to reassure him. I'd tell him later what Santo really wanted.

He gave me a small terse nod then gestured for me to go back to the front. I knew he was coming off as being overbearing, but he was playing the part of a macho Italian man who was in charge. I was uncharacteristically playing the part of the submissive woman. I hoped he realized this wasn't how I'd be acting once this whole nightmare was over. I was my own woman and I wouldn't be dictated to about what I could or couldn't do.

Beau came with me as Gabriel retook his seat and got back on his phone. "Santo must have a death wish. Why else would he try that where Gabe can see him?" he uttered.

"I don't think he thought about what he was doing. He wants to meet with me somewhere private so we can talk. I told him there's nothing we have to talk about and that it's not possible," I explained.

"As if that's ever going to happen. The man is a moron. Gabe can tear him apart in seconds. That man is lethal."

I stared at Beau stunned. I knew that Gabriel was not a man to fool around with and that he had to be tough to do what he did, but the way Beau made it sound, he was an animal.

"Could he really do that?"

"Gemma, do you want me to lie and make you feel better or tell the truth?" he asked gently.

"The truth. I always want the truth."

"Gabe was a Navy SEAL. He was trained on ways to take people apart not only physically but mentally. He's done a lot of dangerous work over the years. He, Sean, Mark and Griffin aren't men you want to mess with. They take their assignments seriously, but this one is even more serious because of you. There's no way that man is going to let someone hurt you or take you from him. He's a goner on you, babe. Just accept it," he said with a wink.

"I don't know about that. Sure, he seems to like me and he wants us to explore being in a relationship, but that might not work out."

"If he asked you to be in a relationship, he's going to do everything under the sun to make it work. I've worked for them for two years. I've gotten to know all of them really well, except Mark, since he hasn't been back that long. They're like the men in my brother-in-law's club. They don't mess around when they claim a woman and they don't stake a claim without thinking it through. Face it, you're stuck with him." He elbowed me lightly, and I saw the smirk on his face.

I smacked his arm. "Behave. Shouldn't you be looming menacingly over them or something, instead of talking to me?"

"Nope, Gabe is doing my job right now."

I looked past him to see that he was right. Gabe's gaze was firmly fixed on Santo and his men. A part of me wanted to wait and see if laser beams would shoot out of his eyes. With the way he looked, I wouldn't be surprised.

The opening of the front door grabbed my attention. I turned to greet whoever had entered. A lone man was standing there. He was searching the room. Something about the way he stood and was checking everything out reminded me of Gabriel and Beau. An instant later, Beau was headed for him. I watched as they greeted each other with a man hug. This told me this had to be our second bodyguard. After a quick greeting, Beau brought him over to me. By then, Gabriel had gotten up and came to stand beside me. He reached out to shake the unknown man's hand.

"Thanks for getting here so quickly. I appreciate it. This is Gemma. She's my woman. You'll be guarding her and me. Gemma, this is Benedict, or Ben as we call him. I'd love to explain more right now, but the enemy is among us. The last table on the left in the back," Gabriel told him in a low voice.

Ben reached out to take my hand. I was taken aback when he raised it to his mouth and kissed the back of it rather than shake it like I thought he would. "Hello, beautiful Gemma. It's a pleasure to meet the woman who stole Gabe's cold heart. You'll have to tell me how you did it."

I couldn't help but laugh at his description of Gabe and the smirk he wore on his face as he said it. "It's a pleasure to meet you too, Ben. Thank you so much for coming to help us."

Gabe took my hand out of Ben's and held on to it. "That's right, she's mine so no more putting your lips anywhere on her. Understand? I'd hate to have to call for a replacement when you go missing."

"Gabriel, behave, he's only being nice. Lord, you'd think every man we meet is after me with the way you act," I chastised him.

"They are, *Principessa*. You just don't recognize that they are. That's why you need me. I'll protect you from the wolves. Well, all but me, that is," he said before he kissed me.

I swear the man could make me forget everything and everyone with his kisses. They made my brain go fuzzy and I got instantly aroused. He kept this one short, but it was no less intense than his others. When he let go of me, I was slightly breathless. He had a satisfied smirk on his face.

"Ben, Beau, I think I'll need you to keep this wolf away from me too," I joked.

"That's not possible, *piccola*. Ben, why don't you join me and we'll leave Beau up here to guard Gemma? Tonight, after we get to the house, we'll talk about what the next few days will look like. Right now, we have too many ears and eyes on us."

"Later, Gemma," Ben said with a nod before he followed Gabriel back to his table. I saw that Santo and his men had their gazes glued to them. Santo didn't look happy. Good. Let the bastard worry.

The next hour ran smoothly. More customers came and went. Santo and his crew were their usual selves until finally they stood up to go. As they approached the front, Beau stepped in front of Santo. Santo stopped to glare at him.

"Yes, what do you want?" he asked through gritted teeth at Beau.

"You forgot something, didn't you?" Beau asked calmly.

"No, I didn't."

"Oh, I think you did. You haven't paid your bill. Gemma, please get their bill rung up so this gentleman can pay for lunch."

"We don't have to pay here. This is our place," Santo spit back at him.

"That's where you're wrong. This place belongs to the Marra family, not you. Everyone who comes in here must pay. You and your men drank a large amount of their best wine and ate a ton of their food. They can't be expected to keep the doors open if they give their food and drinks away for free."

"I'm not fucking paying for anything! Get the hell out of my way. Who are you to tell me what to do? You're nothing but the hired help," Santo snapped. His men were standing behind him.

"Beau is simply following my orders. There will be no more free meals here, Santo. If you and your men come here and partake of any drinks or food, you pay just like everyone else. If you don't like it, you can find someplace else to hang out and eat," Gabriel said from behind them. His tone was hard and unyielding. Santo and his guys all swung around to face him. That's when I saw him.

He was standing there with his arms relaxed at his sides. His jacket was open. Ben was beside him, mirroring his stance. Both of them looked like they were calm and ready to tackle anything. My heart sped up. What if Santo or one of his men decided to pull a gun? It would be three against eight.

"Listen, Gabe, you can't come in here and decide to change how we do things. Sure, we're forming an alliance, but that doesn't give you control of our territory," Santo growled back.

"You're wrong. Everything here can be changed if I deem it necessary for this to work for both sides. Having you eating and drinking for free isn't how we do things. We don't abuse our people like that in the Rizzo family. In addition, since this is for all intents and purposes my family now, there's no way in hell I'm letting you or anyone else steal from them. Pay the fucking bill and leave. Remember what I said. If you don't like it, don't come here." There was no give in Gabriel's tone or stance.

"*Principessa,* get their bill ready," he told me gently.

As it happened, I always kept track of what they ate and drank, even if I knew they wouldn't pay for it.

It was my way to keep track of potential revenue lost. I hurried behind the counter and rang it up. The staring contest between Gabriel and Santo continued for a minute or more before Santo backed down.

"Fuck it," Santo said, as he threw a credit card down on the counter. I ran it through and handed him the receipt to sign. He scribbled on it then flung it at me before stomping out with his men. I sagged in relief when the door closed behind them.

"They're going to retaliate for that," I told the three of them.

"He'll want to. If he's smart, he won't. If he's stupid, then we'll be ready. How much longer until you can leave?" Gabriel asked.

I glanced at the clock. My evening hostess was due any minute. She'd work until closing.

"I should be ready to go in a half hour at the most."

"Good. I'm ready to get out of here. Finish up and I'll have Beau get the car ready for us. Ben, you can stay here with us. Beau, this time, bring the car to the front to pick us up instead of the back. I doubt he's had time to get someone out there to shoot us, but in case he did, they won't expect that."

"Shoot us?" I gasped.

"It's just a precaution. Don't get upset. Nothing will happen to us. Make sure to use the blanket," he informed Beau, who nodded and left the restaurant. I had no idea what a blanket would do. They left me to go back to his table. The rest of my time was a haze as I greeted the new hostess and got her up to speed on reservations and such. My gut was tight thinking of leaving here and what might happen.

Gabe:

I knew the confrontation with Santo had unnerved Gemma. She was used to doing whatever made him happy to keep the peace. Those days were gone. I wanted to push him to the breaking point. Not because I wanted to increase the danger, but so I could find an excuse to take him out. If I did it without a perceived cause, I'd have to deal with his men at the same time. If I could show he was the one to fuck up, they might think twice about jumping into the fight. This would save me a headache. Yeah, eventually they'd all fall, but I'd rather it was when I wanted it, not when they forced it. An all-out war in Toms River was the last thing I wanted.

When it was time to leave the restaurant, I could tell she was tense and scared. I wrapped an arm around her. "Everything is going to be okay. Just do what I say. Keep close to me. Beau is bringing a blanket in with him that we'll wrap around our upper bodies and heads. Once we're in the car, we'll be on our way."

"What good will a blanket do against a bullet?"

"This is a special one. It's made of bulletproof Kevlar. The car is bulletproof as well."

"What about Beau and Ben? They'll be exposed."

"They're wearing Kevlar vests. It's much harder to make a head shot than most people think. Most people are trained to go for a center mass shot."

I didn't know if my words made it better or worse, but I was trying to be honest with her. Sure, there was an off chance someone on Santo's or the Grecos' payroll had been a sniper and could make such a shot, but I doubted it. I could do it and so could Beau and Ben.

When Beau entered with the blanket, I knew we got a lot of attention from the customers and staff, including her family who were standing around watching us. I didn't give a shit. Making sure she was fully covered, Ben opened the door. I hurried her out and to the waiting car that was running right in front with the back door open. I hustled her inside then shut the door. Moments later, both guards were safely in the car too.

She was quiet during the ride to the house. I didn't disturb her. She needed time to think. I knew when she was ready, she'd ask me questions. I was prepared for them.

Being with a man like me was going to be a big adjustment for her. I knew that. I wanted to make it as easy as I could for her, however, there would be things she'd learn I wouldn't compromise on. Her safety was one of those. When it came to that, I was the one who would make the decisions and insist she follow my lead. In other things, I could compromise. Or at least I thought I could. I hadn't been in a relationship since I was a teenager and those hadn't been normal ones.

Overall, I was a dominant man. I'd respected my leaders while I was in the Navy, although if I thought they were wrong, I had spoken up. I'd found ways to do it politely, even if it had almost killed me. Just because you were in command in the military didn't make you a good leader. It had its own corruption and cliques and sometimes it was who you knew rather than your merits that got you advanced.

Those were a couple of the things Mark, Griffin, Sean and I had grown tired of and it led to us getting out. We were on track to do twenty or more years, but we walked away early. The money hadn't been worth it to us. That's why we formed the Dark Patriots. We were the ones making the rules.

At the house, Beau parked the car in the garage and we waited until the door closed all the way before getting out. He went first to unlock the small inner door and shut off the alarm. When we were all inside and the alarm reengaged, we went to the living room. All the blinds were shut. I had insisted we leave them like that so we didn't give anyone a way to see inside. The lights were turned on.

As Gemma took a seat on the couch, I grabbed her a drink. Knowing she rarely drank alcohol, I got her a bottle of flavored water. It was one she'd put on the grocery list. Ben and Beau helped themselves to regular water like I did. I sat down beside her.

"Okay, I know you have questions. First, let me finish your introduction to our newest member. Ben works for my company. He's an operative like Beau is.

What's kind of funny is Ben is in the same situation as Beau."

"What situation is that?"

"Ben's sister is also married to a member of the Warriors MC. His name is Blade. That's how we met."

She gave Ben a surprised look. He grinned and nodded.

"Yep, it's true. One of those damn bikers laid the charms on my sister and that was it. She was a goner. Goddamn him. I threaten to kill him every time I see him, but it doesn't seem to scare the bastard. So, I've given up fighting it. I'm glad I was able to come help you out on this assignment. They filled me in at corporate on what was happening here. Sounds like fun."

"Fun? You think this is fun?" she asked incredulously.

"Hell yeah, it is. Better than my last job. That almost bored me to death."

"Speaking of your last job, I thought you were supposed to be on that assignment for a few more weeks?" I asked.

"I was, but then they decided they didn't need protection anymore, so I was let go. It was perfect timing to come here. Otherwise, I think you'd have ended up with a Warrior or Punisher. I'm much better company and better looking than they are."

I couldn't help but laugh. None of our biker friends were soft and even I could admit they were attractive men. They didn't have any trouble finding the ladies. Beau rolled his eyes as Ben smirked.

"Don't listen to him. He's ugly as hell and he knows it compared to them. Although, for this bodyguard duty, we don't care what he looks like. Even if he couldn't string two words together, I'd take him. He's got talents and knows how to use them. I just don't tell him often or it goes to his head," I explained to Gemma. This only made Ben laugh.

"So, the intense guy at the restaurant is the main pain in the ass we're going to be dealing with, right? He looks like he's just an inch or two away from going over the edge. I thought he was going to burst a blood vessel in his forehead when Beau stopped him and said he had to pay and you backed him up."

"Yeah, that's Santo. He's the main *capo* around here. For some reason, the *capos* who've been here much longer than him defer to him. His men are the worst about treating the people like shit. They've never paid once when they've come into the Mia Bella Rosa. They use it like it's their personal meeting place. Also, he thought Gemma was his. He's not happy to find out he was wrong. He's a ticking time bomb. I just want to ensure we're the ones to dictate when or how that bomb goes off."

Ben whistled. "Damn, no wonder he's so pissed. You've made him look weak in front of his men and the community, and stole the woman he thought was his. The man will for sure want you dead, Gabe. You sure know how to stir up a hornet's nest, don't you?"

Gemma moaned, hearing him say Santo would want me dead. I tugged her over until she was pressed up against me. I ran a hand through her hair.

"*Amore mio*, don't worry so much. We're taking precautions. I know what I'm doing. Men like Santo aren't as unique as you might think. He's not the first of his kind I've gone up against nor will he be the last."

"What if he does kill you? I don't want to lose you. Plus, that leaves the whole community and me at his mercy."

"You and the community won't be left at his mercy. Even if he were to kill me, my friends would make sure to finish the job and free your entire town. As for you, they'd take you to somewhere safe, like I originally wanted to do. No one is going to be allowed to hurt you," I told her. I gave her a gentle kiss on the mouth. She sighed and sank into me.

"Hey, I didn't mean to worry you more, Gemma. Believe me, Gabe is too mean to kill. Okay, so what's the plan? You know that we were followed here. They now know where you're staying," Ben added. Gemma jerked in surprise.

"I know. I caught the tail like you did. They weren't good at hiding themselves, fucking amateurs. I have no doubt he'll post someone to watch us day and night. Expect to be followed everywhere we go."

"How can we protect ourselves when it's just the three of you? You can't be everywhere all the time. You have to sleep. If both Ben and Beau stand guard during the day, how can they stay awake at night?"

"Gemma, they're not the only help I have. There are other eyes watching us and this community. I have help who's staying in the background. You won't see them unless it becomes necessary. Just know they're there. Trust me."

I didn't tell her that the other men watching us were the Rizzo family's men. She'd only be upset. She had no trust in that connection and I wasn't ready to tell her why they were helping me or why I knew they wouldn't betray us. It was in their best interest not to let me get killed.

She didn't probe more, which I was glad about. I knew I'd soon have to tell her more, but I was putting it off as long as I could. Our relationship wasn't where it was supposed to be. Which reminded me, we had something else to discuss. I looked at the guys. "Will you excuse us for a few minutes? There's something I need to talk to Gemma about in private."

"Sure, take your time," Beau said.

I got up and helped her to her feet. I took her to my room and closed the door. She gave me a quizzical look. I sat down on the edge of the bed and had her join me.

"We need to talk about something and I didn't want to put you on the spot in front of the guys. You were right, they both will need to sleep at night since they'll be out and about all day with us. In order to make sure they're well rested, we need to figure out the sleeping arrangements. This house has only three bedrooms. I wasn't thinking at first we'd need a second guard. I want you to move in here with me, so Ben can have your bedroom. I'm not trying to rush you. I swear, I'll keep my hands to myself. I won't force you to do anything you're not ready to do, but we need to do this, Gemma."

She didn't say anything for a minute or more. I was ready to scream by the time she responded to my request. I didn't want to make it an order, but I would if I had to. The guys needed a good bed and there was no way in hell she'd sleep on the couch. As for me taking the couch, it was too short for a man like me to sleep on.

"Gabriel, I have no worries that you're not a man of honor and would force me to do something I wasn't ready to do. I haven't known you very long, but my gut tells me that. I understand Ben and Beau need their rest and I'd be selfish to refuse to give up my bed just because I'm nervous. I'll move in here with you. All I ask is that we see how things go. I'm more than a little attracted to you, but I'm not a woman who sleeps around with men."

"Thank you, *piccola.* I won't rush you, I promise. I know you're not a woman who sleeps around. Any man you've been with had to be someone you had feelings for, I don't doubt." I hated the thought of her being with another man.

Her face flushed as she looked away from me then back. She took a deep breath before speaking. "The thing is, I've never been intimate with a man, Gabriel. I've never felt that close to one to allow it to go beyond some kisses. I have no clue how to do this."

Her confession blew my whole world apart. I sat there gaping at her in shock. The one thing running through my head was how happy I was that no other man had been with her. I'd be the only one.

Gemma: Chapter 10

By the look on Gabriel's face and his silence, I knew that I had stunned him with my revelation. It had taken all my courage to tell him that bit of truth. Who ever heard of a twenty-five-year-old virgin in this day and age. God, it made me sound like a loser. How could I have gotten to this age without ever having sex before? I wondered if he was reconsidering his choice.

"I understand if this changes things between us. You're used to women with experience. I know that. I promise, I'll stay and help you take down the Grecos even if you just want us to stay friends," I hurried to assure him.

In a flash, I was flat on my back on the bed and he was hovering over top of me. "You think that I'm going to let you go just because you're a virgin? Oh, *Dea*, you don't know me yet, but that fact doesn't turn me off even a tiny bit. In fact, knowing no man has ever been inside of you, has never made love to you, makes me fucking ecstatic. I can tell you right now, it'll be my absolute privilege to teach you anything and everything you don't know. And I vow that I'll be the only man who ever gets the honor of making love to you and knowing you in that way."

He ended his speech by taking my mouth in one

of those mind-numbing kisses of his. I raised my hands to grip his hair as we attacked each other's mouths. Lips, teeth, and tongues battled each other. Pants and whimpers, those came from me, were plentiful. My panties grew wet as my nipples grew hard—my standard reaction to his kisses.

I whimpered in need as his hands slid to my waist then underneath the bottom of my top. So far, he hadn't touched me anywhere other than my mouth or his hand on my back or arm. I prayed this meant he was going to touch me where I yearned to be touched. Or at least in one of the spots. If I was going to see where we were going with this, I had to be bold. I took one of my hands and laid it on the one he had on my waist. I slowly pushed his hand under the edge of my top then let go.

He moaned into my mouth then started to slowly run his hand up my stomach. His hands were rougher than mine and it felt so good against my skin. I shivered in delight. Goosebumps erupted all over my skin. He took his time, running his fingers all over my stomach then my ribs. By the time he made it to my breasts, which were in my bra, I was in tortured agony. I had to have his hands on my bare breasts. He broke the kiss, and I chased his mouth with mine.

"*Tesoro*, can I please touch your breasts? I'm dying to touch, taste and see them. Please give me one of those things." His voice sounded guttural.

"You can do all three if you want," I whispered back.

His face showed his surprise. He must have seen

I was serious by the expression on my face, because after pausing a few moments, he pushed up my top until he could remove it. His hands found the clasp on my bra around my back and released it. Grasping it, he took it off and flung it to the end of the bed. My hands automatically came up to hide myself from him.

He took a hold of my hands and shook his head no. "No, there's none of that. I need to see you."

I relaxed and let him lower my hands. His gaze greedily took in the sight of my bare breasts. I wasn't the biggest woman in the world when it came to mine, but they weren't tiny either. I was a nice full C-cup. Would that be enough for him? I was proud that they were pert and didn't sag.

After examining me for several heartbeats, he let out a deep groan. His hands came up to cup my breasts and his thumbs swiped across my hard distended nipples. I moaned at the bolt of shock that went from my breasts to my pussy.

His eyes hungrily met mine. "They're the most *bellissima* breasts I've ever seen. *Dio*, I could look at them all day and die happy. Can I taste you, my sweet Gemma?"

I nodded my head because my voice wouldn't work around the knot in it. His words and the sincerity I heard in them had left me speechless. I watched as he lowered his head then moved one of his hands so he could suck my nipple into his mouth. He sucked deeply and lashed it with his tongue. I cried out at the pleasure that simple move gave me. His mouth was so hot and wet.

Hearing my cry, he increased the suction and gripped my breasts tighter but not enough to hurt. While he sucked and licked the one, his other hand was busy teasing the other nipple and kneading my breast. My panties were flooded with moisture. My breathing grew ragged. I felt like my whole body was going up in flames.

As I gasped, he switched sides to give the same attention to the other breast. I was so lost, I didn't realize at first I'd hiked his shirt up and was running my hands eagerly up and down his back. Even his muscles there were defined and hard. I wanted so badly to see his chest. I wanted to know where he had tattoos and what they looked like. I'd seen some on his arms and I loved them.

It was like he read my mind. He reared up and tore off his shirt. He grabbed my hands and placed them on his chest. I gazed at him and couldn't believe what I was seeing. His chest and stomach were ripped with muscles. I could outline every single one of them. His chest and upper arms had tattoos scattered all over them like I'd imagined. His nipples were dark and small although I could see they were hard. I couldn't resist teasing one with my fingers. He shuddered. I swear his nipple got harder.

"Fuck, that feels so good. There's nothing I want to do more than stay here like this with you for the rest of the evening and tonight, but we have two other people in this house. Don't hate me for this, but we need to stop. Believe me, that's the last thing I want to do.

I swear, after we have dinner and settle for the night, you and I will be back to exploring each other like this. I want more. I need more. Goddamn it, being fucking responsible sucks," he growled.

I couldn't hold back the laugh that bubbled up inside of me. I was thrilled he hadn't found me lacking and he wanted to touch and taste me more. I wanted the same. Although I wanted to say the hell with Ben and Beau, I knew we couldn't. I'd feel weird if they were out there wondering what we were doing in here for this long. Nodding my head, I pushed at his chest.

He reluctantly stood up. He found my bra and handed it to me then gave me back my top. His gaze never left me. Once I was covered, he put his shirt back on. Getting up from the bed, I went to the bathroom to try and tame my hair. No need to make it obvious we'd been fooling around. Once I felt as presentable as I could, I let him lead me back into the living room. I had no idea how much time had passed, but it was more than a few minutes. I expected to get knowing looks, but they only gave us nods. I relaxed.

In order to take my mind off my desire to go back to the bedroom and start over with what we'd been doing, and to distract myself from worrying to death about whether there were men outside watching the house waiting to attack us, I decided I'd fix dinner tonight.

I enjoyed cooking. Who wouldn't after being raised in a restaurant? There were many times I had to step in and cook when one of our cooks had been out. It wasn't something I wanted to do all the time, but it was fun and I found it relaxing.

"Does everyone like Italian food? If not, tell me what kinds you do like. I want to make dinner. I can make other types of food, although we all know Italian is the best," I teased.

"Are you sure you wanna cook, Gemma? It's not a problem for us to order something or I can cook. I doubt I'm at your level, but I won't kill anyone and it'll taste decent enough. And look at me. What self-respecting Italian doesn't like the food of his homeland?" Gabriel said, with a grin.

"I can help. I make a good sous chef. I love just about any kind of food," Ben added.

"I suck in the kitchen. Bryony banned me years ago from even trying, but I can chop stuff and set the table and I know how to clean. Italian sounds great to me," Beau chimed in with a grin.

"I don't mind at all cooking. It relaxes me. Why don't we see what we have and I'll whip something up."

I quickly took an inventory of the various sources of food we had when I got to the kitchen. I chose a favorite of mine. It was always a comfort food for me. I organized the various ingredients and got started on it. It was called penne rustica. It was a penne pasta dish made with shrimp, grilled chicken, smoked prosciutto, and parmesan in a creamy gratinata sauce with garlic and various herbs and spices. You baked it in the oven.

I smiled to see the three of them gather around the kitchen island to watch me. Gabriel opened a bottle of wine and poured all of us a glass. It felt so homey. We all chatted about non-serious things. We'd been talking enough for the last several days about the situation in Toms River and our plans. Tonight, we needed to forget it for a little while and relax.

You can't have Italian food without bread. It was like a rule, I think. We picked up several loaves of crispy bread when we got groceries. I'd serve it with olive oil and balsamic vinegar for those who liked that. I was one of the weird people who didn't like balsamic vinegar. My family often told me I was an oddball.

I took my time and by the time it was ready to eat, we'd spent a good two hours getting to know each other. I found out a lot more about Beau and Ben's families and the time they spent in the military. I was envious that Beau had four brothers and a sister. Ben talked about his best friend, Heath, who had served with him. He now worked for Gabriel's company too.

As we ate, I told them more about my family and how they ended up in the restaurant business. It was all due to my mamma. She'd been an amazing cook, and everyone who ate her food raved about it and told her all the time she should open a restaurant. Eventually, my *papà* and my uncle decided to do it.

The guys were very vocal about how delicious the meal was, which made me happy as well as a tiny bit embarrassed. I wasn't used to hearing praise like that. With my family, it was just expected that I'd be good at it. They were always quick to point out that I wasn't as good as my mamma had been.

"Why're you so shy about someone praising you, Gemma?" Beau asked when I waved away their compliments.

"I guess because in my family, I was expected to be a decent cook, however, they were always telling me how much better my mamma's food was. They said I had a long way to go to be as good as her."

"The more I hear about your family, the more I want to knock the hell out of them. It's ridiculous the way they've tried to beat you down mentally all these years. They should be thankful they had someone so giving and loving as you," Gabriel growled. I could tell he was truly upset for me.

"*Tesoro*, don't get upset. It's just their way. I'll be honest. I do fear that my cousins will never find a woman who can stand them. If they do, I pity the women. They'll forever feel inferior. My cousins don't seem to like strong women."

"That's because they fear them and feel inferior to strong women. They're not secure in their manhood. I wouldn't be able to handle a totally submissive wife who I had to make every decision for. It would drive me crazy," Ben admitted. Gabriel and Beau both nodded their heads in agreement.

I loved discovering this about Gabriel, about all of them. Inside, I was much stronger than I'd been allowed to show. It was great that I wouldn't intimidate him. I didn't see myself being happy in a relationship where the man was always the decision maker or pointing out my supposed flaws.

Beau jumped up to do his part when we were done eating. He cleaned the kitchen and put away the leftovers. They were already making plans to have it for lunch tomorrow. As we went to the living room to sit and see if there might be a movie we'd like to watch, I thought about how wonderful this was. I was more relaxed with them than my own family, which was a shame. Gabriel sat on the couch with me tucked under his arm. I was in heaven.

Gabe:

I enjoyed the evening with the guys and Gemma. To see her smile, laugh, and appear so relaxed was wonderful. Hearing more about how her family didn't truly appreciate her and how they treated her was the unenjoyable part. It only made me want to shake them, beat the hell out of her cousins, and ask them what the hell was wrong with them.

After the movie, I made the excuse that we needed to shower and get some sleep. It wasn't really that late, but I wanted to get Gemma alone in our room. I was hoping we might go back to the foreplay we'd been doing earlier. Calling a halt to it had almost killed me. While she went to move her things to my room and take her bath, I stayed to talk to the guys for a while. We chatted more about the movie and what we had planned for tomorrow, then I reminded them about the need for sleep.

"Try and get some sleep tonight. The house will be safe. Between the alarm and the eyes I have watching us, we should be fine. Just keep your weapons handy. You know the drill."

"We will. You try to get some sleep. Don't stay up all night romancing your woman," Beau told me with a smirk.

"Don't tease like that around her. She's shy about anything like that. I'm not rushing her into anything. However, if down the road, you hear anything, keep your mouths shut," I warned them. The last thing I wanted was for them to let their crude humor embarrass her. They both held up their hands and nodded. Figuring I'd given her enough time to move her things and to shower, I bid them goodnight.

When I got to the bedroom door, I paused and knocked. "Gemma, is it alright if I come in?"

"Yes, come in," she called back.

Opening the door, I took in the sight in front of me. She was lying in bed under the covers. I couldn't tell what she was wearing, but it had thin straps. She was showing more cleavage than she usually did in her regular clothes. It made my hands itch and my mouth water, thinking of how beautiful and responsive her breasts had been earlier. I was hoping to get another taste and touch before we went to bed.

I went to the dresser and pulled out a pair of shorts. I usually slept naked, but I didn't see that happening yet. I'd work her up to it. Maybe I'd get lucky and she'd do the same one day too. With the shorts in my hand, I went over to the bed and dropped a quick, brief kiss on her mouth. "Let me grab a shower then I'll be back. It won't take me long."

"Take your time. The water was nice."

Pulling myself away from her, I went to the bathroom and closed the door. Underneath the water a couple of minutes later, I let my mind wander and I pictured what it would be like when she was comfortable enough for us to progress our relationship all the way. While I was willing to give her the time she needed, I was dying to be with her. When she admitted earlier that she was a virgin, I'd wanted to shout it to the world that she was mine and only mine. Knowing she was untouched fed some deep-seated caveman tendency I didn't know I had.

To be honest, I was astonished she was. Not only because of her age, but because of how beautiful and wonderful she was. How in the hell had no man put in the effort to win her? I wasn't complaining, I just didn't understand it. She should've been one who had lots of guys pursuing her. I wondered if her father and cousins had prevented it.

My thoughts had the side effect of making me hard, which was the last thing I wanted. I couldn't go out there sporting an erection. She'd likely run from the room, thinking I was going to press her for more. I switched my thoughts to thinking about all the things we had yet to accomplish to take down the Greco Mafia. That had the desired effect of making me go soft.

True to my word, I was back at her side, climbing into bed, fifteen minutes later. She smiled shyly at me. "I forgot to ask. Do you have a preference for which side of the bed you sleep on? I should've asked. I don't," she told me.

"I do and you already got it right. I like to be on the left so my right hand is free and closest to the nightstand."

She gave me a puzzled look. “It's so I can reach my gun quicker,” I explained.

“Oh, I never thought of that. It's weird for me to think of you handling a gun. I don't know why. I figure you did it all the time in the SEALs. I guess it's because in my family, they never had them. However, with the way the world is, I think it's a good idea to have one and know how to use it.”

“Do you want to learn? I'll gladly teach you. Honestly, I'd prefer if you knew how to safely use them, but I won't force you to learn if you have an aversion to them. The one thing I can't do is have none in the home. It's not possible.”

She was quiet for about a minute as she thought it through. Finally, she nodded. “Yes, I do believe I'd like that. I guess Cassidy and Sloan know how to shoot?”

“They do. Sloan was a Marine and with Mark as a brother and her dad being the protective sort who he was, there was no way Cassidy was ever going to get away from learning.”

I moved closer to her. I was happy when she wiggled even closer to me. She laid her head down on my chest. Feeling her soft skin against mine made me say the hell with talking guns. We could do that another time. I lifted her chin so she had to look at me.

“I don't wanna talk about guns tonight. I want to hold you and feel you against me. If you're still willing, maybe we can revisit what we were doing earlier. If not, that's fine, as long as I get my kisses.”

She answered me by lifting her mouth to place it against mine. That's all the encouragement I needed. Our mouths instantly began to devour each other. It took no time for me to be hard and tear myself away to kiss down her slender neck to her upper chest. I paused there.

She raised her hands and slid the thin straps of her top down, which let the upper half covering her breasts fall to below her breasts. I groaned. They were just as succulent and gorgeous as I remembered. I eased her onto her back so I could hover over her and give them the attention they deserved and were begging for.

Her nipples were hard beads. They were dark. She fit my hand perfectly. I kneaded one as I teased her nipple, and I sucked on the other. She buried her hands in my hair and tugged me closer. She wiggled underneath me and moaned. She arched her upper back off the bed, pushing her breast deeper into my mouth. I feasted.

Needing to feel more of her pressed against me, I gently pushed her legs apart and lay down between them. This allowed me not only to enjoy her breasts but to also kiss and touch her stomach as I eased her nightgown down more. She was fit but not hard. She was soft, which I loved compared to my hard muscles. I didn't want a woman who was all ripped muscle or was waif thin. I wanted one who looked like a woman. There was no doubt she was all woman. She had an hourglass shape that made me desperate to see the rest of her naked.

I knew it was too soon to go past this stage, but I had to ask. I wanted so badly to see, touch, and taste her in her most private place, that it was making me a little crazy. I finished teasing her belly button which made her jump then I glanced up at her. Her eyes were slumberous, and she was breathing heavily like I was. Her hands were clenched in the sheets.

"I have to ask, but you don't have to say yes. I'll understand if you're not ready, Gemma, but I want so damn badly to see the rest of you. To touch you and maybe even taste you. Is that something you want tonight?"

I hoped to God I wasn't putting too much pressure on her. Having her submit without wanting it or enjoying it would kill the pleasure for me. I ran my fingers lightly up and down her ribs and across her stomach as I waited to see what she said.

She curled a finger at me, like she wanted me to come closer to her face. I rose then leaned up and forward. She grasped my face between her hands and gave me a kiss. I was over the moon that it was a passionate one. She used her tongue as well as her lips. She broke it off too soon. I wanted more.

"Yes, Gabriel, I think I'm ready. I want you to show me more, but I'm nervous. I don't want to disappoint you. This is all so new and you know I don't know what I'm doing," she whispered softly.

"*Amore mio*, you could never disappoint me. My biggest fear is pressuring you into something you don't want yet. Don't let me do that. I can promise you, if you enjoy what we do, then I'll enjoy it."

She dropped her hands from my face and relaxed against her pillow. "Then I'm yours. Look your fill and if you want to touch or taste me, do it. I'll let you know if it's too much or if I want to stop."

"Please do."

Taking her at her word, I pushed the covers down with my feet and sat back on my heels between her legs. I could now see that she had on a short nightgown. It hit mid-thigh on her. I reached for the hem and eased it up. She lifted herself so I could remove it. This left her in a pair of panties. With the way her legs were spread, I could see the crotch was damp. She was excited, which was great. I caught the scent of her pussy. It made my cock harder. I knew if she looked, she'd see my erection pushing against my shorts. I couldn't control it. Not when she was lying here like this.

I grasped the sides of her panties while raising my eyebrows at her, as if to ask, *are you ready*? She nodded. Slowly, I eased them down her legs. I didn't look at her until I had them all the way off. Then I got my first look at her. I couldn't hold back the growl that rumbled in the back of my throat.

Her lower lips was wet with her cream. She had a small patch of hair running down the center of her pussy, but the rest of her was bare. Reverently, I ran a finger across her mound then between her lips. She jerked then moaned. Easing her open with my finger and thumb, I saw her hard clit. It was begging to be touched and tasted.

I rubbed it in a circle, varying the pressure I applied. She wiggled her ass and pressed harder against my finger. Taking my cue from her, I began to tease her from top to bottom. As she spilled more of her cream and moaned, I knew I had to tell her how gorgeous she was. I had to taste her soon or I might die.

"*Principessa*, you are so fucking gorgeous. I'm a very lucky man. Look at how responsive your body is to touch. You were made for this, my own personal *dea*. I could worship you all day and night. Does this feel good?"

"Yes," she gasped as I sped up my rubbing.

"Can I taste all this lovely cream you're spilling?"

"God, yes, please," she whimpered.

I didn't wait to be told twice, I lightly attacked her with my tongue. That first taste was like an explosion on my taste buds. I groaned and lapped more of her cream up. Working her harder, I knew I wanted to make her come. And as she came, I wanted to feel her tighten. With this goal in mind, I slipped one of my fingers into her pussy. She momentarily stiffened. I slowly worked it in and out until she relaxed.

She was tighter than any pussy I'd ever felt. I tried to imagine what she'd feel like gripping my cock. I could feel the precum running down the head of my cock and dampening my shorts. If I wasn't worried about scaring her, I'd take my cock out and jerk myself off as I got her off. As she eased up on my finger a little, I inserted another one.

Sucking on her clit, laving up and down her folds and fingering her pussy, it wasn't long before her cries grew louder. I knew she was close, so I increased my licks and thrusts. Within seconds, she was coming. Her cream flooded my mouth and fingers. Her tight pussy was like a vice around my fingers. I couldn't help but groan as I made her come for me.

She slowly came down from her peak. When she relaxed, I reluctantly lifted my head and removed my fingers. I sucked them clean as I watched her face to see what kind of reaction she'd have. She was flushed and breathing hard. I was breathing a little fast myself. My cock and balls ached.

"I hope that was as good for you as it was for me, *piccola*. You taste like ambrosia from the gods."

"It was nothing I'd ever imagined, Gabriel. Oh my God, I think my brain melted."

Her reply made me feel ten feet tall. I couldn't help but wish I could show her even more, but this was enough for tonight. She'd let me take things much further than I'd dreamed she would this soon. I eased from between her legs and lay down on the bed beside her. Her eyes landed on my erection. They widened.

"What about you?" she asked shyly.

"What about me?"

"I can see you're hard. You have to want to come too."

"I do, but I'll live. I can take care of it myself if it

gets to be too much. I told you. I'm not going to rush you. This was more than I expected tonight. Thank you."

She didn't say anything for several moments then she took a deep breath and replied. Her reply shocked the hell out of me. "I'm not sure if I'm ready to do what you did to me, but I do want to see you and maybe touch you. Can I do that?"

"Are you sure, Gemma? You don't have to. I swear."

"No, I want to. Please. I've never seen a man's, you know, in person. I'm curious."

I wanted to laugh at her not being able to say the word cock. I did wonder what she meant by not seeing one in person.

"What do you mean, you haven't seen a cock in person? Where have you seen one?"

She blushed bright red. She glanced away from me then back. "I've seen a few pornos. I admit, I was curious about what a man looked like naked. What I saw, I don't know if that's real or all for show. The things they did were a little wild."

"Oh, we're going to have to talk more about what you saw that was wild. Every man is basically the same. Some are circumcised and some aren't. We vary in size. That's not only in length but in thickness. Are you sure you want to see me?"

"Yes," she said definitively.

Not waiting for her to get nervous and back out, I lay on my back and took off my shorts. I watched her as I did. She sat up and leaned over to get a closer look at me. I saw fascination and curiosity on her face. Hesitantly, she reached toward me then stopped. I took her hand and brought it the rest of the way, placing it on my cock. I groaned at the feel of her soft hand on me. I jerked under her touch. She gasped.

"Touch me. Stroke it if you want, but I warn you, if you do too much of that, I'll come."

"I don't want to hurt you. What if I grip you too hard?"

"Here, I'll show you how hard you can do it." I wrapped her fingers around me. She couldn't fully reach, but it still felt wonderful. I squeezed her hand tight until it was at the perfect intensity for me. I slid her hand up and down my length a couple of times, then let go. She took over from there. She started slowly then as she gained confidence, she sped up.

"The head is more sensitive and so are my balls. If you concentrate right here, that drives me crazy," I told her hoarsely, directing her hand to the underside of the head. She was a quick learner and soon had me panting and on the edge of coming. She'd even teased my sac. I grabbed her hand.

"Shit, if you keep that up, Gemma, I'm going to come," I warned her.

Her eyes were feverish as she met mine. "Do it. I want to see you come."

I let go and she continued to stroke. It took less than a minute for me to shoot my load. I groaned and grunted as it squirted out and over her hand onto my stomach. She gasped but kept stroking me. I was amazed at how hard I came and how much cum I produced. When I became too sensitive for her to continue, I stopped her.

"*Piccola*, you have to stop. I'm too sensitive. But *Dio*, that was amazing," I panted.

The smile and look of satisfaction on her face was brilliant. I jerked her up so I could kiss her. I took my time then reluctantly ended the kiss. "Come on, let's get cleaned up. I think you've had enough lessons for tonight. Any more and I might have a heart attack."

She laughed. I helped her off the bed and into the bathroom. This was an excellent start to our physical relationship. I couldn't wait to see how soon we could take it further. Back in bed, minutes later, she snuggled into my chest. Exactly where I wanted her, in my arms.

Gabe: Chapter 11

After last night, I wanted nothing more than to stay in bed with her all day and explore each other, but I knew we couldn't do that. Instead, we had to get up and begin our day. Today, we'd be going our separate ways for a while. I had a meeting with Santo to talk to one of their guys who ran a couple of the illegal gambling dens. I wasn't excited to have her out of my sight, but I had to do it. At breakfast, we decided Ben would go with her today to run errands and to check on the restaurant. Beau would be my bodyguard.

The update I got when I woke up was that two of presumably Santo's men had watched the house all night. They walked around the outside, but didn't attempt to get in. I wasn't surprised. I knew Santo would be plotting.

Ben and Gemma took her car. I wasn't excited about it, because it wasn't bulletproof, but the guys argued if any of us needed that kind of protection, it would be me. Santo was much more likely to want to kill me than her. Beau and I followed to make sure they got to the Mia Bella Rosa alright. Before leaving, I went inside with Ben and Beau to check that the restaurant was secure. I gave her a big kiss before I left and I made sure to do it out where we could be seen. Everyone needed to know she was mine.

As much as I worried about her, I had to clear my head and be alert and at my best for this meeting. I couldn't get sloppy and let Santo get the upper hand with me. The address he sent me for us to meet at was on the opposite side of town from the restaurant. We pulled into an unassuming part of town. It wasn't the nicest but it wasn't the slums either. There were a variety of small businesses there. The one with the address we were looking for was of all things a Mexican restaurant. No one would look twice at people entering and staying for a while. Santo was waiting outside when we pulled up. He had his usual crew of five guys with him. I didn't know why he traveled with so many. Was he that worried about someone trying to take him out? Or was it to show how powerful he thought he was?

Beau got out and scanned the area before opening my door. I got out with the air of a man who owned the world and knew it. I knew exactly how to act. I sauntered over to Santo slowly. I could tell by the way his mouth tightened, he was pissed. I didn't tell him good morning or shake his hand. Those days were past. I gave him a curt chin lift.

"Let's get this started. I have lots of things to do today besides following you around. I want to know the number and location of all the gambling sites. I want to make sure we don't need to relocate any to better and safer locales. I know the Rizzos will want to add more. Not in Toms River, but nearby. In order to know where to put them, I need to know where you have them."

"Wait, I thought we were just going to visit here

and one other one? I didn't warn the guy who manages the other two locations that we'd be coming today."

"Why must you warn him? Does he have something to hide? I find it better to surprise those who work for me. It keeps them on their toes and they're less likely to double-cross you or steal from you. He'll have to live with a surprise visit. I don't want any of you to text him ahead of time," I ordered him arrogantly. His fists clenched.

As we entered, Beau made sure to keep a safe distance between him and the other men. I'd keep Santo in check. It was still early, so the restaurant wasn't busy. A large middle-aged Italian man came hustling over to us. He was sweating and eyeing me with trepidation. Santo made the introductions begrudgingly, I thought.

"Gabe, this is Leonardo Carbone. He's been with the family for many years. He runs this location and another one. Leo, this is Gabriel Barbieri. He's the one I was telling you about that the Rizzo family sent."

"It's good to meet you," Leo said. He held out his hand. I didn't shake it. I merely nodded.

"I hope I see good things today. Lead the way. I have a lot of decisions to make," I told him dryly.

I could tell that made him more nervous. We were led through the back into the outer part of the kitchen. There was a stainless-steel cooler door. The kind you saw in most restaurants where they would store their items needing to be refrigerated. There was more than one around the kitchen, I noticed. Leo opened it and took us inside. There was produce in it, however, in the back corner there was another door. He entered a code and that door opened. I walked in to find their gambling den. For so early in the day, it was half full. Men were hunched over various tables. They checked us out when we entered. Some exchanged concerned looks.

They had a variety of games. I saw blackjack, poker, roulette, craps, and slot machines. It wasn't a huge space, but I knew they made money on it. Anything bigger would attract unwanted attention. I listened as Santo and Leo rambled on about what they did here and how they staffed it. I interrupted them after a few minutes.

"That's all fine and well, but I want to see the books. Also, how do you ensure none of the patrons narc you out to the feds or local cops?"

"They know what'll happen to them and their loved ones if they do. Plus, we have a few men on the force in our pockets," Santo stated arrogantly. I grunted in reply. I glanced at Leo.

"Oh, come with me and I'll show you the books. Right this way." He took us to a small office in the very back. I could tell Santo wasn't happy with me looking at their books. It made me wonder why. I quickly pursued it before nodding my head.

"I think I've seen enough. Take me to the other location you oversee, Leo."

From there, it was a short drive. This time, we ended up outside the city limits. There was an industrial-looking warehouse. It wasn't huge. The signs said it was the location of a farming equipment store and a welding business. Like the restaurant, they had a hidden area upstairs in which they had the gambling den. It had the same setup. I made them show me the books here too.

After that, it was a repeat as we left Leo and went to visit another man. His name was Carmine Piras. He oversaw two more gambling sites. One was in a storage unit place and the other was in the back of an adult sex store. Again, I gave the impression I was in charge and Santo answered to me. Carmine seemed almost as nervous as Leo had.

By the time I was done with those two places, I was ready to be away from Santo and his goons. I told him I'd contact him in the morning with what I wanted to do tomorrow. He tried to get me to tell him what it was, so he could have everything ready for me, but I refused to say. Hopefully, it would keep him and his men scrambling all night, trying to clean up things for my visits.

I'd stayed in contact via text with Ben and Gemma the whole time I was gone. I couldn't help but worry. Every time I did, they answered me promptly to tell me everything was fine. She'd run out to do a few errands with Ben and was now back at the restaurant.

Before heading over there to meet them, I made one more stop. It was at a local PO Box that I'd set up to receive packages. I was expecting something I'd asked Sean to get and send me. He and the guys all had access to my house and my safe.

Inside, I was happy to see the package had

arrived. I took it back to the car and directed Beau to take me to Gemma.

"What's in the package? Or should I not ask?"

I took it out and showed him. He glanced back over his shoulder then whistled. "Damn, that's something, Gabe. This is going to be fun," he said with a laugh. I chuckled.

When we pulled into a parking spot in front of the restaurant, we went through the usual routine of checking out our environment before heading inside. It was afternoon, so the lunch rush was over and the dinner rush hadn't started yet. I was hoping Gemma didn't have to stay and cover for anyone today. I wanted to take her home and out tonight. Staying cooped up in the house wasn't what I wanted to do. Sure, we had to be careful, but not act like we were hiding. That would make me appear weak and vulnerable to Santo.

I caught sight of her as soon as we entered. She was talking to a customer at his table. She was smiling. The customer was a man. I guessed him to be around my age, thirty-six. He wasn't a bad-looking man by most standards. What really caught my attention wasn't his look or age, it was how he was looking at Gemma.

She seemed not to realize, as I got closer, that he was flirting with her and checking her out. My hackles rose instantly. Ben was standing not far away, with his back to the wall, watching the man. I came up behind her as she responded to whatever he'd said.

"Henryk, yes, I love horses, you're right, but I can't

go to your farm to see them. I'm too busy with so many things to do. Maybe one day, I can manage it. I haven't been riding since I was a kid."

"But, Gemma, you have to come. It's so peaceful and private. I'll make it worth your time. You can ride them and see how they're trained," he said smoothly. He was giving her a charming smile. One I bet worked for him in most cases to get women to do what he wanted.

She shook her head. "No, I'm sorry, I can't. Thank you though. I appreciate the offer. Is there anything else I can get you today? How about dessert before you go?"

Before he could make a witty reply, I wrapped my arm around her. She startled and glanced over her shoulder. When she realized it was me, she relaxed and smiled. I leaned down and gave her a kiss. I made sure it had tongue and Henryk could see it. Out of the corner of my eye, I saw his shock.

"Hello, *Principessa*, I missed you. How has your day been?"

"Hi, *tesoro*, it's been good. I got everything I wanted to do finished. How was your day?"

"It was rather boring. I'm happy to be done. Are you ready to go home?"

"Give me a minute."

"Who's this, Gemma? I know almost everyone around here and I don't seem to know you," Henryk said. I could hear the edge of dislike in his tone.

"I'm her fiancé, Gabriel Barbieri. You are?"

"Fiancé? I didn't know you were engaged." He glanced at her bare left hand.

"It's recent. Her ring is being sized. I had to snap her up as soon as I knew she was the one, which didn't take me long."

"What brought you to Toms Creek? What kind of business are you in?"

"I'm here checking it out as a possible location to expand my company into. We do a variety of investing and property management. I'm so thankful I came. I'd have missed out on meeting *amore mio*."

He tried to chat and get more information out of me, but I kept my answers short and vague. I didn't bother to ask him what he did. I didn't care. Eventually, he got up to leave. As he left, his expression darkened when he saw Beau and Ben. Why he hadn't noticed Ben before, I don't know. They were obviously bodyguards the way they were acting. He gave me a nervous look before rushing out the door.

"Did you have to be rude?" she asked with a sigh.

"I did. When I come in and find a man trying to get my woman to go to his private farm with him, I don't like it. He was trying hard to get you out there so he could put the moves on you, Gemma."

"No, he wasn't," she protested, as we joined Ben and Beau.

"Yes, he was," they both said at the same time. She rolled her eyes like we were crazy. I didn't waste time convincing her to finish up and to say her goodbyes. As usual, her father was there. He didn't speak to me. I saw Emmet but not Elijah. All he did was glare at me. I resisted giving him the finger.

Gemma:

It was a relief to get home. Today, I hadn't been able to get into working at the restaurant like I usually could. My mind kept going back to Gabriel and what we'd done the night before. Even if I was a virgin, I had experimented with self-gratification. A woman had needs even if she did choose not to satisfy them by sleeping with a man. I hadn't ever been one who could feel comfortable just having sex with someone for the sake of sex only. Hence, why I was a twenty-five-year-old virgin.

Gabriel said it didn't bother him, that he actually really loved that I hadn't been with anyone. I hoped he wouldn't regret it later. I was willing, I think, to be open to trying things in the bedroom. You wouldn't know if you liked something unless you tried it, right?

While I'd watched porn and used a vibrator to pleasure myself, I knew there was a whole host of things out there to experience. The only positive of me using the vibrator was I ended up removing my hymen myself. I'd expected it to hurt way more than it did. Most women I'd been around talked like it was the worst pain in the world. Maybe I was weird.

However, those women had been mostly the older generation and from their other conversations that I'd overheard, they weren't women who were happy in their marriages. They saw sex as a chore to have children and couldn't wait until their husbands left them alone. I prayed that would never become me. I wanted to desire my husband and for him to desire me until we were too old to do anything anymore.

Some of them had old-fashioned arranged marriages, so that might be why they were so unhappy and unfulfilled. People thought those were a thing of the past, but not necessarily in all families. Bloodlines seemed to be very important to some Italian families. I knew of a few where their families forbade the couple from getting married because they felt the partner was from inferior stock. I thought that was crazy in this modern age. We weren't still back in Italy in the eighteen hundreds or earlier.

The orgasm that Gabriel had given me last night had far surpassed any I'd ever given myself. It made me yearn to experience what else we could do together. I loved touching him and seeing that just my hand could bring him to completion. I was nervous and hoping I wasn't rushing into this, but I burned to experience more with him.

Although most of our elders knew their children and grandchildren didn't wait for marriage to have sex, they expected us to wait. Or I should say, they expected it from the women, but not the men. I knew there were some who would judge me for having sex with Gabriel before marriage if that's where we ended up. I prayed that we did. However, I didn't care what those narrow-minded people thought. This was my life and I wanted to live it. I had been living for other people all my life.

Ben had been a champ about doing errands with me. He was on constant alert, which in turn, made me more aware of my surroundings and people. It wasn't a terrible way to be, but I thought it would get exhausting after a long time.

Driving back to the house after work, I thought about how Gabriel had been convinced that Henryk was trying to lure me to his horse farm so he could take advantage. Maybe he was, but I had news for him, that wasn't ever going to happen. For one thing, I didn't feel any spark with him. He was a good-looking man and successful. I knew lots of women who wanted him. For me, he could have been a brother or a friend. I was hoping he didn't see me as more.

Secondly, no one impacted me like Gabriel. I didn't notice men other than him. I might dimly realize they were fit or attractive, but they weren't meant for me. I wondered if he was the same with women. The thought of him being with me and still being attracted to other women bothered me. I hadn't caught him checking anyone out, but it could happen.

Thoughts like this made me worry, what if we couldn't stay together? What if he decided he wanted someone else? What if, God forbid, he cheated on me? The idea of any of those things made me sick to my stomach and I wanted to cry. I didn't see myself as the one wanting someone else. I hadn't for the last twenty-five years, so why would that change? I was caught up in these thoughts when we pulled into the garage behind Beau and Gabriel. Ben turned off the car and turned to me.

"You've been awfully quiet, Gemma. What's wrong?"

Even if we'd just met, I could tell he was genuinely concerned, but how could I tell him my worries? He was Gabriel's employee and it seemed like they might be friends. It was times like this I wished I had at least one close female friend. However, my life hadn't lent me time to make that type of connection. When you always had to work, people who wanted to hang out with you tended to fade away.

To answer him, all I did was shrug. "I just have a lot on my mind," was the lame excuse I gave him.

I saw Gabriel walking over to get my door. Before he got to us, Ben quickly said, "If you need to talk, I'm a good listener. I'll keep what we talk about between us, unless it threatens your safety or Gabriel's."

"Thank you, Ben, that's really sweet of you."

I didn't get to say more because Gabriel opened the door. He gave me a quizzical look. "*Piccola*, are you alright? You seem to be tense. Where's that gorgeous smile of yours?"

This made me smile as he held my hand to assist me out. "It's here. I didn't realize I looked tense. I am glad to be off work for the day. I have a feeling a few staff members are thinking of quitting or calling off."

We all headed into the house. Beau had already gone ahead to check that it was secure. Gabriel frowned and shook his head at my observation. "Why do you say that? Why do you have to be the one to fill in if they do?"

"It's just the funny way a couple of them are acting. I've seen it before with past staff. If I don't fill in, who will? We don't have extra people just waiting for odd shifts."

"Then your father or your two cousins will have to figure it out. Gemma, they can't keep taking advantage of you. What are they going to do when you move away? After this assignment is over, I don't intend to have you live all the way up here. I need you with me."

"You haven't exactly told me where you live, Gabriel. All you said was you live on the East Coast. That's a big area."

Beau and Ben went off to their rooms after resetting the alarm. Gabriel and I took a seat in the living room. He immediately captured one of my hands in his. He raised it to his lips and kissed my knuckles. "I didn't, did I? I'm sorry. I'm so used to protecting information like that."

"If you're not comfortable telling me, that's fine," I said, although it really wasn't. If he didn't trust me, how would this ever work between us?

"No, it's not. I want you in my life. Being here and me living in Hampton, Virginia, which is over a six-hour drive, isn't going to cut it. In case you didn't know it, I'm crazy about you. Last night should've shown you that I want you with me every day and night. I'm not talking about sex, although there is that too. I mean, I just want you beside me. Holding you in my arms and sleeping with you was amazing. I've never craved that with a woman. To be honest, I've never had a woman spend all night in my bed or me in hers."

Thinking of him with other women didn't excite me, but I knew we had to be able to discuss things like this. He got his experience by having sex. Conversations like this would pop up occasionally.

"Does it offend you that I spoke about being with other women?" Something in my expression must have given that fact away.

"It makes me uncomfortable and I'm trying not to let it bother me. I know you've had a life before me and that involved women. My only request is that you never compare me to them in a negative way. Compliments are one thing, but pointing out how one of them was better than me would hurt and piss me off."

"*Cristo*! Christ! I would never do that. Any man who would needs the hell knocked out of him. For me, I only anticipate finding out over and over how much better you are than any of them. You already are. Not a single one ever got me to ask them to marry me. You did."

"But that's just part of your cover, not real. I mean, we're trying to make a relationship work, but telling people we're engaged helps with this undercover assignment."

He frowned and emphatically shook his head no. "*Dio* no, I meant it. I do see us marrying, *Principessa*. I know this has been backward and I apologize. I need to treat you like my woman. That's why I've made reservations for us to go out tonight. I want a chance to wine and dine you and show you off."

"You don't have to do that. I don't need those kinds of things. I appreciate the gesture, but it's too dangerous for us to go out anyway. You know Santo has people watching us. I don't want to give them more chances to do something to us."

"He needs to see us going about our lives. If we hide like we're afraid of him, it'll only make me appear weak. I've already started to establish in his mind and the others that I'm in charge. They should defer to me and fear me, not him. I have to keep pushing that. It'll help us do the job and come out on the other side safely."

"Okay, if you think it'll help, then let's do it. How long do I have to get ready? Is it a fancy place?"

I had a few nicer dresses, but nothing terribly high end. Although Toms River didn't have a really upper-end place, there were a couple of nice restaurants that were considered fine dining.

"We need to be there by seven o'clock. So if we leave here by six-thirty we'll have more than enough time to get there. You don't have to go all formal. You look good in everything. I saw you brought some dresses with you when we brought your things here. I've been dying to see you in one. Seeing those stunning legs of your last night, I want to see more of them. Just nothing too short. I can't have men ogling you more than they already do, or things will get ugly."

I smiled and shook my head at his silliness. It was four-thirty already. That gave me two hours, which usually would be way too much time, but I wanted to wow him. I gave him a kiss, which he quickly returned.

It was hard to break it off.

"I need time to get dolled up. Are you alright with me taking over the bathroom in your room for a while?"

"You can have it as long as you want, but you don't need to do anything to be beautiful. You just are. And it's our bedroom, not mine. Take your time. I'll use the one in the hallway that Ben and Beau use."

He waved me off. I wondered what he'd do. He wouldn't need long to get ready. I hastened to our room to start the process. A long soak in scented water was number one. Then I'd have to make sure everything was shaved and smooth. As we talked, I came to a decision. Tonight, I wanted Gabriel to make me his completely. I was done being cautious and worrying about what if. It was time to live that life I wanted.

Gemma: Chapter 12

I smoothed my hands down my dress. I was feeling nervous. Would he like how I looked? I'd gone all out for our special night. My long hair I'd washed, dried then curled it. I swept those curls up on the top of my head and pulled a curl down in front of each ear. I thought this style showed off the lighter streaks in my hair and made it look pretty.

I didn't have any fancy jewelry, so I wore the simple diamond solitaire earrings and necklace that had belonged to my mamma. *Papà* had given them to me when she died. He said she wanted me to have them and pass them down to my daughter one day. I loved the idea of family heirlooms like this rather than always getting new things. It was one of two things he'd bought her after Mia Bella Rosa had become a success. He'd insisted on burying her with her wedding band and engagement ring on. I didn't blame him. Despite everything, he had loved her and she loved him.

The dress I chose was one that hit just below mid-thigh. I thought it showed off my legs and Gabriel would love it. I did have nice legs, even if I did say so myself. They were toned and shapely. The three-inch peep-toe nude heels I paired with my dress only made them appear longer. The dress was red. I'd bought it a long time ago but hadn't ever had a reason to wear it. It screamed, *look at me*. Something I usually didn't want. However, tonight, I wanted him to have only eyes for me.

It was a wraparound dress with a decent V-cut in the bodice. My breasts and cleavage showed without being vulgar. A silver belt nipped in the waist. There was no denying I had curves and they were on display. I hoped this wasn't too much and Gabriel would like it. Thankfully, it was summer, so no need for a sweater. I transferred a few items to a nude clutch purse I had that matched the shoes.

My makeup I'd done carefully, so it looked like I wasn't wearing any even though I was. It helped enhance my olive skin tone and made it glow. My cheeks I kept free of blush. My lipstick was a glossy neutral color. My eyes were where I did the most. I used shadow and liner to darken them, making them appear smoky. I was blessed with naturally long eyelashes, so a quick curl and they were good. I didn't even need mascara. Something more than one woman had commented on over the years. They always told me how lucky I was.

My last thing was to spray on a few squirts of my favorite perfume. It was Cashmere Mist by Donna Karan. I loved the scent of it. I didn't wear it all the time, but it had a floral scent without being cloying. Taking a deep breath as I checked in the mirror for the last time, I left the bedroom in search of my date.

I'd heard him while I was in the bathroom come get clothes. After I'd gotten out of the bath and was in my robe, he'd come in to get his personal care items. He'd checked me out and growled, before giving me a kiss and leaving.

As I came down the hall, I saw Ben first. He was standing in the opening between the kitchen and the living room. He was facing the living room. He glanced at me then I heard him whistle and say, "Damn, I don't think Gabe should take you out looking like that."

"Why? What's wrong with it?" Was it too much or not enough? The whistle suggested he liked it.

"Nothing, other than he'll spend all night defending you," he said with a big grin. Beau popped around the corner from the kitchen. He stopped and whistled too. I couldn't help but be pleased. I hoped Gabriel felt the same as they did.

It was at that moment Gabriel moved from the living room to where I could see him. He took my breath away with how handsome and sexy he looked, as cliche as that sounded. His dark hair was combed back and looked perfect. His dark blue suit and light blue shirt made his blue eyes pop. He'd foregone a tie and left the top two buttons open. He had the relaxed though classy dressed look down pat. I watched as his eyes ran from my top to my bottom then back up. When his eyes met mine, all I could see was a deep burning yearning in them. My whole body came alive.

He held out his hand to me and ordered, "Come here, *amore mio*."

I walked to him as if in a trance. When my hand met his, he tugged me to him and dropped his mouth down on mine. His kiss was the hungriest I'd ever gotten. He was devouring me and I loved it. I worked to kiss him back just as intensely. I'd have to reapply my lipstick, but it was so worth it.

His tongue was dueling with mine and his teeth kept nipping my bottom lip. It was a while before he let me go. When he did, I was flushed, panting, and wanting to drag him straight to the bedroom for the night. My nipples were hard. I hoped no one could see them through my bra. My thong underwear were damp. I'd worn those to keep from having panty lines.

"Fuck, you look so damn exquisite, they're right. I'll be lucky if we're not mobbed by men tonight. That dress is absolutely stunning on you, Gemma. And that color is made for you. However, your legs are going to be the death of me."

All his complimentary words made me feel like a million dollars. I felt beautiful, sexy, and very desirable.

"Thank you, but I think I'm the one who needs to worry. You in that suit will have the ladies swooning."

"Thank you, *piccola*, but I'm nothing compared to you. Good thing I have my gun and I'm not afraid to use it."

This remark made me laugh, although I knew he wasn't kidding about carrying one. He always did, along with the guys. Thinking of them had me turning to look at them. They were both dressed in nice suits which showed off how handsome they were, but theirs were much more sedate. Ben was in black with a white shirt and Beau had on a dark gray suit with a lighter gray shirt. I knew that was to help them fade into the background. There was no way Gabriel would risk us going without our bodyguards.

"Are you ready to go, *Principessa*?" he asked, as he bent his arm and tucked my hand over it.

"I am. Lead away."

He led me out to his car. As he opened my door and waited for me to get in, the guys secured the house then joined us. Gabriel was in the back with me and they sat up front. The drive wasn't a long one, but all of them were alert. As we got closer to downtown, I took out a mirror and my lipstick to repair the damage he'd done. I was more than happy with how he responded to the dress and my look.

Gabe:

I couldn't take my eyes off Gemma. I hadn't lied. She always looked drop-dead beautiful to me, however, her hair, makeup and that dress, somehow made her even more so. She thought we were kidding about fighting off men, but I wouldn't be surprised if we did. I knew at a minimum there would be several getting an evil glare from me. Now that I had her, I wasn't going to let anything or anyone take her away from me.

Her legs and cleavage kept drawing my gaze back to them. My hands wanted to touch and my mouth wanted to explore. Shit, tonight when we got back, I hoped like hell she'd let me do what I did last night. Only this time, I'd spend more time and make sure she came more than once. I wanted her begging me to let her come until she can't take anymore. I couldn't resist rubbing a hand on her thigh under the bottom of her dress. I watched her shiver and her breathing pick up. Oh yeah, she was feeling it too. As much as I wanted tonight's date, I was praying it passed quickly, so I could take her home and get her naked.

Ben was driving and he parked the car as close to the restaurant as he could. The plan was he'd stay with the car and Beau would be inside with us. I wasn't going to leave our car unprotected. The place I chose had a ton of positive reviews online praising the food. I hoped they were right. It was considered a fine dining spot and I lucked out to get a reservation.

As always, I was a gentleman and helped her out of the car. Beau went ahead of us and opened the door to the restaurant while Ben covered our backs. Once we were inside, Ben went back to the car. The hostess was at a small desk. She smiled as she asked if we had a reservation. It was very busy from the looks of the inside and the parking lot.

"Yes, we have a seven o'clock reservation for Barbieri," I informed her.

I saw her eyes widen and she glanced down. She seemed to tense up. What the hell was up with that? What did my name mean to her?

"O-oh, Mr. Barbieri. Right this way, sir. We have your table ready and it's set up per your instructions. Enjoy your dinner," she politely rattled off. You could tell she said it from rote.

The table I had requested was one that placed us in a more secluded area. I could face most of the dining room and see who was coming. Beau could rest not too far away against a wall. I'd checked this place out ahead of time. The darker area made the candles and a bouquet of flowers pop. I didn't go for the standard red roses. For her, it was a mix of more exotic flowers you find mostly in other parts of the world. They were a bright explosion of color.

I'd ordered ahead of time a special champagne to be served too. I was nervous about whether she'd like what I had done, or would she think it was too predictable? I'd had dinner with women in the past, but it hadn't mattered to me if they felt wanted or not. I wanted Gemma to feel and know how damn special she was to me.

I called her *amore mio*, but I hadn't come out and told her I loved her. I wanted to, and it was hard to hold back. My fear of rushing her was what stopped me. Tonight, I was going to tell her. Our hostess laid down our menus as I pulled out Gemma's chair then scooted her closer to the table.

"Your waiter will be right with you," the hostess parroted before scurrying off to the front.

Beau didn't say a word as he took up his position against the wall. People were staring at us. I think it was for a variety of reasons. One was Gemma herself. She was a stunning woman and men and women alike turned to look at her as she passed. I wasn't oblivious to the fact women found me attractive, so I also got attention. I wondered if any of them knew who I was in association with Santo and the Greco family. It was likely. The town wasn't that big, and they seemed to have a lot of people helping them or being threatened by them.

The vibe was one of unease and curiosity. The unease better not ruin this for us. The other thing I think that caught their attention was we had a bodyguard. No one seeing Beau could doubt what he was here for. This had the other diners wondering who we were and why we needed a bodyguard.

Deciding to ignore the other people, I brought my

attention back to my date. She was gazing at the flowers in awe. She looked across the table at me. I took her hand that was on the table and caressed her fingers.

"Gabriel, these flowers are breathtaking. You didn't have to do this, but I love them."

"Gemma, I did have to do this. I want you to have no doubts how much you mean to me. You should always have beautiful things."

Before either of us could say more, our waiter came to the table. He was a younger guy, maybe in his early thirties. He gave me a short bow. He was carrying the champagne in a bucket of ice. The glasses were already on the table.

"Good evening, sir. May I open and pour your champagne for you and the lovely lady before you decide on any other drink orders?"

"Yes, please," I told him. As he worked to remove the cork, I asked Gemma what else she wanted to drink.

"If I could just have some water with lemon that would be great," she said to the waiter. He nodded. I ordered the same.

It wasn't long before he was pouring the champagne. After he did, he told us, "Take your time looking at the menu. If you have any questions, my name is Anton. I'll be back shortly with your waters and to check on you."

"Thank you, Anton," I replied.

As he walked away, I thought how well he had his

spiel down. If he was attentive, I bet he made good tips. I lifted my glass and Gemma picked up hers.

"I want to make a toast. To the unforgettable vision in front of me. Thank you for giving me a chance to grow old with you. I hope to give you a life of happiness. Cheers." I touched my glass to hers.

She was smiling from ear to ear. "Cheers and thank you, Gabriel, for coming into my life and showing me everything I was missing."

"*Piccola,* it's all my pleasure. Now, I hope you're hungry because I heard this place has great food and large portions."

"Oh Lord, I think you might have to eat some of mine," she said as we opened the menus.

There were the expected selections of filet mignon, lobster, other seafood, and lamb. As we tried to decide, Anton came back with the water and brought us a basket of warm bread with honey butter. I buttered a piece for her then one for me. She took a bite and moaned.

"I love this butter. You know, I feel guilty eating this and poor Beau and Ben have to watch and starve."

"Gemma, they won't starve, I promise. They told me what they wanted earlier and there's already an order in for when the time comes for us to leave. I can be an asshole, but I'm not that much of one. Besides, if we ate here and they didn't, they might mutiny on me."

She burst out laughing. We carried on a relaxing conversation about the food. After Anton came to take our orders, we started to talk about growing up. It reminded me there were things I still had to tell her. I planned to, but not tonight. This evening was all about happiness. The stuff in my past was dark and at times ugly, so I only shared a few of the good times.

It sounded like her mother had been her best friend growing up and when she died, it left Gemma adrift. Her father hadn't been one to be loving and she suffered alone. I ached to hold her and tell her that'll never happen again.

As the evening passed and we got our food to eat, I became more nervous. I planned the next part and was praying it came off the way I wanted. Even though we were having a great time, I kept an eye on the comings and goings of our fellow diners. The staring settled down a little, which I was thankful for.

We'd just gotten our main course, and she'd taken a bite of her seafood when my cell phone beeped. I had to check it in case it was important. As I took it out of my suit jacket and read it, I knew things were about to get messy. It was from Ben with Beau responding since he sent it to both of us.

Ben: Heads up, Santo and a few of his goons incoming.

Beau: Roger. Watch your back.

Ben: I will. Let me know if you need me inside.

Me: Stay alert and don't take risks. We've got the inside covered.

Both of them acknowledged me then went silent.

As they did, the front door opened and in marched Santo and three of his usual sidekicks. His eyes were scanning the dining room. He knew we were here. Not only had he probably seen Ben, but his body language told me this wasn't an accidental meeting. Someone had informed him Gemma and I were here.

Truthfully, I'd been waiting for him to explode and make a scene soon about Gemma. He'd lost her, and I knew it was a very hard thing for him. He was used to always commanding and getting what he wanted. She would forever be the one who defied him and dared to go to another man. When his eyes met mine, I saw him stiffen and the hate on his face increased.

"Gemma, remain calm. Don't engage Santo, no matter what he says. He's going to come over here and likely make a scene. I'm sorry, *tesoro*," I told her softly. I could tell she was a little scared. I gave her a wink.

She tried to smile. "I'll do my best. Why does he have to do this? Just get over it."

"You don't have a clue how unforgettable you are. I wouldn't be able to just forget you. Now, keep eating and act like you don't have a care in the world."

She nodded, and we went back to eating our delicious meal. I wasn't going to let it go to waste because of that asshole. To my surprise, he didn't immediately come over to us. Instead, he and his guys were seated by the hostess at a table that had a direct view of ours. The way the hostess was talking and her body language—even though I couldn't hear what was said—told me she knew Santo and was likely the one who told him we were here. Hmm, I wonder what hold he had on her?

I'd done the typical man thing and ordered a filet mignon wrapped in bacon with whiskey peppercorn reduction sauce. It was one of the best I'd tasted. As we ate, I could tell Gemma was struggling to eat and not look around at Santo. I decided the hell with it, I was going to stick to the plan I prepared. Finally, we finished our meal.

"We have to get dessert. I heard they make this decadent layered chocolate cake. You'll love that."

"Gabriel, I don't know if I can. I feel full, although it's tempting. Okay, if you'll help me eat it then bring on the cake. I can't say no to chocolate." She sighed happily.

Waving to get Anton's attention, he rushed over and I told him what we wanted. He assured us it would be right out. I knew it would because I'd already ordered it before we ever came. It was all part of my romantic night.

I could feel Santo and his men's stares practically burning holes through me. I was hoping he'd stay away from us until the next part was over. Within a few minutes, Anton was back carrying a plate with a huge piece of chocolate cake. As he set it down, Gemma gasped. Sitting next to the cake was a small royal blue velvet-covered box. She glanced over at me. Her mouth was open as if she was about to speak, only she didn't. I took pity on her.

"I know this is kind of out of order. We announced to people we're engaged and the ring is being sized, but the truth is, I had to get it. I want the world to know that you belong with me. Please accept this ring as a symbol of my commitment and love for you."

I got up and came around the table. As she slowly opened it, I kneeled in front of her. She gasped when she saw the ring. I took it out of the box and as she held out a shaky left hand, I slid it onto the all-important fourth finger. It fit like it had been made for her. Another sign to me that she was the one.

"Gabriel, it's just so gorgeous. I don't know what to say. It's way too expensive. You shouldn't have spent this much money on a ring. The vintage look is my favorite. It looks like someone's heirloom jewelry."

The ring was impressive. It had a large old European-cut diamond in the center. It was almost two carats. Surrounding it were smaller topaz stones. They shone in the gold setting. My mother had been unique and her ring reflected that.

"It is an heirloom. It belonged to my mother. It was left to me to give to my future wife one day. I didn't think I'd ever give it to anyone until I met you. You're my future." I raised her hand to my lips and kissed the ring.

"Gabriel, I know it's crazy, but it seems we're crazy. I want you to know that I love you too. Even if it's too soon to feel like that. I'll wear your mother's ring with honor and I'm so happy that you feel that way about me. I never expected you either."

I raised up to my feet and was about to give her a real kiss when Beau moved closer. I knew what that meant. Santo was coming. “He’s coming,” I whispered to her. I slowly turned to face him.

The expression on his face left no one in doubt he hated me and wanted to kill me. His gaze was locked on me. All three of his goons were right behind him. He stomped up and stood directly in front of me. His fists were clenched at his sides.

“What the fuck is this?” he hissed. His gaze was now fixed on the ring on her hand.

“I don’t like your tone. I’m trying to have a romantic dinner with my fiancée and you come over here disrupting us, asking stupid questions. What does it look like? I got her ring sized and was presenting it to her again. I’d appreciate it if you’d leave,” I growled at him.

“She can’t marry you! She’s mine. It’s me she’s supposed to be with. I don’t know why the two of you are pretending to be engaged unless you’re trying to piss me off for some reason. I warn you, if you don’t take that ring off her finger and let her come back home, I’ll speak to the Grecos about us not going through with this deal. I no longer think it’s beneficial for us,” he hissed lowly. He was trying not to let people hear what he was saying. He shouldn’t even be talking about our alliance in public.

I leaned closer to him, which made him take a step back. Good, he was afraid of me. “This isn’t the time or place for this conversation. I’ll talk to you tomorrow. Meet me at Mia Bella Rosa at noon. However, I want to assure you that this is no sham or to piss you off.

Gemma and I are in love and she's going to be my wife. That ring stays on her finger. You had three years to win her heart. I can't help it if you couldn't do it." I smirked when I said the last part.

His face turned so red, I thought he might have a stroke. He was shaking. One of his men must have clued in that I'd tear Santo to shreds if he attacked me because he came closer and said to his boss, "Santo, we need to leave. There's too many people here. We'll finish this tomorrow. Come on." I recalled that he was called Fausto. He was watching me warily.

"Listen to your man. If you take a swing at me, I'll put you on the ground. If you keep this shit up, chasing after Gemma, I'll put you in the ground. The deal can survive without you, Santo. Remember that. But it can't and won't survive without me."

He warred with himself for a minute then, swearing loudly, he whipped around and marched out of the restaurant. People were whispering and staring at both of us. I chose to pretend I didn't notice. I went to sit back down, but then I saw Gemma was shaking and had tears in her eyes. Instead, I grabbed my chair and brought it around the table to sit beside her. When I sat, I pulled her into my arms. I gave her a gentle kiss.

"Don't cry. He's gone and I promise you'll be safe."

"I'm not worried about me. I'm worried about you. You saw his face. He hates you and wants you dead, Gabriel. He won't stop until he kills you. I won't survive that. Please, you have to leave here," she pleaded. A tear ran down her face. I wiped it away with my thumb and brought it to my lips. I tasted the saltiness of it.

"Shh, *piccola*, please, Seeing you cry is killing me. I'm not leaving. Believe me, Santo is going to be handled. I can't say when or exactly how, but it'll happen. I swear to God that he will. What I want is for you and me to work on our life together like he doesn't exist, because he doesn't. He can bitch and moan all he wants, but he's just jealous that I have you and he doesn't."

She sniffed and carefully wiped another tear away. Finally, she made eye contact with me and gave me a tiny smile. "I'll try my best, but I won't be able to stop worrying about you. I'll be praying for you and that this whole mess gets resolved really soon."

"Good. Now, I don't know about you, but this cake is calling my name. If we don't eat it, I think Beau is going to come over here and eat it. I saw him eyeballing it like a hungry wolf," I teased. I said it loud enough for him to hear me. He grinned then made a growling noise like a wolf. Gemma burst out laughing. That broke the tension and got us back to enjoying our night together.

Once we finished our dessert, we were ready to go. I paid, and they brought out the orders for my guys. I texted Ben to let him know we were coming out. I escorted her out with her carrying her flowers. Beau brought up the rear. This time, the car was waiting at the door with the engine running. We hustled into it.

As I was rounding the car to get in on my side, Ben whispered to me, "Santo left two guys to watch. They're going to follow us home. I have a bad feeling, Gabe. They're going to try something soon."

"I have the same feeling. All we can do is stay alert. The extra protection is still here."

"Are you going to tell us who they are?"

"Nope. It's on a need-to-know basis. Right now, you don't need to know."

He rolled his eyes but didn't say anything else. I got in the car then he did. The ride back to the house was filled with moans from Beau and Ben about how delicious the food smelled and how hungry they were. Gemma teased them by telling them how good her food was. They were telling her she was cruel. The relaxed way they interacted told me she was going to easily fit in with my friends. I couldn't wait for her to meet Cassidy and Sloan.

Gabe: Chapter 13

I'll admit, I was still worrying about Santo when we made it back to the house. I distracted myself at first by watching the show Ben and Beau put on as they ate their dinner. The way they carried on, you'd think they never had good food. When Gemma told them that, they both told her why.

"The food in the service is far from good. The officers eat much better than the lowly enlisted guys like us. If we were lucky, we might find a decent, cheap place out in town to eat, but it was never of this quality. We didn't make enough then to eat like this. Only maybe on a really special occasion we might spurge. This place is awesome. I could eat this every damn day," Ben said, as he looked at me.

"Don't expect it every day. We might go there again before we head home. We'll see. I agree with the quality of the food in the service. I carried around a bottle of Worcestershire sauce to use on stuff to either kill the taste or to give it some. I had to retrain myself that I didn't need it after I got out."

"I used hot sauce like that," Beau added, as he swallowed another piece of steak.

"It's a shame they don't feed you better. You're there defending your country and others, and to be fed that way." She shook her head.

"Don't feel too bad for us. It made us tougher," Beau said as he held up his arms and flexed.

This got them off on another conversation. As they chattered, I walked over to peek out the window. I wanted to see if I could see Santo's men. They didn't strike me as very slick. Scanning the street, I saw three houses down a dark sedan with dark windows sitting along the street. Since we'd moved in, I made it my business to know the vehicles of those living on the street. This wasn't one of them. It had to be them. I snapped my fingers to get the guys' attention. They both immediately came to me.

"See the car down the street? That's them I bet. You know, this is a quiet street and we watch out for each other. I think someone should call the cops and report there are suspicious men lurking around and there are children who live on this street."

They both grinned. It wouldn't get rid of them forever, but it would be fun to fuck with them. They flipped a coin to see who got to make the call. Gemma was observing us with a smile on her face as she shook her head. I winked at her. Ben won the toss, so he placed the call.

From that moment on, we watched the street, all four of us. It wasn't more than maybe fifteen minutes before we saw a cop cruiser show up. Two officers got out and approached the car. The conversation lasted a good five minutes or more, before the car left and the cops got back in their car and left.

"Keep an eye open. I doubt they'll stay away long. Hopefully, the cops will increase their patrols to make sure they don't return. I know this isn't a solution, but it'll shake them up. The more uncertain they are, the more likely it is they'll screw up," I told them.

Over the next hour we tried to relax. As soon as it was ten o'clock, I called it quits. I had to have alone time with my woman. She was still in that dress and wearing those heels. My ring was on her finger. I was hard, and I needed to strip her naked and hopefully feast on her lush body.

As Gemma said goodnight to the guys, I did one final walk around. I knew we'd checked all the windows and doors when we came home and the alarm was on, but I was still paranoid enough to want to double-check. Throughout the night, I bet the guys would do the same.

I held her hand as we walked to our room together. As soon as the door was shut, I pressed her to the wall next to it and captured her mouth. She moaned as I made a meal of it. By the time I called it quits, her lips were swollen and she was panting like I was. I slid my hand down to the hem of her sexy red dress. Inching it up slowly as she stared into my eyes, I told her what I wanted to do to her.

"I want to tear this dress off and see what it's hiding. Then I want to lay you down on that bed and kiss and lick your whole body. I'll pay special attention to your gorgeous breasts and your amazing pussy. I want to make you come over and over again on my mouth and my fingers. One day soon, I hope it'll be on my cock." I pressed my erection into her soft stomach.

She surprised me when her hand cupped my aching cock and gave it a squeeze. "Then why don't you take this dress off me? I'd prefer you not tear it, because I love it. Then when I'm naked and on the bed, you can explore all you want. Make me come, Gabriel. I want to come on your fingers, on your tongue and on your cock. Give me all of them, as long as I give you equal pleasure."

It took my lust-filled brain a couple of moments to understand what she said. When I did, I had to clarify. This was too important to misinterpret. "Did I hear you right, Gemma? Did you just give me permission to give you my cock anyway I want, even in your sweet pussy?" I was afraid to breathe as I waited for her to respond.

"Yes, Gabriel, you heard right. I'm ready. I need you to show me more of that mind-numbing pleasure you gave me last night and then I want you to show me even more. I want to know what it feels like to have you inside of me."

I think I lost my mind and turned into a slightly crazed beast who was focused on making her mine and making her scream my name. I swept her off her feet and took her to the bed. I sat her down on her feet at the edge of it and stripped her dress off.

Her sexy bra and barely there thong that was the same color as her dress made me groan. I turned her around, and I palmed her lush ass cheeks in both hands and squeezed them. She moaned too, so I gave her a light smack on one cheek. She jumped and gave me a startled look, but she didn't tell me no.

I gave her another one, only it was harder. She jerked, and I heard her hiss but she pushed her ass toward me. Shit, she liked getting spanked. There were so many things we could do to satisfy that need. I leaned over her shoulder to nibble on her delicate ear as I hoarsely told her, "We're gonna explore your apparent liking of pain from a spanking. I want to see what else you like, but that's for another night. Right now, I want to look at you and taste. Lie on the bed on your back. Put your arms up toward the headboard and spread your legs, so I can see your pussy."

She didn't say a word. She just climbed on the tall mattress and lay herself down exactly as instructed. It exposed everything to me. I ran my gaze up and down her body as I quickly got rid of my shoes, gun, and clothing. When I was as naked as she was, I fisted my cock and stroked it a few times.

Her gaze zeroed in on what I was doing. I was as hard as I ever remember being. The head of my cock was a ruddy color. Precum coated the head and was even running down my shaft. The veins running the length of it were visible. My cock was anxious to feel her wrapped around it, but that would have to wait until I made her come a few times. She licked her lips. *Wait, maybe there would be a change of plans.*

I walked closer until my knees were pressed into the side of the mattress.

"What does *amore mio* want? I can see that look in your eyes. Do you want to taste my cock? You got to touch it and get me off last night. Do you want more tonight? If you do, I'm all yours."

In a flash, she wiggled around and lay on the bed with her head level with my cock. The bed was at the height that it would take nothing to slip my cock between those lips and into her mouth.

She licked her lips then tentatively reached up and over to grasp my cock in her hand. I let go. She pumped up and down like she did last night. "Gabriel, I don't know what I'm doing, but I'm dying to taste you. Please, tell me what you want, so I can make this good for you," she pleaded prettily.

I rubbed my fingers across her lips. She took it into her mouth and sucked on it before letting go. Jesus, she was so damn sensual and didn't have a bit of experience. What would she be like once she knew more? I'd have a damn femme fatale on my hands.

"Lick it, stroke it like that. Play with my balls. Remember how you touched them last night. That was perfect. If you want, you can put as much as you can in your mouth and suck on it. It's up to you. Any and all those things will give me immense pleasure."

One quick adjustment of her head and she was able to swirl her tongue around the head of my cock. I almost shouted, it felt that good. She was licking me like an ice cream cone. Seeing her pink tongue swirling around me, it made me hotter. She moaned but didn't stop. She did it again as she pumped my cock and my hips jerked, causing my cock to slip deeper into her mouth.

"Shit, I'm sorry, it was a reflex," I told her, as I pulled back. Her hand tightening around me made me stop. She shook her head. With her eyes staring into mine, she slowly sucked me deeper. As she did, she kept swirling her tongue where she could and pumping. My knees weakened. In no time, I felt the back of her throat. I ran my hand through her long hair. She'd taken it down when we got home.

"That's it. You're doing so well. It feels wonderful. Now, we can stay like this, or you can go back to licking me. Just be warned, you do much more and I'll come. You'll have to decide if you want to swallow my cum or not." As I explained her options, my hips kept flexing. My cock was thrusting back and forth in her incredible mouth. She might not have technique, but she could make me come. Her untutored movements were a major turn on for me.

She moved her head and I popped out of her mouth. She kept stroking me. "I want you to come in my mouth. I've watched porn and I've seen women take men deeper, like down in their throats. Does that feel good to you? Is it better that way?"

I groaned. "*Piccola*, I won't lie. It does feel incredible, but that's not necessary and it can be scary. You won't be able to breathe when I'm that deep. I'd never let you smother, but it might feel like it. If you want to try that, it can wait."

I was edging closer to blowing my load. I wanted back in her mouth when I did. Her admitting she wanted to swallow my jizz made me harder. I loved coming in a woman's mouth, but a lot of them hated it. They said cum tasted nasty. I wouldn't force her to take it.

"I want to try now," she said softly, then I was swallowed and this time, when I got to the back of her throat, she took a deep breath then tried to let me in deeper. I didn't get far, but the fact she did it and the tight constriction around the head of my cock was so damn wonderful, I had to cry out.

"Fuck, that feels fantastic. Swallow again," I instructed. She did it. I moaned as I held it for several seconds then I slid back to let her breathe.

"You're incredible, Gemma. Thank you, *piccola*. Do you want me to do it again?"

She nodded eagerly. Slowly I pushed deeper and this time I slipped a bit further down her throat. This set up repeated steps of me going a little deeper each time, holding it longer and the sensations increasing. In no time, I was thrusting in and out in a haze. My sac kept caressing her face. She'd play with my balls as she gave me what was turning out to be one of the best blow jobs of my life. I was there, and I needed to warn her in case she'd changed her mind about swallowing.

"Gemma, I'm there. I'm gonna come. Push me away if you don't want this load in your mouth," I grunted. I was gritting my teeth to hold on. She didn't let go. The minx sucked harder and that was it. I cried out her name as jet after jet of my cum filled her mouth. She was a trouper and worked to swallow it all as she kept stroking my cock. By the time I stopped coming, I was so sensitive I had to beg her to stop.

"Stop, stop, *Amore mio*, I'm too sensitive," I hissed as I withdrew. She kissed the head of my cock after it passed her lips. Knowing she still would taste like my cum, I bent down and tongued her mouth. She gripped my head and sank her fingers into my hair as she eagerly returned the kiss. I tasted myself for the first time. It didn't taste that bad to me. However, it didn't taste half as good as her pussy did, which got me thinking of eating her out.

I said nothing to her. All I did was crawl on the bed and over her body until I was between her legs. I pushed them further apart and lay down so I could have enough room to get to my meal. With one hand, I lifted her ass up and, with the other, I put a pillow underneath her ass. She was now raised so I could more easily reach all the places I wanted to explore.

She was soaked. That told me she had definitely liked giving head. I stuck out my tongue and swiped it from her entrance to her clit, where I twirled it around her hard nub then sucked it. She cried out this time. For the next several minutes, I kept busy licking, sucking all up and down her folds and using my fingers to simulate what my cock planned to be doing shortly. Her sweet cries as she tightened down on those fingers and came was incredible. She flooded my mouth with her cream.

I didn't stop after she had her orgasm. Instead, I kept going. I wanted her to come again. She was crying out, "Oh God," over and over which made me proud. I don't think she knew how loud she was. Beau and Ben couldn't help but hear us. I didn't give a damn. All I wanted was for both of us to be sated.

When she came for a second time, producing even more cream and her whole body shaking, I knew I had to be inside of her. Simply eating her pussy had gotten me hard again. My cock was begging me to be inside her pussy. I knew from how she gripped my fingers and the fact she was a virgin, she'd be tight. Fuck, I'd never been with a virgin. I had purposefully steered clear of them. Look at me now. Rising up, I rolled off her and over onto my back.

"I think for your first time, you need to control the speed and how deep I go. I want you to straddle me and ride my cock, Gemma."

She got to her hands and knees then straddled me. Her wet pussy slid over the head of my cock. We both groaned. I held my cock upright and notched it at her entrance.

"Take it slow. It's going to hurt."

"I don't think it will. I don't have a hymen anymore, Gabriel."

"What?" I asked in shock.

She smiled and shrugged. "A woman has needs. Even if I am a virgin, it doesn't mean I never got horny. I've watched porn and I played around with a vibrator. I accidentally went too deep one time and removed it. It hurt but not like some people said it would."

"Well then, what're you waiting for? Ride me, cowgirl," I teased to relieve her tension.

Smiling, she began to slowly press down. I held myself in check to prevent myself from thrusting all the way into her. As she took more of my cock inside, I got lost in how incredible she felt. I was right. She was tight as a vise and so wet. The heat from her pussy felt like it could scorch my cock. I groaned long and deep as she worked me inside of her. I kept watching her face to make sure it wasn't hurting her. She showed some discomfort but no signs of pain.

"Take your time," I whispered. As much as I wanted to be all in there, I didn't want to hurt her. My hands were gripping her hips. I heard her take a deep breath, then suddenly she bore down and took the rest of me to the root. I cried out while she moaned and ground her hips in a circle.

"*Gesù Cristo*!" I cried.

It was like something inside of her broke. As I worked to catch my breath, she lifted herself and then dropped back down on me. I'd never seen a woman ride like she was. Again, her natural sensualness was showing. She not only rode my cock, but she also made circles with her hips, ground down, and flexed her inner muscles. I didn't know what porn she'd watched, but I wanted to send the company or the actors a gift. My virgin soon-to-be-wife fucked me until we were both shouting our bliss as we came. As I squirted pump after pump of cum into her pussy as she milked it out of me and kept coming, I realized something.

We hadn't talked about birth control. I was inside her bare. Something I'd religiously made sure I never forgot to wrap up. Even if she said she was on birth control, I protected myself from catching an STI or getting a woman pregnant. I was shocked to realize this realization didn't scare me. I wasn't feeling panicked or trapped. A sense of peace and even happiness filled me.

If she wasn't taking anything, which was likely, and this resulted in her getting pregnant with my child, I'd shout it from the damn rooftops. I had no doubts I wanted her to be the mother of my children and I didn't give a damn when it happened. The sooner the better was my thought.

Finally softening all the way, I reluctantly slipped out of her. She moved to lie on her side facing away from me. Concerned she might be upset or that I'd missed a signal that she hadn't enjoyed it as much as I thought, I moved to spoon her body with mine. I kissed her neck then her cheek. Her eyes were closed, and she wore a serene smile on her face. I felt ten feet tall and invincible. All because I knew I'd gotten my woman off her first time.

"Gemma, tell me that you're alright. That it was as fantastic for you as it was for me. You blew my mind."

It took a few seconds before she opened her eyes and answered me. "Gabriel, my whole body is humming. I'm still having what I think are mini orgasms. God, I never imagined it would feel like that. My vibrator sure never made me feel like this."

I chuckled. "Well thank *Dio*, it didn't. If it did, you'd have no need for me."

She smiled at me tenderly and ran her fingers

back and forth over my lips. I licked them as she did.

"There's no contest. You have nothing to worry about. Despite the fact I'm still floating here, I can't stop thinking of doing it again. I think you might have created a monster, Gabriel."

"Oh, we can do that although we do need to talk about something. We should've done it before we got carried away. Before we go for a second round, I need to know. Are you on birth control?"

Instantly, she shot up into a sitting position. Her face paled and she looked like she was going to faint. She clutched her hands to her breasts.

"Oh my God! How could I forget that? I'm so stupid. Gabriel. I swear, I didn't do this on purpose. I assumed we'd use condoms when the time came. Except when it did, I lost my mind and totally forgot to ask you to use one. I'm sorry."

She gave me a beseeching look. I hauled her into my arms then onto my lap since I was now sitting up too. I rubbed her back.

"*Piccola*, you don't need to apologize. I'm as much at fault as you are. Hell, more so because I have experience. I've never in my life went without protection. You made me just as crazy."

"Okay, fine, we're both at fault, but that doesn't help us. What if I get pregnant?"

"Then you get pregnant. It's going to happen. I know you want kids. I want them. We might start on the first one sooner than we thought, but so what.

Hell, Mark and Sean didn't waste time having their first babies, especially Mark. I think he got Sloan pregnant the first time they had sex."

"Why are you so calm? You're the man. Aren't you supposed to be panicking and running out to get the morning-after pill or something? Or shouting at me for letting you forget and for me not being on anything."

"Hell no. Why would I do any of that? You and I are getting married. We're going to have a family. That's the bottom line. If you do get pregnant, then I know you won't run off and leave me."

"What? I could take one of those pills they have."

I scowled at her. "Like hell you will. I might not be practicing my faith, but in my family, we don't believe in that. If others want to, that's their business but not us. Do you want to take it?" I dreaded her answer. It was her body after all. She had the right to decide what to do with it.

"I don't want it. I only mentioned it because I thought I should. I don't believe in using that for this reason, which doesn't leave us much of a choice. We can wait and see and make sure we use condoms from now on or we say the hell with it and let mother nature decide when and if."

"Which way do you want to go? I don't care. It's your body that has to carry a baby for nine months."

"Don't be mad at me, but I think we should use condoms. Maybe we dodged the bullet. I'm not saying that because I don't want your baby. I do. I love children and was thinking I might never have any. It's only because of the situation with Santo. Until he's taken care of, I'd be terrified if I got pregnant and he found out what he might do. He's not entirely sane."

As much as I didn't want to do that, I understood her fear. He wasn't right in the head. I nodded. "Okay, we'll use condoms until Santo is out of our hair, which is hopefully soon. Once he's gone, I'm going to do my damndest to get you pregnant. I think barefoot and pregnant, serving me dinner every night, as you rub my feet after work, would be perfect."

I knew as I said it, she'd have something to say. I laughed as she swung a pillow at me and whacked it up against my head. Somehow, that led to a pillow fight. By the time we were done, we were both in need of a wash and some sleep. I had plans and they included me waking up later to have her again. Once wasn't enough. I doubted it ever would be. Minutes later, we were cleaned and snuggled in bed. I was already half asleep.

Gemma: Chapter 14

The insistent ringing of a phone dragged me from my deep sleep. It took a couple of seconds for me to realize it wasn't my phone. It was Gabriel's. He was already talking urgently into it. My bleary eyes looked around the bedroom at the clock. It was two o'clock in the morning. We'd only been asleep for over an hour. After my spectacular introduction to sex and our silly pillow fight, we'd gone to sleep. I felt out of it. He appeared to be totally awake and functioning. I hated people like that. I was one of those who took a few tries to fully wake up. Hence, why I set my alarm early because I knew I'd hit snooze at least twice.

His words jarred me to full wakefulness. "Have them taken to you know where. I want at least one of you to come into the house and tell us the details. How the hell did they get that close?" he barked into the phone before he hit end. His face was furious.

I sat up and touched his arm. His gaze darted to look at me. "What's wrong? Take who where?"

"It's nothing. I'm sorry we woke you. Why don't you go back to sleep? I'm awake and need to get up for a bit."

"Don't treat me like the little brainless woman you have to protect or lie to, Gabriel. I'm not. If you don't want to tell me, then tell me that," I snapped back. I had enough men in my family treating me like I didn't have brains. I didn't need it from him nor would I tolerate it. I threw the covers back to get out of bed. He grabbed my arm before I could get up.

"I'm sorry, *piccola*. I don't think you're brainless. I just hate having to involve you in this shit more than you already are. You should be able to sleep and know that you're safe."

"So, something happened to threaten our safety, is that what you're trying to say?"

He sighed and rubbed a hand along his jaw before he nodded his head. "Yes, that's what I'm saying."

He was going to say more, but a knock at the bedroom door stopped him. He quickly threw the covers back up over me, although I wasn't naked, and made sure I was covered before hollering to enter. The door opened and there stood Ben and Beau. I was disgusted. They looked wide awake like Gabriel. Hadn't they been to bed yet? Or was I the only one who had this issue? I noticed they were dressed in loose shorts and had no t-shirts on. Even if I was all into Gabriel, I'd have to be blind not to notice they were physically fit men with yummy muscles and tattoos.

"Got the alert. Everything okay?" Beau asked.

"Yeah, they got them, but we need to get up. Someone is coming in to talk to us. Give me a minute to get dressed. I'll meet you in the living room."

They both nodded and Ben shut the door. Gabriel

got out of bed. I followed him.

"I guess it would be too much to expect you to stay here?" he asked.

"It would. If you want me to be your partner in life, Gabriel, that means when it involves me, I know everything too. No keeping secrets. I understand when it comes to your job, that there might be times you can't tell me everything. I get that, but not in something like this."

He wearily nodded his head but didn't say more. I got out of bed and threw on a pair of shorts, my bra, and a t-shirt. No way was I going out there without a bra. He pulled on a t-shirt to go with the shorts he already had on. When we went to sleep, he'd put them back on. Something told me it was more for my comfort than his. I bet soon he'd be asking me not to wear anything to bed. I wasn't sure how I felt about that, but it could wait until he asked. Right now, I wanted to know what had happened and who was coming to speak to us?

He held my hand as we went to the living room. The guys had on shirts now too and were standing around. They looked relaxed, but I knew that wasn't the case. We hadn't gotten any more than out there when there was a knock at the door. Ben, Gabriel, and Beau all pulled out guns. I gasped. I hadn't even seen Gabriel pick his up.

He gave me a comforting look then went to answer the door. I went to follow, but Beau grabbed my arm and shook his head. He positioned himself in front of me. Ben was off to the side but between me and the door as well. A low murmur of voices came from the entry then a few moments later, Gabriel came back. Behind him was a man who I had never seen before.

He was tall and had a dark complexion, very much like Gabriel's. He was muscular and gave off this dangerous vibe as well. His eyes immediately took in the room. I doubted he missed anything. I shifted a little to the side, so I could see him better. His gaze zeroed in on me. His eyes stopped not far from me.

"Is this what the big stink is all about, *amico*?" he asked Gabriel, as he stared intently at me.

I was comforted a little by the fact he called Gabriel friend and that Gabriel felt safe enough to have his back to him. There weren't a lot of people he would do that with.

"Yes, Tristano, this is what all *la puzza* is about. Gemma, come here, *amore mio*. I want to introduce you." He held out his hand, so I edged around Beau and went to him. He hugged me close to him as he made the introduction.

"Gemma, this is a friend of mine, Tristano. Tristano, this is Gemma Marra, my fiancée."

"Hello, it's nice to meet you, Tristano," I said, as I held out my hand.

He took it. "Oh, believe me, *tesoro*, it's my pleasure to meet you. When I heard Gabe had found himself a woman and was claiming her, I didn't believe it. I thought it had to be a lie. I've been watching you and I can see why he's been ensnared. You're beautiful, smart, and kind. No wonder Santo is going crazy over losing you. I would too. Keep her close, or someone will surely steal her, maybe even me," he told Gabriel with a wicked smile.

"Friend or no friend, if you try to do that, I'll gut you and you'll never be found again. You can let go of her hand now. Let me formally introduce you to my men."

Before he could do that, I interrupted him. "I'm sorry, Gabriel, but what does he mean by he's been watching me?"

"I'll explain in a second, Gemma. Let me get the rest of the introductions out of the way."

I settled down and waited. He quickly introduced Ben and Beau. Once that was done, Gabriel started to explain who Tristano was and why he was here in the middle of the night.

"Let's all sit down and grab a drink, so we're comfortable. Gemma, water for you? Tristano, we have water, soda, and beer. I can make coffee if you want. It's one of those fast single cup maker deals."

"Water will be good for me, Gabe," Tristano told him as he took a seat. I nodded yes to Gabriel's offer of water. Anything with caffeine would keep me awake and I didn't like beer. As he grabbed water for the three of us, Ben got a couple for him and Beau. They all took their seats.

"I know you're anxious to find out what this is all about. I told you, I had other eyes watching us, Santo, and the other Greco members. Tristano is one of them. Tonight, he was here, helping to watch the house with another one of his guys. We knew those men we had the cops run off would be back. Well, they did come back, only not in a car. Somehow, they snuck into the neighborhood on foot without being seen. They were almost to the house before they were spotted and apprehended by Tristano and Sergio."

"What happened to them?" I asked.

"They were secured and Sergio took them somewhere they'll be checked out further," Tristano answered calmly.

"Checked out further or tortured and questioned?" I asked back. Call me crazy, but I didn't see Gabriel or this man just checking into anyone who worked for Santo. Torturing them until they spilled their guts, yes.

Tristano smiled at me. "Why would you think that, Gemma?" His attempt to look innocent didn't fool me.

"Because I'm not stupid. There's more to me than great hair and boobs. There's an actual brain in this head. I thought you said I was smart?" I immediately flung back at him. Gabriel snorted, and I heard the others choke on their laughs.

"*Dio*, please say you'll give her to me. She's perfect. With her by my side, I'll have no problem working my way up into a better position," he sighed.

"Forget it. She's mine and that's the way she

stays," Gabriel growled at him.

"Not if I kill you myself and then take her. I bet it wouldn't take me long to console her and show her that I'm the better choice."

In a flash, Gabriel was up and over to Tristano. He had his head in a headlock. "Do you think you can kill me? I wouldn't let the past twenty years fool you. I haven't gone soft."

Tristano patted Gabriel's arm and he let go. Tristano rubbed his neck as he laughed. "I'd never think that, *mio fratello*. I'd hazard a guess that you're more deadly than you ever were."

Gabriel retook his seat and calmly took a drink of his water. I was caught on Tristano now calling him brother. How did they know each other?

"Gabriel, who is Tristano? I know you said he's helping to watch and protect us, but why? Who is he to you?"

"Maybe I should've given you his full name. This is Tristano Rizzo. He's part of the Rizzo family."

His bombshell shocked me. One of the Rizzo Mafia family was standing watch over us. Although they hid it, I knew Beau and Ben were probably as shocked as I was.

"To be fair, I'm just a Rizzo cousin, not one of the big main five who run everything. I'm not a big deal like my uncle and cousins or like Gabe here. The family wanted to make sure this goes off without a hitch. It's too important to all of us for it to fail."

"That's something I don't fully understand. If your family doesn't hope to gain territory, why help Gabriel? What's in it for you?"

Tristano gave Gabriel a mysterious look then answered me, without really answering me, which frustrated me. "The repayment of an old debt is what's in it for us. Rizzos always repay their debts, especially one like this."

I went to ask more, but Gabriel stopped me. "I know you want to know more, but this isn't the time or place, Gemma. I promise you, I'll explain when the time is right. Just know, the Rizzo family means it when they say they won't double-cross me on this."

I harrumphed but didn't say anything.

"I don't want to leave her here with just one guard. They might send others when they don't hear back from those two you captured. I'll have to arrange to come speak to them later today," Gabriel told Tristano.

"I thought of that. I moved a couple more men over here. They'll stay here with her and one of your men while you and the other come with us. I doubt it'll take long to find out what you want to know if they know anything. They didn't strike me as the sharpest knives in the drawer. I doubt they know much about what Santo is planning. They're a couple of his lesser men, not the handful that he seems to always have with him."

I knew Gabriel was contemplating whether to go or not. I took his hand in mine and squeezed it. "I'll be fine here. You should go. Get this over with just in case they know more than you think. We can't afford to delay in making moves. I want this over with as soon as possible."

He was silent for a minute then he nodded his head. "You're right. We need to not delay. Tristano, as soon as your extra men are here, we'll go."

"They should be here any minute. Why don't you go get ready? I doubt you'll want to go out dressed like that. I'll sit here and get better acquainted with the *bella* Gemma."

"Ben, Beau, watch him. If he tries anything with Gemma, shoot him," Gabriel ordered as he stood. The two of them got evil looks on their faces. Tristano snorted. Gabriel gave me a kiss then headed off to our room. I sat back to wait and see what Tristano would say or ask next. I found him to be rather engaging. His flirting I didn't take seriously. He was trying to get a rise out of Gabriel.

Gabe:

After leaving Gemma at the house with Beau, it was about a half hour drive to get to where the two men were being held. It was an out-of-the-way old barn that when we set this up, the Rizzo family somehow knew about. They had assured me that the owner wouldn't ask questions or open his mouth. I didn't bother to ask why not. Knowing them, the owner owed them a debt or was in their pocket somehow. The less I knew about their dealings the better.

As much as it killed me to know they were a Mafia family and I should be working to take them down, not working with them, I knew I couldn't. There were reasons that I couldn't change. It helped to keep both sides honest. As long as they never betrayed me or strayed too far into the darkness, I'd leave them alone. There were a ton more Mafia and mob families out there who were a hundred times worse than them.

It was dark as pitch when we pulled up outside the dilapidated barn sitting in a field out in the middle of nowhere. Tall weeds and grass grew all around it. The place looked like it might collapse any moment. I hoped it would stay standing until after I was gone. There was a faint light shining from the inside. An SUV was parked off to the side of the barn. Ben whistled as we got out of the car with Tristano.

“Damn, this place is about to fall in. Are you sure it’s safe to go in there? I’d hate to die this way.”

Tristano grinned at him in the light of the flashlight he’d turned on. His ghostly face looked demented. “You’ll just have to live dangerously, I guess.”

He nonchalantly led us to the door. He gave a complicated knock. A few seconds later, the door swung open, and we were admitted. Inside, there were actually three men in addition to the two captives. I knew Sergio. He was Tristano’s brother. The other two I didn’t know by name. I greeted Sergio and then the others as they were introduced as Noé and Zeno. They were more distant Rizzo cousins. The damn family bred like rabbits.

Our two captives were gagged and hanging by ropes from the beams in the top of the barn. They had been stripped down to their underwear. I could see they had a few bruises on them. I raised a brow at Sergio. He shrugged at me.

“What could I do? They fought us and we had to subdue them. Bruises happen. They’re fine. Their mouths still work.”

“I hope so. If not, then I’m wasting my time here and you know how I hate to waste time, Sergio.”

He winced. He and I had gone rounds in the past when I got pissed off or bored and he was dumb enough to stand up and go at it with me.

“Yeah, I know. Okay, let’s get down to business. So far, they haven’t told us anything, but we haven’t pushed since I knew you'd want to be here for this."

"Their names are Heinz and Heinrich Koch. I know who they are. They're Greco *soldatos*, although very low standing ones. They are mainly drones. Santo often sends them out to do his bidding when he doesn't want to use his main guys. I think they're considered expendable," I explained.

I'd made it my job to find out the names and information on as many of the Greco crew as I could. Unlike a lot of the men they had working for them, the Koch brothers weren't Italian. They were of German descent. If you were going to be in the upper levels of the organization, the Grecos insisted on using only Italian men. How they found these two, I had no idea.

They took exception to me saying they were considered expendable. They began to thrash around and grunt, trying to speak through their gags. I nodded to Zeno. He went over and tore off both gags.

As soon as he did, Heinz shouted, "We're not fucking expendable, asshole. When Santo and the others get done with you, you're gonna wish you walked away and gave up the bitch to him. Let us go and maybe he'll go easier on you."

"Yeah, a piece of tail isn't worth blowing a deal over," Heinrich added.

Hearing them refer to Gemma as a bitch and a piece of tail pissed me off. They were so far beneath her, they shouldn't even be breathing the same air as her. I walked up to them. Their ankles had been tied together to make it harder for them to kick. Drawing back my fist, I drove it first into Heinz's stomach then into Heinrich's. Both of them cried out in pain and groaned.

I began to pace around them as I spoke. Ben was standing quietly, watching and waiting for my instructions. He wouldn't act unless I needed him to. Right now, he was playing his role as my bodyguard to the hilt. Some might underestimate him and think he was all muscle and no brains. If they did, it would be their mistake. He was a very lethal and calculating man, just like Beau. We only hired the best at Dark Patriots. We didn't need or want mindless sycophants or drones. We had men and women who could think.

"I'd watch my mouth if I were you. This can go one of two ways. With you telling us what we want to know without a lot of pain and blood or you telling us what we want to know with lots of pain and blood. It's purely your choice," I said, sounding bored.

"We're not telling you anything, you fucking arschlöcher," Heinz said, as he spat at me.

I didn't think he knew that I knew he'd called us assholes in German. I'd grown up around enough German-speaking people to pick up enough to follow, especially the swear words.

"The only assholes I see here are the two tied up like sacrificial offerings. We weren't the ones dumb enough to get caught. Did you have fun talking to the cops earlier this afternoon?"

"Fucker, you called them? Santo was pissed," Heinrich shouted.

"I bet he was. Enough of the chitchat. Let's get to business. I don't have all night. My woman is at home waiting for me."

I took a pair of leather gloves out of my pocket and slid them on. They were for two purposes. One, they wouldn't leave prints and two, they would protect my hands as I beat the hell out of these two morons. I doubted they'd have much to tell me, but it would be a way to get some of my frustration out. I wanted this to be over with, and me back in Virginia, introducing Gemma to my friends and starting our life together.

They eyed the gloves warily then grew more nervous when they saw Ben and Tristano pull on theirs. Sergio, Noé, and Zeno already had theirs on.

"I want to know what Santo told you to do. Why were you watching us? What was your plan if you got in the house tonight?"

Both of them remained quiet. This time, the punch was a right hook to their jaws. I made it hard enough to hurt but not hard enough to break their jaws, even though I could do it. The clicking of their teeth crashing together was loud along with their cries of pain.

I landed a few more punches, this time to their kidney and another to their stomachs, in the exact spot I hit them before. When I landed the stomach punches, Heinrich puked. I got out of the way just in time.

"Disgusting and pathetic. Can't even take a few punches. What kind of *femminellas* does this Santo hire?" Sergio snorted. I could tell by the blank look on the Koch brothers' faces, they had no idea he'd just referred to them as pussies.

"From what I've seen, Santo surrounds himself with a lot of pussies like these two," I told them with a smirk.

"Cocksucker, we'll show you pussies when we get done with you. Santo is going to kill you and take that bitch, Gemma. She'll be trained to do everything he wants. She'll spend the rest of her life on her back or knees. When he's done with her and the rest of us get tired of her, she'll be sold to a brothel. She'll die there," Heinz yelled.

Fury burst through me, hearing what was planned for her. I knew Santo wanted her, but would he really give her to others when he was done? I wasn't sure of that.

Before I'd left the house, not only had I brought my gun, but I'd brought with me one of my favorite knives. It wasn't the most wicked looking one, but it was sharp enough to cut through paper like it was nothing. It was an MK3, the preferred knife of most Navy SEALs. The blade was a decent six inches long and one side of the blade had small serrations. I took it out of the back of my jeans from the holder I had it in underneath my shirt. I held it up to the light.

"This might not seem like that big of a knife, but in the hands of a man like me, it's lethal. I not only can give you so much pain that you'll gladly tell me what I want to know, but I can gut you and chop you to pieces in no time. What kind of man do you think knows how to wield this expertly?"

They didn't say a word. Ben was the one to answer. "Isn't that the knife you carried when you were a Navy SEAL? The one you've used on countless insurgents and terrorists, plus the assholes who you've taken out since then?" His tone sounded like he was making a casual observance.

Heinrich and Heinz became more uneasy. They glanced at each other then back to me. Sergio and his cousins smiled and nodded their heads.

"You're right. It is. This knife has tasted the blood of many people. It's been a while and it's thirsty, so if you don't want to be the ones to slake that thirst, start by telling me what I want to know. What were your orders?"

Neither said anything, so I lashed out. In a flash, each had an angry, although not excessively deep cut across their chests. I knew it would still hurt. They cried out. I raised my hand again and they broke.

"Stop! We'll tell you what you want to know. No fucking job is worth dying over, not like this. Santo has gone off the deep end. Everything is about her and not our jobs with the Greco family. I don't know how he's getting away with this without the bosses finding out. Even in jail, they've always known what the hell is going on," Heinrich said.

"If you're waiting on Matteo, Carlo, or Anthony to send help or to reel him back in, you'll be waiting a long time. I don't know how you haven't heard, but they killed each other in prison over a month ago. They must've gotten into a fight and all three shanked the other. The Greco territory is dying. Soon, there won't be any territory left," I informed them.

Shock appeared on their faces. They shook their heads in denial. "No, that can't be true! Santo is still getting orders from them," Heinz gasped.

"Santo is lying. Is he the only one who communicated with them or did some of the other *capos* speak to them?" This was something I'd been trying to find out.

"Santo is their mouthpiece. It wasn't like that years ago, but once he came, it changed. The other *capos* aren't happy about it," Heinrich added.

"Does anyone know why he's been given the lead *capo* position and why someone who no one heard of before three years ago, did it out of the gate?"

"The rumor is that he's got something over them and when he came into the organization, they had no choice but to make him the head honcho. I don't know if that's true or not, but the others were told to do as he said. Communication came from them in jail telling the others to do as Santo said. That he was going to be their main contact from then on," Heinz offered up.

"So, the other *capos* and some of their men don't like Santo," I observed.

"They hate him. He has the power they want. All of us who work for him know it. That's why me and my brother made sure to stay on his good side. He's not a man you want to cross. If you do, you'll be found dead," Heinrich answered.

This information confirmed what I'd suspected. Santo had a hold over the Grecos and with them gone, he was running things as if they were still giving him orders. I wondered what he planned to do when the news of their deaths came out. Someone would find out it had happened a while ago. I'd have to find that out somewhere else. These two wouldn't know.

"Back to the house tonight. What were you going to do if you got into the house? Did Santo order you to break in or was that your brilliant idea?"

"It was Santo's order. He's tired of waiting for a chance to get Gemma alone. He said to go in and kill you and your men then take her. We were to call him when the job was done and he would tell us where to meet him," Heinz replied.

Now that they started to talk, they were spilling what they knew without me having to threaten them. I found it a little disappointing. I'd been looking forward to working off more of my frustration. I'd have to keep it for when I got my chance at Santo.

"Why only send the two of you? I mean, really, two against three doesn't sound fair."

"He said that you were used to acting big and bad, but he doubted you ever got your hands dirty, or if you did, it was long ago. As for your bodyguards, a gun would eliminate them quick enough," Heinrich answered with a tilt of his head.

Tristano laughed. "Santo is a *bischero*, an idiot. Gabe here is one of the deadliest men I know and that was before he was ever a SEAL. I can only try and imagine how much more deadly he is now. I wouldn't go up against him without an army and even then, I might not win. You guys were sent on a suicide mission. Your boss is either stupid or insane."

"He's been talking crazy ever since this one popped up on the scene. When he came out and claimed Gemma was his, that crazy talk became total insanity. She's all he can talk about. He wants revenge on Gabe for taking her and he talks about his plans when he gets her back. He's been letting work slide as he plots and has us watching them," Heinz agreed.

"He thinks he'll use him to get this deal with the Rizzos then he can have him killed. I think he sees himself running a huge territory. If the Grecos are dead, then he's planning to make a move to become the top boss," Heinrich stated.

"He is. What can you tell us about who works for him and his routes and distribution network?" I asked.

Over the next hour, they told me what I asked, which unfortunately, wasn't anything I didn't already know. It was apparent Santo kept that information close to his chest. His foot soldiers were just that. In the end, because they had cooperated, I gave them both a quick death. A knife to the heart did it.

As Noé and Zeno worked to untie them and wrap them in plastic with Ben's help, I talked to Sergio and Tristano. "I need to bring more guys in to watch over

Gemma. Do you have any more? If not, I can get them from some friends."

"I think we should be able to. Let me find out. You need to not underestimate this man, Gabe. The insane ones are unpredictable. I think you're more at risk than your woman is," Sergio stated before turning to his brother. "Is she as beautiful in person as she looks from a distance? Did you tell her there are better men out there and she should check us out?" This was said with a grin on his face. I should've known he'd do something like this. He was as bad as his brother.

Tristano grinned back at him. "She's even more beautiful, sassy, and sexy as hell. She's not dumb either. I tried, but he seems to have her tied up in him. It's unfortunate. I could become a king with a woman like her."

"What the hell, you become a king? I thought we were both going to be kings? We could share her," Sergio said.

"Listen, I don't need to hear about what the two of you do in your personal lives with women. All you need to know is mine isn't going to be yours. The death threat I gave you, Tristano, I meant."

This got both of them laughing. We teased and argued for a few more minutes then got on the road home. The sun would be up soon. I knew Gemma would be awake and worrying. As Tristano took Ben and I back to town, I sent her a text to let her know I was on the way and was safe. I laid my head back and closed my eyes. It was going to be a long day, and I hadn't gotten a chance to make love to her for a second time like I planned. Santo had a lot to answer for, the fucker.

Gemma: Chapter 15

When Gabriel and Ben returned, I was disappointed. They didn't know a whole lot. The most interesting was the part about the rumor Santo had something over the Grecos and that was why they'd put him in charge. It made me want to know what it was that they had feared. Gabriel was more interested in the fact Santo's men were saying he was insane about me being with another man and everything now was geared toward that and not business.

I couldn't understand it. Sure, he'd chased me, but there was nothing about me that would make a man lose his mind over me to the extent Santo seemed to have done. When I mentioned that, Gabriel had assured me I was more than worthy of a man being obsessed with me. Beau and Ben merely chuckled. I chose to ignore his remark. I wasn't interesting or gorgeous enough to warrant it.

Afterward, we'd laid down to try and get a couple of hours of sleep, but I only drifted in and out. When we got up, Gabriel tried to convince me to stay at the house today. He explained more men would be watching over me. I refused. I'd go insane if I did that. I had to do something. Going to the restaurant was at least something to do. He was concerned about what Santo might do when his men didn't report in. He hadn't confirmed they were dead, but I knew they were.

That had been a few hours ago. It was now lunchtime. Every time the door opened, I was nervous it would be Santo. Gabriel stayed at the restaurant rather than arrange to go somewhere or do something with Santo. He said things were going fine, but I knew he was worried about Santo's reaction too. He, Ben, and Beau had taken over a table in the back of the dining room and they kept watch over me. If I went to the back, two of them went with me. Gabriel was always one of them. I felt so loved and protected even if I thought two was overkill.

I was busy rolling more clean silverware into cloth napkins when Elijah came up to me. I was behind the hostess stand, working on a table we had there for that reason. The noon rush was slowing down.

"Gemma, this has to stop. Enough is enough," he barked at me.

"What are you talking about, Elijah?" I asked, mystified. He and Emmet hadn't spoken more than one or two words at a time to me since I blew off Santo. They were both at the restaurant, doing nothing as usual.

"Don't act all innocent with me. You know what I'm talking about. Having that man and his goons sitting around the restaurant every day is bad for business. People are scared of them. Tell them to stop it. You don't need them here while you work."

"Gabriel and our bodyguards are here for my protection. Not a single customer has said a word about being afraid of them. It's not bad for business. In fact, I think our business has increased. Maybe the customers feel safer having them here. That way when Santo and his goon squad come in, they don't have to be afraid of them."

"That's another thing. How long are you going to play this game of yours with Santo? He's not going to remain patient forever. You're supposed to be his, not Gabe's. I don't know why you keep fighting it and pissing him off. He's going to take it out on us and the restaurant if you don't stop it," he hissed.

I laid down the silverware I had in my hands and put my hands on my hips. "All you're worried about is your own neck and how much money you might lose. Let's be honest here. You couldn't give a damn about me. As long as Santo and his kind don't hurt you and keep paying you along with the profits you get from here, you don't care. It's time for you and Emmet to wake up and take responsibility for this place. When I leave, *Papà* won't be able to do it on his own. You'll have to jump in to work. That'll be a change for you two. No more riding along on my hard work, while you laze around, earning your share of money you don't do a damn thing to work for," I snapped back. I was done with their attitudes.

He reached out and grabbed my upper arm. His grip bit into my arm. I jerked on it to make him let go, but he didn't. An instant later, a hand wrapped around his wrist and squeezed. He cried out and let go of me. Gabriel was standing there looking furious.

"Don't ever touch her again or I'll tear your fucking head off. Do you understand me? She's never to be hurt. What the hell is going on over here?" I saw Ben and Beau were behind him. In the back of the room, Emmet was hovering, watching the scene. I bet he put Elijah up to this. Emmet was too weak to do it himself. Elijah tended to be the braver one.

"It's okay, Gabriel. I was just explaining to my dear cousin how you guys don't scare off the customers and are here for my protection. I also don't give a damn what Santo wants and that he and Emmet need to start working, since they'll be the ones left to do it when I'm gone. He didn't like that."

"Where the hell do you think you're going? This is a family business. You have a responsibility to work here," Elijah said, hotly.

"Why? You and Emmet don't. I work and *Papà* does what he can, but it's mainly me. I'm going to be moving away to live with Gabriel soon. When I do, who's going to fill in for staff when they call off? Who's going to keep up with the ordering, paying bills, payroll and the thousands of things I do around here? It'll have to be you guys, or else you'll have to hire more people. We know you won't like that, since it'll cut into your profits."

Emmet had slunk up to join us. His face looked aghast when he heard what I said. I fought not to laugh at their looks of horror. "You can't just abandon your family," Emmet cried.

"I'm moving on to start my own family. I have no intention of living separate from my husband and Gabriel doesn't live in New Jersey."

"Where the hell does he live? We haven't given

you permission to marry him. As the men in your family, that's our duty. We don't like him for you. You can't marry him," Elijah said, as he puffed out his chest.

I laughed in his face. "What century do you think we live in, cousin? The days of the men in a family determining who the women could or couldn't marry are long gone. I don't need your approval or permission. Gabriel is my choice. As soon as the wedding can be arranged, we'll be wed. As for where he lives, that's none of your business. You won't be invited to the wedding or our home."

The flabbergasted looks that they got were comical. They really thought they had a say in how I lived my life. How had I not realized it, and how had I let them get away with using me for so long? I'd been blind or maybe I ignored it since there was nothing I wanted to do more with my life. Gabriel had brought a world of change with him.

"I'd listen to your cousin. She's mine and I won't allow her to be used or hurt, not even by her family. I suggest you two start observing the various positions around here, so you can be ready to get your hands dirty," Gabriel sneered. Throwing him a scared look, they both scurried away into the back. I knew they were probably going right out the back door to their cars.

He rubbed my arm. "Did he hurt you?"

"It's sore and I might have a bruise, but it's okay. Aren't you guys bored to death, yet?"

Gabriel didn't look happy to hear it might bruise, but he let it go. I didn't want to dwell on my unloving family. It only made my heart hurt. After Gabe gave me a kiss, they went to take their seats again. He had been working on his laptop and phone on and off, so it wasn't as if he wasn't doing anything.

I felt the sorriest for Beau and Ben. They kept their eyes on me and the people in the restaurant the whole time. Usually one would stay with the car, but today, Gabriel insisted he wanted them both inside. He said there would be others to watch the car. Before I got caught up in doing more silverware, I asked one of the waitresses to please see if they needed anything. She happily agreed.

I was back at my boring task for maybe five minutes when the door opened. I pasted on a smile to greet whoever it was. My hostess was busy doing something else. I hated to make people wait to be seated. I fought to hold onto my smile when I saw Santo and his entourage. Out of the corner of my eye, I saw my guys stand up and begin to make their way to me.

"Good afternoon, right this way," I said without an ounce of recognition in my tone. I began to pick up menus. Santo was instantly in front of me.

"I'm not here to fucking eat. I want to talk to that bastard Gabe," he snarled. His expression looked crazy to me. I couldn't help it. I backed away from him. Before I could say anything, Gabriel was there.

"Anything you have to say to me, can wait until we're in a more private setting. I won't have you come in here and disturb the customers. You can wait until we're done for the day, then I'll let you know when and where we can talk. Don't ever come in here again and boss around my woman," he arrogantly told Santo.

"Your woman! That's rich. You stole her from me. She's mine. I'm going to have her back and if that means you have to die, then so be it," he practically yelled. I heard gasps around the room. Those closest to us had no problem hearing his threat.

Gabriel grabbed him around the throat and leaned in until they were nose to nose. "Get out, now. I'll contact you when I'm ready." He shoved Santo away from him. He glanced at the men with Santo. "If you know what's good for you and him, get him outta here. There's too many people around for this. He knows better," he told them softly.

They must've agreed with him or knew he wasn't going to take a no for an answer, because all five of them started talking to Santo. In the end, when it became clear he wasn't going to listen, they had to manhandle him out of the restaurant. People were openly gawking and whispering as they watched. I saw a few holding up their phones and taking video of it. God, this wasn't going to end well.

"I think you need to wrap things up for the day, *piccola*. I want to get you home. We'll decide when to have this urgent conversation Santo wants."

"Gabriel, he's not going to wait long. He's out of control," I warned him.

"I know. Let me worry about him. Finish up, please."

As I rushed to check with the staff before leaving, he and the guys remained on their feet, watching through the windows. Gabriel had his phone out and was texting away on it. It took me ten minutes to be ready to leave. Luckily, the car was right out front again. Ben ducked out, then came back in with the Kevlar blanket. I hated that thing. He and Beau hustled us out and into the car. They didn't waste time zooming off toward home. I held on to Gabriel's hand with a death grip the whole way there. I was too scared to even try to carry on a conversation. My gut was churning at the thought of how volatile this whole situation was becoming.

When we arrived at the house, it was straight into the garage, then shutting the door. Both Ben and Beau got out and hurried inside to check the house out after disabling the alarm. Gabriel kept me in the car, rubbing my hands soothingly. "Everything is going to be okay, Gemma. I hate to see you so worried."

"I can't help it. You're not invincible. You can be hurt or killed. He's not a sane man. There's no telling what he'll do."

"You're right, he's not sane, but I'm not underestimating him. I have more people arriving as we speak to help protect us and to get this assignment over with. It's time. I think I have enough to wrap up all lines of the business and to take down the people who need to be removed. Hang in there. I just need a week or two max, then we'll be off to start our life together. I can't wait for you to get to know my real family and all our friends."

"I can't either."

We didn't get to say more because Ben was back. He nodded and waved for us to come inside. In the house, the first thing Gabriel insisted we do was get changed into more comfortable clothes. I admit, being out of dress clothes and in my shorts and a tank top was better. We came back and sat in the living room. I anxiously waited to see what he'd say.

"Gemma, I know you're wondering what the next step is, after the way Santo acted today. He's quickly unraveling, which makes him dangerous, but it also makes him sloppy. He's going to miss stuff. His authority is already being questioned by his men and I can guarantee you, the other *capos* and their men are doing the same."

"I agree. What're you going to do about meeting him? It should be somewhere private enough no one overhears you, but public enough, he's less likely to ambush you," Beau asked.

"I've been thinking about that. First, be assured, more men have already been dispatched here to watch over all of us. Otherwise, I wouldn't leave Gemma here, not even with both of you. No offense, but I have no idea how many men will follow Santo's orders. I plan to take Ben with me and leave you here with Gemma, Beau. It's not that I don't trust the ones watching her, but she knows you and will be comfortable having you here."

"Not a problem. I understand," Beau said nonchalantly.

"The spot I think I should meet him is that large park at the edge of town. After dark, it'll be mostly deserted. You can see in every direction, so no one can sneak up on me or hide. There are no trees. It's in town, so any gunshots or commotion will most likely bring the cops. It's the best I can do, I think."

"I've spent time checking out the town, just like you have, and I can't off the top of my head think of a better place. We don't want to be out of town in an isolated location. My worry is we can't hide men either and we have no idea how many men he'll bring with him. He was pretty crazy at the restaurant. He's not going to back down on Gemma being his, Gabe. You have to be prepared that although it's relatively public, he could lose it," Beau warned him.

I felt sick to my stomach. Nothing they were saying was reassuring me that Gabriel and Ben would get out of this alive.

"Don't do it. It's too dangerous. Have him come to the restaurant tomorrow. I'll tell my family that we have to use it for a private meeting. We don't open until ten, so if you have your meeting say at eight o'clock that should give you plenty of time. He can't hide men there and outside there are places not only for his men to hide but ours too," I suggested in a hurry.

I could tell by the expressions on their faces, they were taken by surprise at my suggestion and that they were considering it.

"*Piccola*, I actually like that idea a lot, only there's one thing. If he goes off, the Mia Bella Rosa could get destroyed," Gabriel warned me.

"Better it than you guys. We have insurance if that happens. My family might bitch and moan, but I don't care. You mean more to me than the restaurant."

Gabriel took me in his arms and kissed me. He made sure it was a thorough one before he let me go. "Thank you. That means more to me than you know. I'll do that instead."

I sagged in relief. Ben piped up, "Just a warning. He might not wait until then. He was a mess today. We need to be prepared for him to hit us again tonight."

"I've already thought of that and we're covered."

"Is it more guys from the company or the Rizzo family?" Ben asked.

"Both, plus a few bikers we know. Believe me, Santo and his men better think twice before they mess with any of them."

All three of them laughed. I didn't know any of the people he mentioned, so I didn't know their capabilities. Even if I did, I was too stressed to laugh. With this decided, Gabriel excused himself to make more arrangements and to contact Santo about the meeting. Ben and Beau said they were going to walk the house. This left me with nothing to do, other than to get lost in cooking. It would distract me some and we had to eat. It was a win-win in my book.

After doing my prep work and getting everything going, I had time to let my family know about the meeting in the morning. I didn't ask them for permission. I stated it as a fact. To minimize the arguments that I knew would arise, I sent them a group text.

Me: Heads up. Before the restaurant opens in the morning, we'll be using it for a private meeting. It will start at eight and be done in time for us to open. I'll need all of you to stay away until it's over.

It didn't take long for the texts to start rolling in.

Emmet: What the hell does that mean? A meeting? With whom? Why?

Elijah: No one asked our permission to use our place for a meeting.

Papà: Are you sure this is a good idea? Who is the meeting between? I assume Gabe will be there.

Me: Yes, Gabriel will be running the meeting. He's meeting with Santo. They needed someplace private yet still public. I offered them Mia Bella Rosa. It's perfect.

Elijah: That's bullshit! You can't do that without our permission, Gemma.

Emmet: Elijah is right. And why do we have to stay away? It's our place.

Me: That restaurant is as much mine as it is yours. I don't need permission. You never asked mine when you held your after-hours parties with your friends and wrecked the place and I had to clean it up for business the next day. It's happening and if you try to come, you'll be escorted off the premises. I'm done arguing. Goodnight.

They were pissing me off. They used it several

times for their own reasons. Why couldn't I? Just another example of how they didn't see me as their equal. Moving away was looking better and better. More texts came in from them, but I ignored them. I'd said all I was going to say. I got back to preparing our dinner.

I barely slept all night. I was waiting for Santo to make a move on the house. I wasn't the only one. Gabriel got up several times and I heard Ben and Beau walking around the house. I was dragging this morning.

We got to the restaurant early. I went straight to the espresso machine. Customers loved it, but I rarely drank it. I needed the extra energy the caffeine would give me today. When I started to hand out cups of it, the guys blew me kisses while Gabriel gave me a real one. "Thank you, *Principessa*. This is just what we need. I'm sorry if I kept you awake last night."

"You didn't. I couldn't get my brain to shut down. I was worried about them hitting the house. When I wasn't worrying about that, I worried about this meeting. I should shoot Santo myself for causing me so much stress. All those texts from my family didn't help either."

My family hadn't let up on the text messages. They tried calling me several times, but I didn't answer. I couldn't turn my phone off, since staff would call me if they had issues, like if they were calling off.

"Yeah, that was annoying as hell. Do you think they'll turn up?" Gabriel asked.

"I have no idea. They might. Or they might be too scared to do it, since they know Santo is going to be here."

He scowled. He hated how my family treated me. He tried not to say negative things about them to me, but it was hard for him not to, I knew.

On the way inside, I hadn't seen anyone. It made me nervous. Gabriel assured me that his men were there. With time to burn, I straightened tables and smoothed out the linen tablecloths on the tables. I checked that we had enough silverware wrapped. Anything I could do to be ready for the day. Although we'd be closed, the cook would usually come in at nine. There were things she'd have to get started on before the doors opened. I'd reminded them of this. Gabriel asked if I would mind doing it, so no one innocent would be in here. I agreed. I'd done it plenty of times in the past. It was decided that I'd stay out of sight in the kitchen. Ben and Beau would stay put in the main dining area with Gabriel.

"You're going to leave her in the back all alone? I know the door will be locked, but I still don't like it," Beau muttered.

"Hell no. You should know me better than that. I have her bodyguard coming any minute now."

"Who?" both men asked at the same time.

He grinned. "You'll see."

Five minutes later, there was a hard knock at the front door. Gabriel went to answer it. When he opened it, two people I'd seen before walked in. It was Undertaker, I mean, Mark, and his wife, Sloan. I was shocked to see them here. Ben and Beau greeted them as I stood there not knowing what to do. Sloan was the one to break the ice. She came rushing toward me and engulfed me in her arms.

"Girl, we're gonna have so much fun today. I'm thrilled I got to come and meet you. While these guys play who's the baddest *mafioso*, we'll get to cook and talk. Cassidy is so jealous."

"Don't get caught up in talking and cooking and forget what you're here for," Undertaker said gruffly. He was eyeing me.

"As if that would ever happen. Calm your tits. I don't know why you insisted on coming along."

"I came to make sure that fine ass of yours didn't get shot and to help this dumbass not get killed."

Gabriel slapped him on the back. "I'm glad to have you, although I can protect my own ass. You just can't let your woman out of your sight. Admit it. And stop looking like you're about to kill someone. You're scaring Gemma."

He was right. Undertaker's scowl did scare me. I watched in amazement as the scowl melted away and he smiled. It transformed his ruggedly handsome face into a beautiful one. Suddenly, I was engulfed in his arms and he gave me a hug. I felt like I was being hugged by a grizzly bear. I hung on and waited to see what else he would do.

Gabriel: Chapter 16

I had wondered when I got word that Sloan would be joining us if Mark would tag along. I thought he would. Although she did go on assignments without him, he preferred to go when it was a particularly dangerous one. In fact, she'd stopped doing some of them at his insistence. When they both were working, Cassidy would keep their little one, Caleb, along with her and Sean's son, Noah. Caleb was nine months old and Noah would be two years old in a few months.

I didn't blame Mark. I'd be the same way if Gemma worked with us. I didn't see that happening, but if it did, I'd want her to stay in the office. Sean tried to do the same with Cassidy, but it didn't always work for him either.

After Mark got done shocking the hell out of Gemma with a hug and greeting her, she went to the kitchen with Sloan. I knew Sloan would be armed to the teeth and anyone trying to come in there after Gemma was a dead man.

It was wonderful to have one of my brothers-in-arms here for this. We worked seamlessly together. It wasn't bad with Beau and Ben by any means, just not the same. Mark and I had years of working together to perfect our moves. We could read each other's thoughts.

That could save your life.

"Why don't we just kill the fucker when he comes through the door? If his men object, kill them too. If they don't, then use them to shut this shit down then do whatever with them," Mark grumbled. His years in an outlaw MC had changed him. He was rougher and less forgiving in some ways.

"Believe me, I'd love nothing more than to kill this bastard. He's a threat to Gemma and that's enough reason to kill him. However, I still need him to close this shitshow down. If I don't have him, it'll make it more difficult, but not impossible."

"You should've seen him yesterday, Mark. His men had to drag him out of here. He was practically frothing at the mouth. He's totally lost it over Gemma. Santo is convinced she's his and he can get her back," Ben told him with a roll of his eyes.

"Yeah, he's batshit crazy," Beau agreed.

"Those are the most dangerous ones. He'll feel like he's invincible and has nothing to lose. You two keep an eye on the guys he brings with him. Old Santo is mine," Mark ordered. I didn't mind his idea, so I let him give them the order.

They took up their positions around the room. They found the best vantage points with cover if they needed it. I was the most exposed. I would be sitting at a table in the middle of the dining room. The most I could do was flip over the table to use as a shield. All of us were wearing Kevlar vests. I'd even insisted Gemma wear one, although it was hot and heavy. She hadn't argued, which told me how scared she was.

Five minutes before eight, the front door came swinging open. I knew it was them, because I got a text a few minutes before telling me they were walking toward the front door. I sat relaxed in my chair, looking as if I didn't have a worry in the world. When Santo came marching in like he owned the place, I wanted to take out my gun and shoot him. Who the hell did this little fucker think he was? He had his standard five bodyguards with him.

If he wanted to play with the big dogs, we'd play. "I'd appreciate it if you'd knock before coming into one of my places. It's only common courtesy to announce yourself. You'll get shot doing that shit," I snapped.

His gait shuffled awkwardly for a moment then he kept coming. I didn't bother to rise or offer him my hand. He wasn't a friend or colleague. I had no need for niceties with him. I kicked a chair across from me away from the table for him to sit down in. His guys remained standing. I saw them checking out my three guys. They might outnumber us, but each of us could take out two men to one, maybe more.

"Since when is this your place?" Santo snapped.

"Since one of its owners is engaged to me. Let's not play games. You wanted to meet with me. You came in here yesterday yelling. That should never happen in front of anyone. There were customers in here. They could've heard something they shouldn't or called the cops. Also, Gemma was here. I don't talk about business in front of my woman. This shit needs to stay far away from her. I would've thought the Greco family did that. Things seem to be slipping with them in prison. Have you heard anything about when they might get out?"

My question caught him off guard. He hesitated, shifted his eyes then shook his head. "No, I haven't heard anything. Their original sentences were twenty-five years to life, although they might be eligible for parole after serving half their time. That's at least another four and a half years away."

"When was the last time you talked to them? I want to talk to them myself before we complete this deal. I think I'll head over to the prison and see them."

I watched as his face paled. That was hard to do with olive skin. His eyes darted around again then came to rest on me. "They aren't allowed to have visitors. The only way to communicate with them is through a guard. He takes messages to them and brings messages out from them. I hate to say it, but you're not going to be able to talk directly to them. I'll pass along your request."

The only reason I was talking about the Grecos was to throw him off balance. He'd come in here sure of himself and I'd already destroyed that in less than five minutes. Now, it was time to go on the attack.

"I'm not sure what you're used to, but in the Rizzo family, we don't attack our allies. We don't air our laundry in public. We don't start wars over nothing. This whole alliance could benefit both of us, but if you keep this crazy behavior up, I'll have to advise the others that you're too volatile for us to work with. We need steady and reliable people at the helm, not ticking time bombs. Do you want this alliance to fall through?"

"N-no, I don't. My only issue is you came in here to form this with me then you went behind my back and stole my woman. I want Gemma back. You can have any other woman, just not her. Where is she?" He glanced around the room again as if he expected to see her.

"Let me be clear. This alliance was with the Greco family, not you personally. You're just another *capo*. You take your orders from them. Also, I didn't go behind your back and steal anyone. Gemma was a free woman. She wasn't yours. You weren't dating, living together, and she didn't have your ring on her finger. She was free to be with whomever she pleased. I was lucky enough that she wanted to be with me. I can have any woman I want, but I only want her. Get over it. You're never getting her. As for where she is, she's safe."

His face began to flush red before he came bounding to his feet. His men tensed. I could tell they weren't happy with him or the conversation. Good. His closest men were on the brink of turning on him.

"I'm not gonna let some fucking *soldato* from the Rizzo family come in here and tell me what to do. I'm the head *capo* for the Greco family. I take orders only from Matteo and his sons. I'm in charge. There won't be a deal until you give me Gemma. And I want to know what happened to my men?"

Ah, he'd finally brought them up. I had been waiting for him to do that. I stood slowly. I took my time straightening my jacket and flicking the cuffs on my shirt. Finally, I glanced at him.

"You need to be educated, *ragazzo*. I'm no fucking *soldato*. I'm not a *capo*. I'm the *consigliere* to the Rizzo family. I don't take orders from pissants like you."

Gasps came from his men. Shock was evident on all their faces. That was quickly followed by fear. Calling him a boy was an insult. Informing him I was third in command of the Rizzo family and the main adviser to the Boss was bad news for him.

I knew telling them I was the *consigliere* was a gamble, but the Rizzos would back me up if asked. His men stepped further away from me. They glanced at Ben, Beau, and Mark, who were all wearing their hard-ass looks. Their hands were close to their jackets. It didn't take a genius to know it was so they could go for their guns if they had too.

"*La mia famiglia* is tired of this whole thing. They want to either finalize this and get started on the work to bring the Greco family into our organization or to walk away and we can form an alliance elsewhere. Gemma's status is not to be questioned again. She's mine. Period. Any more outbursts or attempts to take her, like the one the other night at our house, will result in the deal being broken off and you and anyone else helping you being put on a hit list. You have three days to have all the names of your contacts and associates to me. Along with those, each and every location you do business in, including who pays you protection money or launders money for you, will be on that list. I have plans next weekend to be back home, introducing my woman to the family and celebrating our engagement.

Don't fuck that up or you won't like it."

Santo was so angry he was shaking. He was breathing hard, like he'd just ran a race. "You killed my men," he said angrily.

"Of course I did. They attempted to infiltrate my house and take my woman. Did you expect me to slap their hands and send them running back to you? Fuck that. I play for keeps and I always win, Santo. Don't try my patience again. Now, it's time for you to go. The restaurant needs time to get ready to open. Don't come in for your meals or to just hang out. This place is a no-fly zone for you. Remember, three days."

It was obvious it was killing him to leave. His men practically dragged him out again. Only this time, he wasn't saying anything. If looks could kill, I'd be dead. As soon as the door closed behind them, Ben flipped the lock. We had all the blinds still down on the windows. The tension in the room began to fade.

Beau whistled. "Damn, you sure came out the hard-ass. I thought his head was going to explode a couple of times. Forgive me, what's a *consigliere*? I know it's important, but not exactly what it is?"

As he asked, Sloan and Gemma joined us. I put an arm around Gemma. Sloan went to Mark and he hugged her close.

"A *consigliere* is the adviser to the top guy, the Boss. He's third in command. Why?" Gemma asked him.

"Your man here just informed Santo that he's the *consigliere* of the Rizzo family. I thought him and his goons were going to shit their pants. Jesus, you sure know how to twist them in knots. Will the Rizzos back that claim up?"

"They'll back it up. They won't be shocked I told him that. They're ready for him to reach out to them to ask questions about me. Okay, we have a lot to do. These next three days will be busy and the most dangerous. If he's going to make a move against me, it has to be before the deal goes all the way through. He's still fuming over Gemma and he knows I killed his men. He'll want revenge."

"Gabriel, what can we do to make sure he can't touch you?" Gemma asked hoarsely. She was shaking. I hugged her closer and rubbed her back as I placed soft kisses all over her face then her lips. Only when I'd given her what I thought was enough of them, did I answer.

"We're going to head up to our safe house. That means I'm going to need you guys to help with a distraction tonight, so we can sneak away and not be followed."

"Sure thing. It's a good idea. Your communication with him doesn't need to be face-to-face," Mark said.

"I have an idea. Are we going to stay here today or head to the house now, so we can plan?" Beau asked me.

"We're going to the house. As soon as we have the distraction in place, we'll head out. Mark, are you and Sloan headed back home tonight?"

He shook his head. "There's no way I'm leaving you now. This is too important. We'll take you to the safe house. That'll leave Ben and Beau to make sure the distraction worked and we got away clean. Afterward, they can come join us if they can get away without being seen."

I liked his plan, so all I did was nod. I knew it would do no good to argue about them sticking around. Beau's plan to smuggle a covered-up Ben out so they thought it was me was a simple one but I knew they'd fall for it. Further talk was halted by the sound of a key in the front lock then the door opening. It was only nine o'clock according to my watch, so we had time before the customers started to come in. It was Emmet and Elijah. The looks on their faces told me they were surprised not to see Santo.

"What're you doing here? I told you to stay away until ten," Gemma said impatiently.

"You're not our boss, Gemma. We can be here any time we want. Where's Santo? I thought you had a meeting," Elijah grumbled. He gave me a belligerent look.

"Our meeting is over, fortunately. We're leaving for the day," I informed him.

"All of you, including Gemma?" Emmet asked.

"Yes, including Gemma," I answered back.

"She can't. I got a call since she wasn't answering her phone. One of the waitresses called in sick. She has to stay and work. You shouldn't ignore your phone, Gemma. You know it's your job to take staff calls and to handle this kind of stuff."

"What exactly do you two do around here other than sit on your asses and get paid money? Not a damn thing that I see. Well, boys, the days of that happening are over. Gemma is done. She's coming with me and she's not going to be back. Hope you can find someone to fill in. If not, the aprons and order pads are in the back," I informed them.

I gestured to Ben and Beau. "We're ready. Go get the car. I can't stand the smell in here."

They grinned as he went out. Elijah and Emmet sputtered and tried to protest, but I ignored them. Mark and Sloan stood there watching the show with amused expressions on their faces. I was glad to see Gemma looked unconcerned. I knew it would be hard for her not to jump to the rescue. She had been doing it for years. She was the one her family relied on to fix everything so their lives were calm. They were in for a rude awakening when they had to actually handle their own issues.

Within a few minutes, the guys were back and the six of us left her cousins standing in the dining room looking lost. A cautious walk to the car and we were ready to head home. We made sure Sloan and Mark made it safely to their car. They followed us.

Our heads were on a swivel the whole drive. It wasn't hard to spot our tail. God, someone needed to teach them how to tail someone without being seen. At the house, we parked in the garage. Mark and Sloan parked out in front of the house and came in the front door after we got inside. Gemma gave them a quick tour while I got us all a drink. Once they were back, we got down to business.

"You said you had an idea for a distraction. What is it?" I asked Beau without delay.

"I feel like Gemma is getting sick. In fact, she is getting so sick, we need to call an ambulance to take her to the hospital. You'll insist on riding along with her, of course. Once you're there, in the busy ER, it'll be easy to smuggle you out the back door. Mark and Sloan can be the ones to do that. Ben and I will stay out in the waiting area, making sure everyone can see us. They know we're there to protect someone. They won't know for hours you've gotten away."

It was a good idea. He was right that they wouldn't be allowed back in the exam area and we could slip away. All I had to do was make sure the ER staff didn't make me stay in the waiting room. I knew I could intimidate myself in the back with her if I had to.

"What kind of illness do you want me to have?" she asked him.

"Something that's causing you lots of pain. You'll have to be able to cry and carry on like you're in the worst pain ever. The paramedics have to be convinced you need to go to the ER to be evaluated," he told her.

"I can do that," she assured him.

"Are you sure? If you can't, then we'll have to think of something else," I questioned her. The rest of us were used to lying and acting.

As she stared at me, tears welled up in her eyes. They spilled down her cheeks. I reached for her. I hadn't meant to hurt her feelings. Suddenly, she cried out, as if she was in terrible pain and fell to her knees. She bent forward and wrapped her arms around her stomach. She was rocking back and forth, sobbing and moaning. In between, she was stuttering out how bad she hurt and that she needed help.

I sat there stunned. If I didn't know better, I'd think she was really ill. As fast as it started, her tears stopped and she calmly got back up and sat on the couch. She took a sip of her drink and glanced around the room at all of us. "How was that?"

"Jesus, where the hell did that come from?" Ben asked in awe.

"I used to act in school plays when I was growing up. It was a way to live a different person's life. I was always told I was really good at it. If you think that was good enough, then I think we have our plan."

"Good enough? That was Oscar worthy. Shit. Okay, let's run through what we think the next three days look like, then we'll get ready. Do we want to wait until it's dark to leave or do it this afternoon?" Mark asked.

"I'd like to wait until close to dark. It'll give us even more cover when we leave the hospital. I'll inform the others who're watching us what the plan is. They can help run interference if Santo's crew spots us leaving town," I told them.

The rest of the morning and the afternoon passed in a blur of preparation. I had several calls to make to inform the others of what was happening and to get them in place to help us. Besides doing that, we ran through some of the things we'd be getting in place for the final confrontation in three days. Santo and his personal guards wouldn't be ones who were sent to prison. They had to be eliminated.

We packed our bags and took them out to the car in the garage and loaded them in the trunk. Along with clothing and our personal care stuff, we picked up the guns we'd placed all over the house. I doubt we'd be coming back to this place, even though I had rented it for almost an entire month more.

We had leftover lasagna for lunch. As the time got closer, I could tell Gemma was getting nervous. Sloan was trying to distract her with stories about Caleb and how much she was going to love Virginia. Finally, after being tense for hours, it was showtime.

I placed the call for an ambulance. Gemma made sure to be crying and moaning about her pain in the background to make it believable. The dispatcher assured me the ambulance would be there soon.

Ben kept watch and informed us when he saw the ambulance enter our street. They didn't have their siren on but they did have their lights flashing. By the time they got to the door, Gemma had tears running down her face. Mascara was everywhere. She was curled up in a ball on our bed, rocking herself. She looked so pathetic. I was on the bed trying to comfort her.

The paramedics didn't waste time. They got down to business. I explained it had started an hour or so ago and had steadily gotten worse. In between her cries, she described it to them.

"It feels like knives are ripping through my insides. I want to throw up. I think I'm dying. Something's really wrong. Please, help me."

"Ma'am, we will. Just hang in there. Do you have any medical conditions we should know about?" paramedic one asked as he took her vitals.

"No."

"Is it possible you could be pregnant?" the second one asked.

I was taken aback. Did miscarriages look like this? If so, I prayed she never experienced one. As for whether she might be pregnant, it had only been a couple of days since we'd had sex without the condom. It was possible but she wouldn't show positive on a test yet.

"We've had unprotected sex. Yes, it's possible," I informed them. I winked at her when they weren't looking.

Quickly she was assessed, put on the gurney, and wheeled out to the ambulance. As they loaded her into it, Ben, Beau, Sloan, and Mark all followed us and got in their cars. The paramedics didn't give me any grief about riding with them. The only thing was I had to ride in the front.

The whole way there, Gemma gave the performance of her life. I was so damn proud of her. From there, she continued her acting for the ER staff. The only time I saw a little panic was when they wanted to give her pain medicine. She adamantly told them no.

That she didn't want to risk hurting our baby if she was pregnant. They took blood and promised they'd be back soon to do other tests. They told her to rest.

Knowing we couldn't wait and chance them trying to give her meds again or put her through some crazy tests, we waited until they were busy with a new admission. This guy was tripping on some kind of drugs and he was fighting with the staff. That's when we slipped out of the ambulance entrance. Right before we did, I sent a quick text to Mark.

We hid in the bushes beside the building. It was dark and we'd worn dark clothes. A couple of minutes later, I heard a psst sound. It was Sloan peeking around the corner of the building. She waved at us to follow her. Staying in a crouch, we ran as fast we could to her then around the corner. Idling just a few feet away was the car she and Mark had brought with them. We got in the backseat and lay down. He took off. We stayed like that until we were out of town and Mark gave us the all clear. We sat up. Gemma hugged me.

"That was one helluva performance. If we ever need something like that at work, we'll have to call you," Mark said with admiration in his voice.

"She's not going to work with us," I informed him.

"Wait, who said I wasn't? Maybe it would be something I'd love to do," she protested.

"No way in hell I can do that, Gemma. My heart wouldn't be able to take it."

As she tried to convince me it would be a good

idea, the miles sped by. Even though I was talking to her, I kept my eyes on our back trail. I knew Mark and Sloan were doing the same. Just under two hours later, he pulled up to my safe house. This would be the first time anyone other than Gemma had been here. I was a little nervous about what they might think. I directed him to the garage. I got out and entered a code to open the garage door, since he didn't have a garage opener. Mine was in the car Ben and Beau would bring. It would have to stay there until this was over.

Gemma: Chapter 17

I won't lie. I didn't get much sleep again after we made it to the safe house in Mahwah. Even though everything indicated that we'd made it there free and clear, I was too afraid to believe it. We spent time talking to Undertaker and Sloan. It was good, because I slowly began to see the softer side of Undertaker and my mind was able to start thinking of him as Mark. It would take a bit longer to make the flip, but I thought I could get there. It was his obvious love for Sloan and how he cared for Gabriel that did it.

It was late, well after midnight, when Ben and Beau had arrived. They reported on the reaction Santo and his men had when they realized we'd escaped. While they went to search the hospital for us, no one thought to keep an eye on Ben and Beau. They'd slipped away and spent a few hours driving randomly around until they were sure they hadn't been followed. I was happy that they had made it. I had been worried about them. What Santo would do to them once he found out we were gone had preyed on my mind. He was slipping more and more into insanity.

It was barely six in the morning now. I moved to get up and a strong arm caged me in as a gruff voice growled in my ear, "Where do you think you're going?"

"I'm going to use the bathroom then get up and make breakfast."

"No, you're not. You can use the bathroom then I want you back here in this bed with me."

By his tone, I knew it wasn't more sleep he wanted. He wanted sex and I couldn't say no. Since we'd done it for the first time a couple of days ago, he'd been insatiable. Last night was the first time we hadn't had sex after going to bed. I decided to tease him a little once I used the bathroom. I patted his arm and he let me up. I used the bathroom and freshened up then came back to stand at the edge of the bed. He was staring at me with a hungry look on his face.

"I don't know. Maybe I'm not in the mood to do that this morning. We have a house full of people. They might hear us. I think we'll have to wait until this assignment is over."

I squealed when he lunged up out of bed and grabbed me. He was so fast I hadn't anticipated him moving like that. The squeal just sort of escaped. He gently tossed me on the bed and jumped on it to straddle me. He had my arms trapped. I noticed he had taken off his shorts. His cock was hard and ready for action. Instantly, my pussy started to get wet as I imagined him taking me.

"I hope this isn't your favorite," he said.

I gave him a confused look. What was he talking about? I found out an instant later when he tore my tank top down the middle, exposing my breasts.

He growled then attacked them with his mouth. His tongue and teeth had my nipples standing at attention within seconds. I moaned at the sensations shooting from them to my pussy. He lifted his head to give me a wicked look. “Do you still want to go make breakfast or stay here and let me make love to you until you scream?”

I pretended to contemplate it. He growled and attacked again, only this time, my shorts were the victim. He tore them down each seam then tossed the ruined remains to the floor. He tugged off the torn top and did the same. Now I was as naked and vulnerable as he was.

“Seems I have some convincing to do,” he muttered before he licked his way from my breasts to my pussy. I moved my legs apart so he could get to me. “Hmm, it seems like your pussy wants what I want. I think we should change her owner’s mind.”

The first swipe of his tongue up then down my slit made me moan. He chuckled. From there, he set out to drive me out of my mind with pleasure. He fluttered his tongue against my clit then sucked on it hard. When he wasn’t doing that, he was teasing my folds or thrusting his tongue in and out of my entrance. My breath stalled when he slipped his tongue further back and he ran it around the entrance to my ass.

“Does that feel good?”

“I-it does in an odd way,” I stuttered. I knew people had anal sex. I’d just never thought about doing it.

"Maybe one day, we'll see if you might enjoy more fun back here. It can be really good, but only if you're okay with trying. I won't force this or anything else on you, *piccola*."

"I know you won't. I trust you, Gabriel. I'm willing to try some play there and we'll see."

"Good," he said before he went back to paying attention to my pussy. This time, he added his fingers to the mix. It didn't take him long to have me crying out. I tried to muffle it with my hand, since we had so many people in the house. I don't know if I was very successful.

Once I came down from the high of it, he was up and moving me. In a daze, I followed where his hands pushed me. I ended up on my hands and knees. I moaned. So far, we'd stuck to the missionary position or me on top. I'd heard that doggie style would allow him to go deeper. God, would I be able to stand it? He wasn't exactly a small man. It was usually a fight to get all of him inside of me, but when he was, the pleasure was unreal.

He pressed my head and chest toward the mattress, while keeping my ass in the air. His lips skimmed down my spine, making me shiver. I jumped when he nipped each ass cheek with his teeth. "Stay just like this, Gemma. Fuck, I want to fuck you so hard, seeing your ass like this and how wet you are."

"Then do it. I won't break, Gabriel. If it's too much, I'll tell you," I whispered to him. I was dying to come again even though I just had. Nothing compared to getting off with him inside of me. I wiggled my ass to entice him. He growled. I felt the brush of the head of his cock at my entrance.

"Are you sure?"

"Yes," I moaned.

As soon as I said that, he plunged his cock into me in one hard thrust. He didn't give me time to adjust to his size. He gave it all to me. I cried out. I forgot to muffle the sound. So many sensations were flying through my body. When he was fully inside, I felt fuller than I ever had. He felt like he was deeper inside of me too.

"Are you alright?" he grunted.

I couldn't speak, so I nodded my head yes. He let loose and I lost my mind. He drew back and thrust again. Over and over, he pounded his cock in and out of my aching pussy. I gripped the bed sheets and tried to keep my cries quiet. I shouted again when his hand came around to tease my clit.

"Come for me, *mio angelo*, my angel. I need to feel you milking my cock," he growled. He was slamming himself in and out. It was just what I needed to make me come. I screamed as I clamped down on him. Somehow he kept thrusting as I flooded the bed with my release. When I became cognizant again, I realized he was still hard, and he wasn't done with me yet.

"God, Gabriel, I don't know if I can take this. It feels too good."

"You can take it. I want you to fly, Gemma. You're gonna come again," he vowed.

I don't know how he did it, but he somehow sped up more. I held on and tried not to lose my mind as he pushed me toward another orgasm. One I knew would overshadow the one he'd just given me. The slap of our skin coming together, our ragged breathing, and our moans filled the room.

I had no idea how much time passed before I was there again then tipping over the edge into a blinding orgasm. I buried my head into my pillow as I screamed his name. When my scream died down, I heard him swearing, then his pace stuttered and he was coming too. He jerked over and over. As we floated in a world of peace and pleasure, a realization slowly crept in my mind.

The reason he felt so good and I could feel his cum was because he was bare. We'd forgotten to use a condom. Shit. We'd been good at using them since the first time.

Slowly he withdrew and fell to the bed, taking me with him, so he was spooning me. He kissed my neck and cheek. "That was amazing, Gemma. I lost all sense of reality."

"It was amazing. And I know we both lost touch because we forgot something."

I expected him to be upset but all he did was sigh.

"Gabriel, we didn't use a condom. We're playing with fire. I could get pregnant. We agreed, we'd wait until this mess with Santo was over before doing that."

"I know and it is almost over with, Gemma. I

want to do as you wish, but I get so crazy and lost in you that it goes right out the window. I've never been like that. Maybe it's because I love you and I want to have kids. I don't care when, just as long as you're their mother."

He was right. This should all be a bad memory in a few days. If I did get pregnant, we wouldn't know for weeks. What harm could it do? As new as we were and even considering how much we still had to learn about each other, I loved him and wanted to have a family with him.

"Fine, we'll dispense with the condoms. Just be warned, I'll probably be one of those fertile women that all you have to do is say the word pregnant and I'm knocked up. When we're done having kids, we'll definitely have to have one of us get fixed, or we'll have twenty kids. I'm not going to mother that many. I'd lose my mind."

He rolled me onto my back and gave me a kiss full of tongue. When he was done, he smiled down at me. "I promise, no twenty kids. When we're done, I'll go get clipped. Although I do like the idea of at least three. What do you think?"

"I think that's a nice number. At least two, because I hated being an only child."

"I can deal with that. Okay, I hate to do it, because I'd love nothing more than to spend all day in bed with you, but we need to get up. I want to check in and see what's been happening all night."

I groaned but he was right. He slapped me on the

ass and got up, dragging me with him. After a quick shower and some basic grooming, we dressed and went to the kitchen. I found the coffee had been made and Beau and Ben were up. They gave us a sly smile, which told me they'd heard us. I blushed.

"Good morning," I said as I went to the refrigerator. I wanted to see what we had to make for breakfast.

"Good morning, although we don't think ours was as good as yours, or Mark and Sloan's. Unless this house is haunted, there sure was a lot of moaning and other noises," Ben said cheekily. I slapped his arm. He laughed.

"Don't tease her. If you make her self-conscious enough to stop making love with me, I'll kill you. I mean it," Gabriel threatened them.

This only made them laugh more. I was saved from more comments by Sloan entering the kitchen. Mark was right behind her. He had a rare smile on his face. She looked like she was glowing.

Gabriel noticed. "Hey, are you two pregnant again? Sloan is glowing."

Mark jerked to a stop. He ran his eyes up and down his wife. She was merely smiling at him. "Are you?" he asked her.

"I don't know. I haven't checked. I might be."

"Are you guys trying? Caleb is just over nine months old. That would make them a year-and-a-half apart. That's a good age. I've been telling Sean and

Cassidy they should have another one. We don't want Noah to be lonely," Gabriel said as he poured cups of coffee and handed them out so people could fix them how they wanted.

"We've decided to see what fate does. We hadn't planned Caleb and she got pregnant right away. We don't want our kids to be years and years apart. As for Sean and my sister, I've been telling them the same thing. At this point, he'll be two-and-a-half if they have a baby soon. He's a year older than Caleb," Mark observed. You could see the love he had for his nephew on his face.

"That would be fantastic. We could have children all around the same age. They'd have friends from birth. I bet they'll grow up to be best friends," Gabriel observed.

Mark froze, taking a drink of his coffee. He lowered his cup. He was staring intently at Gabriel then he switched to do the same to me. I tried not to squirm under his intent gaze.

"Are you two trying to have a baby already?" Mark asked. Sloan's eyes widened and she started to smile. I swear, I think she bounced up and down on her toes.

Gabriel gave them a sly look and then smirked. "Maybe. Who knows? We'll just have to see."

"Gabe, don't you dare do that to us. Are you or not?" Sloan cried out as she hit him in the arm with a fist.

He laughed then pretended to rub his arm. "Geez,

keep her under control, Mark. She's bruising me. Okay, fine, we've decided we'll do the same and let fate or mother nature decide."

Sloan gasped then I was wrapped in her arms as she hugged me. I could do nothing but hug her back. When the hoopla died down, Beau and Ben were shaking their heads.

"Why are you shaking your heads?" I asked.

"You poor fools. None of you have thought this through. You're all happy at the thought of them being best friends. What if some of them are girls? You could be looking at their future husbands from birth. What're you gonna do if Caleb or Noah or their other sons look at your daughter and want to be with her?" Beau asked Gabriel.

The look of horror on his face and Mark's was hilarious. Sloan and I just smiled. I wouldn't mind it. At least we'd know the boys and how they were raised.

"Like hell. If I have daughters, they are not dating. They'll live with me and their mother. They can take care of us when we're old," Gabriel stated. I noticed Mark nodding his head as if he agreed.

"Like hell. Our daughter or daughters will be free to find their happiness, just like our sons will," Sloan told him hotly. Her hands were on her hips.

"I have to agree with Sloan. No locking up our girls and letting the boys do whatever they want," I added.

"We can't! You don't understand. Guys are horny,

devious creatures. All they want is sex. No, not my daughters," Mark said firmly.

"You mean they're just like you and Gabriel and every other guy we know," Sloan said sweetly.

This shut them up. I couldn't help but laugh. It took me a little bit to get it under control. Gabriel and Mark looked like their hopes and dreams had been destroyed. Ben and Beau were smirking. Just wait. I hoped one day I could be there to remind them of this moment. Sloan and I hooked our arms together and went to work making breakfast.

Eventually they settled and got to work on getting reports about the night. By the time breakfast was ready, they were deep in conversation about those reports. I sat there, quietly listening. It seemed the people Gabriel had on Santo and the other Greco men had all reported that they were a beehive of activity all night. No one seemed to get much sleep. They tore through Toms River searching for us. They had even gone to my family's house. For a moment I was terrified of what they might have done to them, but I had to recall that they would've given me up in an instant. It still hurt knowing how little I meant to them.

"Gemma, your family is fine. They left when they couldn't find you. Someone snuck in and checked on them. They roughed up your cousins a little bit, but they're not seriously hurt. Your father is fine. It shook him up, but that's all," Gabriel told me, as he hugged me.

"Thank you. I know they would sell me out in a heartbeat, but they're all the family I have. I can't help worrying about them."

"That's not unusual. I'm doing everything I can to keep them as far out of this as I can, but they're involved. It makes it hard," he stated.

"I know you are and I appreciate it. However, if we have to pay a price for going along with this terrible family all these years, then we must."

"You won't be. They might. You were a child when they made that decision and by helping me, there's no way anyone will touch you. I made sure of it," Gabriel growled.

I hoped he was right. I wanted to spend my life with him, not behind bars. The thought of that made me sick. They continued to discuss the other reports. There were so many names I didn't know that it was hard to follow.

After everyone was done eating, Sloan and I cleaned up the mess. The guys spread stuff out on the table and were conferring over things. I saw a map of Toms River. Gabriel was pointing to different spots. Mark pointed to others. This was their thing, not mine, so I went to the living room. I was sort of surprised when Sloan joined me instead of staying with the guys. She obviously knew what they were talking about.

"It's hard, isn't it? When you have no clue what they're talking about. I'm sorry. You'll learn."

"Did you learn it or did you always know it?"

"I knew most of it already because of my work with the company and my time in the Marines."

"Maybe Gabriel would be better off with someone like you. I don't think I'll be much help to him or the company. He's not going to be able to bounce ideas off me. I have no experience with this kind of thing. All I've ever done is run a business and cook. If you need a cook, waitress, or a manager, then I'm your girl."

"Don't sell yourself short. We do a lot of different things. You may not think that sort of knowledge comes in handy, but it does. And no one said you have to work for the company. What would you want to do if you could do anything?"

I sat and thought. It had been so long since I'd thought about my dreams. I had them when I was younger when I thought I'd be able to have something outside of Mia Bella Rosa.

"I wanted to go to college and get a degree in business or maybe management. I'd need that if I was to start my own business. I like aspects of what I do at the restaurant on the management side of it, however, I wanted to take that and do something totally outside the restaurant world."

"Like what?"

"Like having a clothing store. One that sells cute, unique clothes you can't get anywhere else. It would be more like a boutique, I guess. I've always loved pretty clothes, even if I didn't buy them. There's a place in Toms River like that and I love going in there and browsing." I was so involved in talking to Sloan that I hadn't noticed that Gabriel had slipped up behind me.

His hands on my shoulders made me jump. He kissed my neck. "If that's what you really want to do, then do it. I'll fully support you in whatever you want to do, Gemma."

"Honey, I appreciate that, but I'm too old to go to college. Plus, if we start having babies, they'll have to be my focus."

"You can do both. I don't expect you to work, not if you don't want to. I'll be there to help with the babies. It won't all fall on you. You can take your time getting your degree. You're far from too old. You have so much practical experience, you don't need to wait to get a degree to open a shop."

"I might not need the degree but I'll have to work and save the money to have a shop. That'll take time. Maybe by the time the kids grow up, I'll be ready to do that."

"I can promise you, you won't have to wait that long. Trust me. There are ways. We'll talk about them after we get this assignment cleaned up." Nodding my head, as if I agree, he smiled at me and went back to the table.

Sloan patted my knee. "Don't think for a minute he won't come back to you about this. If you have a dream or desire, these men will make sure it happens. It's who they are. They want to make their women safe, happy, and fulfilled. It makes them happy, I think. I thought it was crazy when I first met Mark. Here was this big alpha man who had lived the outlaw biker life and had been a SEAL. He couldn't be anyone with softer aspects to him. I was so wrong."

I could see Gabriel in her remarks too. He was constantly surprising me. I couldn't wait to see what else I'd find out about him. I was eager to learn more and to start our life. Hopefully, he was right, and this whole mess would be over within a few more days.

Gabriel: Chapter 18

We were on our second day at the safe house and I was about to climb the walls. I hated not being in the thick of things. Everything seemed to be moving toward the conclusion I wanted. I'd received several calls and messages from Santo.

He was demanding that we meet. I knew he was going crazy over where we'd escaped to. He didn't come out and say he was looking for us, but my spies knew he had his men still combing Toms River and the surrounding towns searching for us. So far, he hadn't found a clue. I hadn't taken any of his calls, but I did text him. The latest was fresh on my mind.

Santo: We have to meet now. I have the list of names and places you want.

Me: Good. You can forward them to me. I'll send you a secure email you can send it to.

Santo: I'm not comfortable doing that, even if the email is secure. This needs to be an in-person handoff.

Me: I can't. I'm busy taking care of Gemma. She had a scare the other night and had to go to the ER.

Santo: I heard. Is she alright?

Me: She's doing much better. I have to insist that

you send me those names. Once I get them, then we can arrange a meeting.

After that, he'd tried a few more times to convince me to meet now, but I held fast. In the end, he begrudgingly agreed to email the information to me. I was waiting for it to come over. As soon as it did, I'd disseminate the information so we had people in place.

We planned to do the takedown all at once. That way no one could warn the others. It was the cleanest way to do it. It would take a lot of manpower, but we had help not only from our friends, but the feds. They loved it when we helped them take criminals off the streets and let them have all the credit. We stayed in the background. It was better that way. It left us free to continue to infiltrate other companies and organizations. If they recognized us, we'd lose our opportunity.

Gemma was a ball of nerves. She was getting more tense rather than less. I knew she was worried about her family as well as Santo. She had told me she was terrified he'd find a way to get away. Her family had been calling and texting her. They insisted she tell them where she was. They wanted to know why she'd left town. The one thing they didn't tell her was that Santo was looking for her. She ignored all of them like I had told her to do.

Sloan helped in trying to keep her mind off things, but she was also busy helping us plan stuff too. She had a great analytical mind, and we needed people like her to make sure we hadn't overlooked anything.

The only time Gemma relaxed was when we made love. I tried to wear her out every night and every morning to take her mind off things. It wasn't a hardship to do it. I craved her like she was an addiction.

In an attempt to get her mind onto something else, I had Cassidy send pictures of my house. I'd been living in it for the past five years. It wasn't a huge mansion, but it was a nice house. She'd come through for me and I had them now. I went to find Gemma. I found her in our bedroom. She was lying down and had her e-reader out, although she was staring off into space. When she saw me, she sat up. "What? Did something happen?"

"Nothing happened. I have some photos here I want you to take a look at." I sat down on the bed next to her and placed my tablet on her lap. I clicked through the photos.

"What are these?" I could hear interest in her voice.

"These are photos of my house in Hampton. I wanted to show them to you to see if you like it. If you do, then I thought you could use these to start thinking about how you'd like to decorate it. I'll admit, it's more of a bachelor place than a home. Cassidy tried, but I wouldn't let her change it. If you don't like the house, then when we get home, we'll start looking for one you do like. I have no real attachment to this one. It's nice and it's been a good house, but I want us to have a home that we love. One that you're comfortable in."

She gave me a stunned look then hugged me. Her

lips landed on mine. I had to kiss her back. It took a few minutes for us to get back on the topic at hand. "I take it you like that idea?" I asked with a grin.

"I love it! Although, so far, I do like this house. Thank you. I know you're all so busy and I'm not much help. I'm trying to stay out of the way. This'll help me do that."

"Gemma, you're never in the way. I love having you here. I don't expect you to plan with us. If we have a question about the town, you're our expert. I know waiting is hell. I hate it too, but I've grown used to it. Just think, the day after tomorrow, this'll all be a memory."

She nodded her head. I sat with her for a little while, going through the photos and telling her more about them. Finally, I had to get back to work. She gave me a kiss and went right back to looking intently at them.

Back in the kitchen, I was hit with more reports. They were coming in like wildfire. The names and places Santo gave me were being staked out and prepared for the takedown. I knew what I had to do next. I took out my phone and dialed. It didn't take long for it to be picked up. He'd recognize the number.

"About time you and I talked. You have your names and locations. It's time to meet," Santo barked into the phone. I guess he still was fighting who was the alpha here.

"I don't answer to you, *stronzo*," I replied. I knew he'd hate me calling him an asshole. It would only wind him up tighter.

"You have no right to call me an asshole," he shouted.

"I can call you anything I want. You seem to forget, I'm in charge. I'm the *consigliere*. You do what I say or else. Are we doing this deal or not?" I snapped back. I knew he couldn't afford to say the deal was off. He had too much riding on it. Even with the Grecos dead, he had to protect his position when that news finally came out. Which it was about to. I had it planned down to the moment I wanted. I heard him cursing under his breath, but he didn't swear at me anymore.

"Now, are you ready to work?" I asked sternly.

"Yes," is all he said. The resentment was clear in his tone.

"Good. I'll meet with you tomorrow afternoon. I'll send you the address of where to go right before the meeting. I want just you and your personal guard there. I'll do the same. We need to get together to finalize this agreement and start producing money. You and your men are going to be richer than you ever dreamed, Santo. There won't be much you can't do." I knew he'd eat that idea up.

"I'm ready for it. This organization has needed to grow for a while."

"Did you by any chance get a message to the Grecos about me wanting to talk to them?" I threw in unexpectedly.

It was quiet for a few moments before he

answered me. Mark, Ben, and Beau were listening on my end. They had grins on their faces. "No, I haven't. Things have been so busy. I'll do it today. Sometimes it takes a few days for that guard to answer. Then he has to find a way to get back to us with their answers. It's different when it comes from them to me, you know. He has to get paid before he'll finish the job."

"Maybe they should look for a new man to be their go-between."

"Yeah, they should, but I don't think it's as easy as that. Anyway, I'll pass your message along today. I'm looking forward to the meet. Send me the location as soon as you can."

"I will. I like to hold off until the last moment because it helps prevent people from accidentally finding out where we are. No use inviting trouble. I'll see you tomorrow. Goodbye."

I didn't wait for him to say goodbye, I hung up. The guys were laughing. "God, the hate that man has for you just oozes through the phone, Gabe. You know, you're gonna have to watch your back at all times with him," Mark stated.

"I know."

"Are you planning to take only Ben and Beau with you?" he asked.

"No, they saw you the other day and knew you were acting as a bodyguard. You're coming too. I want Sloan to stay here with Gemma. As soon as it goes down and we get it cleaned up, we'll come back to get them and head home. I've been away long enough."

"Amen. I'm ready to get out of here. Don't get me wrong, it's an alright place, New Jersey, but it's not home," Beau stated.

"Any new news about what Santo and his guys are doing?"

"No, but it seems the other *capos* aren't running around like he is. I think they're pissed that he's running everything. They're not going to be likely to come to his rescue. That makes our plan even better." Ben smirked.

We had a plan to turn the other *capos* and their men against Santo at the same time we go after them. Honestly, if I intended for Santo to go to prison rather than die, he wouldn't be likely to last long on the inside. One of the other *capos* would see to that.

We spent the next hour pouring over the map, deciding on the best place to have the meeting with Santo. It had to be somewhere private with very little to no people around, even if they lived a distance away. We didn't want to have collateral damage. Once we had the location, I'd let the rest of the team know. I intended to tell Santo at the last minute, so he wouldn't have time to get more of his men there and in a position to ambush us, but the same couldn't be said of my own.

We would have backup at the ready in case we needed it. As we were taking down Santo and his bunch, the other targets we'd identified would be experiencing the same thing. The feds would be taking down the ones who were going to serve jail time. The ones who we'd determined couldn't go to jail would be taken out quietly by our people. They would simply disappear or be found dead from apparent natural or accidental causes. Would the cops and feds be suspicious? Yes, but they wouldn't be able to prove anything. After a while, they'd forget about it and move on. No need to waste time with a bunch of criminals. They had living ones to catch. That was the sad thing. No matter how many bad people we took down, there were always more out there. It meant Dark Patriots had job security, I guess.

It was actually Gemma who found the ideal location. She came into the kitchen to get a drink while we were debating locations. She came over to see what we were doing. When I explained, she immediately pointed to a location not too far outside of Toms River, maybe ten miles max.

"If you want privacy, this would be where I suggest. All the land around it is fields. It has an old, abandoned plant there. It used to make all kinds of molded wire products. Some of them were for production equipment, I think. I remember my *papà* talking about it. It's been abandoned since they built a new one on the other side of town. The company still owns the property. It's fenced in so it's not the easiest place to get into. It would be very private."

"Does it have cameras, alarms, or security guards patrolling?" Mark asked first.

"I don't know about the cameras or alarms. I've never heard of anyone getting caught in there and some people have broken in, so I don't believe there are guards. For most, the fence intimidates them, I think. I wish I knew more. I'm sorry."

"No, don't be. This would be perfect. We'll have it checked out tonight. If it doesn't have guards, we'll be good. Cameras and alarms can be interfered with for a short period of time. We have the people who can do that in their sleep," I said, as I thought of our techs along with Smoke and Everly in Dublin Falls. What our staff couldn't handle, they could.

"Thank you. This is what we needed," I added as I gave her a kiss. She left the kitchen smiling. I knew she felt she wasn't a help. This was a big help. I didn't waste time dispatching people to check it out. The sooner we knew the better. In case we couldn't use it, we found a backup. I made sure to ask Gemma if it would work. She agreed it wasn't as good as the first choice, but it would work.

As the hours ticked by, the tension mounted. No matter how prepared you felt you were for a mission, it was always stressful waiting. When things started to happen, I'd go into a different mode and things would just flow. They didn't always seamlessly happen. We had obstacles we didn't expect that cropped up at times. We planned as many contingencies as we could. It was having multiple plans that saved lives. It was how Mark, Sean, Griffin, and I had survived in the SEALs. I knew it was how a lot of others had too.

By the time nightfall came, we were all hyped up, but we needed to get some rest. My answer was to take Gemma to bed and wear us both out with lovemaking. I'll admit, after the third round, we were both ready to sleep. I held her close as we drifted off. I sent up a prayer.

Please God, let this all go as planned. Keep everyone safe. Watch out for my Gemma. I can't do this without her. Bring me home to her.

The next morning came way too soon. I took everyone into town to the diner for breakfast. We needed to get out of the house. I knew Gemma was going stir-crazy. Luckily, this time there were no run-ins with prior bed partners. We still got a few looks, but I think it was mainly because people around here weren't used to seeing me with other people.

After breakfast, I took them around to show them the town. It was a quiet place. People overall were very friendly. They waved when you passed them. When we had enough of that, it was back to the house. The guys and I had to get the car ready to go with all the equipment we'd already packed. Most of it was weapons.

I planned to text Santo with the location after we were there. I'd give him a half hour to meet us. It shouldn't take even that long from town. The recon from yesterday showed that Gemma's first suggestion was the place. There were no guards. The fence did have cameras, but they could easily be put on a loop so no one would see us. One of the guys went over the fence and to the building itself. He easily broke in. There was no alarm triggered.

When it was time to go, Gemma clung to me. "Promise me you'll be careful and that you'll come back," she whispered. I could see tears gathering in her eyes.

"*Principessa*, I promise I'll do everything in my considerable power to be safe and to come back to you. I love you and I have plans for us that'll take at least the next fifty years to accomplish. Stay alert and do whatever Sloan tells you. She knows what she's doing."

"I will."

I couldn't leave her without giving her one more passionate, soul-reaching kiss. When we parted, both of us were a little breathless. I got in the car with the guys. It was a tight squeeze with the four of us, but we'd decided one car was enough. More than that might attract attention. We weren't taking the highway to our destination. Or at least not on the last leg of it. We'd mapped out secondary roads to get us there. I had no doubt Santo had eyes watching the main roads into town. We waved at the women as we left. Sloan and Gemma had their arms around each other.

"They'll be fine. They're gonna stress, it's what they do. Sloan will keep Gemma safe," Mark remarked. Beau was driving. I was up front with him. The other two were in the back seat. Behind them in the cargo area were all our weapons.

"I know, it's just hard to see her upset."

"Get used to it. No matter what, there'll be times you do upset her and can't do anything about it. It's not always work-related either," Mark replied.

"Are you saying you piss off Sloan on a regular basis?" Ben asked with a smirk.

"Yeah, I do, but she never stays mad for long. She

can't live without me or my cock," Mark flung back at him.

"Damn, I thought she had better taste. When I found out she was hooked up with you, I shook my head in disappointment. There are so many better choices for her. I mean, hell, look at me," Ben quipped. I knew he was using this to break our tension. We all went along with it.

It was a lively debate with lots of colorful threats that made the two-hour drive back to the Toms River area bearable and not take forever. When we got to the old, abandoned factory, we parked the car in the trees, where it wouldn't be noticeable. We were greeted by several men I knew. There was another Dark Patriot operative along with a few bikers.

From our work was Heath. I'd let Ben talk to Heath to get him fully up to speed. From Dublin Falls were Gunner and Sniper. They both had military experience and were single. I was trying not to include many who had wives and kids. From the Iron Punishers, Reaper had sent Lash, Mayhem, and Crusher. They, like us, had prior military training as well.

Sniper, as his name suggested, would be a sniper along with Mayhem. The rest would be scattered throughout the factory and grounds to assist as needed. Surely ten against Santo and his five would be more than enough. I knew he wouldn't leave his main guys behind. We had the advantage and the experience, he didn't. A quick confab to run through everything and then we were ready. I took out my phone and texted Santo.

Me: Come to 100 Ocean County Road 571. You have 30 minutes.

Santo: That's not long enough. I need more time. Give me an hour.

Me: If you're not here in 29 minutes, I'm gone and the deal is off. The clock is ticking.

He didn't bother to reply. Everyone scattered to find their places. That left me with Ben, Beau, and Mark to greet them. I relaxed as we waited. Waiting had been a big lesson I learned in the military. There was always a lot of rushing then waiting. You had to learn not to let it get to you. The motto a lot of military guys liked to quote was "hurry up and wait."

With exactly three minutes to spare, I saw two cars coming up the long, pothole-filled driveway of the factory. I stood relaxed but ready for anything. Nothing guaranteed they wouldn't come out of the car shooting. We were ready if they did. Let the game begin.

Santo was the first out of the front car. He didn't wait for any of his men to get out and check the perimeter. He came strutting up to me, his usual blustery self. I think he truly thought no one could touch him. He was in for a very rude awakening here in a few. His five usual companions rushed to catch up to him. I saw they didn't look very happy.

"About time you and I met. I don't like this over-the-phone shit. Going forward, we'll have our meetings face-to-face or not at all," he spouted immediately.

"I'll tell you when, where, and how we'll have any

future meetings, Santo. I guess you still haven't gotten the message. You're not the one in charge, I am. There was no reason for us to meet before now. I was busy and I told you that."

His face flushed an ugly shade of red, however, he somehow found it within himself not to say whatever he was thinking. His guys exchanged worried looks. They knew better than to test me even if he didn't.

"How is Gemma? Is she better?" he asked. Jesus, the guy couldn't resist thinking about her.

"Gemma is doing great. She's back to her old self. Now, since you were so eager to talk, tell me what it is you wanted to discuss and then I'll tell you what the next steps are."

He glanced around at the factory. It was obvious it hadn't been used in several years. Everything looked old and it was showing it needed work. "What made you choose this place? I didn't even know it existed. How did you?"

"It's private. I don't want to chance having people who don't need to know our business hearing us. There's no one to get nosy and call the cops on us. I'm thinking of buying it. This might be a good place for us to consider setting up making the drugs or packaging them for distribution. We'll need a bigger spot now that you'll be helping move a much larger quantity every month."

I saw the greedy look that came over his face. He was already imagining how much more money he would make. Too bad for him, he wasn't going to make a dime more.

"That's a great idea. You didn't say how you found it?"

"I have resources and connections all over. You'd be amazed at what I know or find out about."

I noticed he got a slightly uneasy look on his face. He slowly looked around us. I wondered if he could feel the extra eyes on him. Was a cold bead of sweat forming at the back of his neck ready to slide down his spine? That thought made me want to smile. His men had been standing there while we talked. They took turns staring at my guys and scanning the area. At least they seemed more alert and aware than Santo did. What I wouldn't give to know what he had over the Grecos to get him this top spot. Hopefully, I'd find out.

I planned to end the others quickly and overall painlessly, if possible. There was no need to extend their deaths. In Santo's case, I wanted to make him suffer. The number of people he'd beaten, killed, and raped had been alarming when I got the full report. Yeah, a few of the others had done those things too, but we wouldn't have forever to question and get retaliation on all of them. I'd have to be satisfied with doing that to Santo.

Yes, I could admit that a big part of it was how he had been arrogant enough to claim Gemma and keep trying to say she was his and not mine. He deserved, as the leader of those men, to pay not only for his crimes but theirs as well. I was determined to find out what he had over the Grecos and why he hadn't revealed they were dead to anyone. In fact, the last thing I would ask right now.

"Santo, I do have something that's been bugging me that I hope you can answer for me."

"What's that?"

"Why have you kept it from everyone, even your own men, that Matteo, Carlo, and Anthony Greco were killed in prison over a month ago? Hell, it's close to two months now. You told me you were sending them a message from me. I know you've told others inside your organization of supposed communications you had with them over the past two months. How is that possible when they're dead?"

The effect was more than I hoped for. His eyes widened and I saw panic fill them. The looks on his men's faces were just as good. They looked stunned and like they didn't believe it.

"I-I don't know what you mean," he stuttered.

"Really? Check this out. It just came out on the news, across the internet and all the social media sites." I held up my phone and clicked to the site I had pulled up for this exact reason. My contacts had timed it perfectly. They leaked the story and it was spreading like wildfire.

The headlines screamed, *Mafia Boss and Sons Found Murdered in Their Prison Cells*. Attached was a photo of the Grecos as seen when they went to prison. The article started out questioning why it had taken almost two months for the story to break. Why had it been hidden? Was there some conspiracy going on?

I read the first few sentences aloud to them. He went pale. His guys began to mutter and send dark looks his way. I'll give him credit, he tried to play it off.

"I don't know anything about this. I have contact with a guard who works there. He's been giving me information. I had no idea it wasn't coming from them," he protested.

"Yeah, I might believe that but further down, it tells of a guard found dead in his home two days after the Grecos were found. An investigation is showing he had huge sums of money in his bank account paid by a shell company that belongs to the Grecos. If he died two days after them, how was he still communicating with you?"

The muttered voices had grown louder. His men moved closer to him. Santo spun around so he could see them and us. He was backing away and shaking his head. "I don't know. Maybe someone impersonated him. I only ever spoke to him on the phone. The voice sounded the same, but whoever it was must have mimicked his voice. He knew the right code words and stuff," he babbled.

"No, I think we all know what happened. You've been lying your ass off for two months. No one has been communicating with you. How do you think the Rizzo family knew it was a good time to make a move? It wasn't because they wanted an alliance to expand their businesses. They want to take over the Greco territory completely. I'm not sent in for measly alliances. I'm sent in for the ones that involve things getting messy. We don't want or need men like you in our organization," I told him coldly.

As I watched his men get closer, the earpiece I had to communicate with the others on overwatch, came alive. Sniper's voice was talking in my ear.

"Gabe, we've got incoming. It looks like three vehicles with at least four or more men in each. They're coming in fast and hard. He's brought reinforcements."

"It's a green light, Sniper." I said loudly. The guys with me plus the others all knew what that meant. We'd set it up as our prearranged code. If he had brought more men or things were going to go south, when they heard the word green light, they would go on the offensive.

Instantly, we pulled out our guns. I dove for cover with the others behind our vehicle. Santo and his men, seeing us moving, all scattered. He went with them. They hid behind their vehicles. The roar of the engines of the cars coming up the long lane grew louder. Shots were fired. By the sound of them, they were from high-powered rifles, the kind Sniper and Mayhem were using. The first car swerved as the tire was shot out. The same happened to the other two.

From there, it became a game of cat and mouse. As Sniper and Mayhem kept the heat on the vehicles, a few men did get out and take cover. More than one hit the ground and didn't get up after they were shot. Lash, Crusher, and Gunner came out of hiding and were adding to the firepower. Beau, Mark, Ben, and I started to work our way over to get to where we could get the men with Santo.

The whole area turned into one big war zone. Eventually, we made it to where we could see them. To my shock, they weren't trying to fire at our men. They were too busy arguing with each other. Scanning them, I realized Santo wasn't with them. Taking a chance, I waved at my three bodyguards and we converged on them.

They didn't even try to shoot us. They immediately threw their guns on the ground and put their hands in the air. Fausto, the main man of Santo's, was the one to say something first. "We had no idea he was lying. I swear. He's been the only contact with them for the past three years. Nothing made us question it. We're willing to work for whoever is in charge."

"Where's Santo?"

"He crawled off in that direction as soon as we hid back here." Fausto pointed behind them. It happened that their car was parked not far from a bunch of trees. From where we had been standing, we hadn't had full visibility of that section. Their cars had blocked it.

I swore. "Son of a bitch, we have a runner. Can any of you take a partner and search the trees off to the right? It seems our guy Santo has pulled a disappearing act on us," I said into my earpiece.

"I can do it. Let me get Crusher. We'll track the little shit," Mayhem said.

"Thanks," I said.

Everything in me wanted to go after him myself,

but we had work to do. We'd catch him and when we did, he was a dead man. It did infuriate me that we'd been right here and he still managed to slip away, but he'd brought twenty men total with him. We had to take care of most of them first.

"Leave Fausto, I might have some questions for him," I told my three guys.

In a blink of an eye, they shot and killed the other four men with Fausto. He cried out when he saw his friends fall dead to the ground.

"Please, I can help you. Don't kill me," he pleaded as he fell to his knees.

"I want to know all the places that Santo likes to hide. If you tell me that, I promise to make it quick and painless. If you don't and I have to torture it out of you, you're not going to like it. I can keep a man alive for days."

As I waited for him to decide, I told Ben to keep an eye on him. The rest of us went to check to see how the others were doing. Most of the shooting had stopped. It sounded like they'd done their job. I was praying the last part would be as quick. I wanted Santo. Also, I needed to check in and see how the cleanup at the various other locations was going with the feds. So much for this being quick and easy. This is why we liked to have contingency plans. I'd have to text Gemma and tell her we'd be delayed in coming to get them.

Gemma: Chapter 19

I'd discovered something that was indisputable about myself. I wasn't a good person at sitting around and waiting. I went not only stir-crazy but found myself imagining the worst scenarios and I turned bitchy. Poor Sloan, she seemed to be so calm and cool. I snapped at her at least three or four times for nothing. I did apologize, but I still felt awful for doing it.

She was such a sweetheart, and she was doing everything she could to distract me and assure me that everything would be alright. I knew she had more experience with things like this than I did, but my gut wouldn't stop hurting or my brain telling me that something was wrong.

Lucky for Gabriel, the safe house had wooden floors not carpet or I might have worn holes in it. It hadn't helped matters that we couldn't see or know what was happening in Toms River. It wasn't like Gabriel or the others could keep sending us updated texts. That would've been nice, but not realistic.

It had been hours and I was ready to climb the walls. The last text we'd gotten almost two hours ago had made my anxiety worse. He had texted to inform us that they'd be delayed coming to get us. He assured me that everything was fine. They were still apprehending all the people they needed to get.

When I texted back to ask him what that meant; he hadn't answered. Sloan even tried to find out from Mark and got the same vague answer as Gabriel had given me. With those still preying on my mind, I was trying to convince her to listen to me.

"Sloan, I think we should leave and head toward Toms River. We can stop somewhere near there, where we're out of the danger zone and wait. Having to wait maybe hours for them to finish then two more on top of that to get here is going to push me over the edge."

"Gemma, I know it's hard. Believe me, I'm dying, not knowing what's happening and wanting to be there too, but Gabriel would kill me if I took you from the safety of this house. No one knows it's here. It's the safest place for you. We have no idea where else Santo has spies. He could have them in other towns outside of Toms River."

"I know, but I'm telling you, something is wrong. I can feel it."

She tried to hide a flash of uneasiness that momentarily showed on her face. If I hadn't been staring so hard at her, I would've missed it.

"There! I saw that. You're worried too, aren't you?" I said excitedly.

"Gemma, don't. It's nothing. I often get weird feelings when Mark is on an assignment and they always turn out to be wrong. I think it's a leftover from when he got shot and was in a coma."

She'd shared with me how Mark had been hurt at the end of their assignment and spent a month in a coma. She hadn't done it to scare me. It was to show how tough he was and that Gabriel and the others were made of the same cloth as him. I'd been shocked and upset to hear it. To think, he woke up after a month and found out he was going to be a father. I bet that had knocked him for a loop. And how much stress it had put on her. I wanted to be as tough as she was one day. I wanted to be worthy of Gabriel.

In order to help pass the time, she's been showing me some self-defense moves. I wasn't the best at them, but I thought with practice, I might be decent. She'd also been showing me her handgun. Gabriel had them all over the place, or he had. I had been too taken up in the task before us, to ask him to show me how to use one. That was something else I wanted to learn.

I didn't want him to have to be the one to always defend me. I wanted to be able to defend myself and our children. Thankfully, although they took most of the guns with them, they had left a few. Sloan handled them like they were extensions of herself. I was envious. I'd told her I wanted to be like her when I grew up. She laughed. That laughter was now forgotten as I argued with her.

"Please, I can't stand it. My stomach is getting worse. I feel like I could throw up."

"God, you're not going to stop, are you? Fine, if we haven't heard from them within the next half hour, then we'll slowly start to make our way there. I'll determine where we stop. I swear, if Mark and Gabriel beat our asses for this, I'm blaming you."

"Would Mark really beat you?" I asked aghast.

She smiled and shook her head. "Not like you think. He'd do it in a sexual way that stirred me up and then the bastard would hold off letting me come until it hurt. Only then would he give me what I want. He can be inventive with what he likes to call my punishments." The dreamy look on her face as she told me about that told me whatever he did, she was totally okay with it.

I wondered if Gabriel was into punishing like that. Would I like it? I didn't know. I had nothing to compare it to, but I was sure I'd be willing to find out. As long as it was nothing that involved horrible, lasting pain or actual injury, I had the feeling that man could talk me into trying anything.

She laughed. "I saw where your mind went. You're trying to imagine Gabe doing that to you. Honey, if he does, then look out. You'll be in for the night of your life. Those alpha military men can be the biggest pains in the ass, but they can also be a good pain in the ass, if you know what I mean." She wiggled her eyebrows. I blushed bright red.

"Okay, no need to tell me if you have or not, but if not, I can say there's a lot to be said for anal sex. There's some pain, I won't lie, but the end result is awesome."

"God, stop. If you keep this up, I'll never be able to face you again or look at Mark. He scares me enough, now to be wondering inappropriate stuff about you and him. No, I'd have to bleach my mind," I protested. This only made her laugh harder. I threw the cushion on the couch at her head. She easily ducked it.

"I can't wait for Cassidy to be able to join us for a girls' night. We're going to have a blast. We'll leave the men to watch the kids and we'll get drunk and let all our secrets out."

"I don't have any. I'm an open book. All you have to do is look at my face, apparently."

"True. We'll have to work on that with you. Cassidy and I have been waiting for Gabe and Griffin to find someone. There are others at the company we'd like to see settled, but especially those two. They're Mark and Sean's brothers-at-arms. Can I ask you a question?" When she asked that, I nodded. Hell, why not.

"Why do you call him Gabriel instead of Gabe like everyone else?"

"Because to me he's not a Gabe. He struck me as what the Archangel Gabriel might look like when I met him. The whole avenging angel thing came to mind. I can't see him as an ordinary Gabe."

"God, that's sweet. Wait until I tell the others. They'll tease the hell out of him."

"Don't you dare or I'll have to kill you! I'll find a way, Sloan. I swear," I warned her.

"Then you'd better be practicing your self-defense moves and learning to use that gun, because I'm sneaky and pretty tough, if I do say so myself," she said proudly. The fact was I knew she was right. She'd be easy to hate if she wasn't so great at the same time. The only answer I had was to shove her away from me.

After that, she started telling me more stories about the various people I'd met. She was the one to finally tell me the name of their company was Dark Patriots. I thought that was an apt name. Although they didn't require their employees to have military experience, it was preferred. The minutes slowly ticked by. I was watching the clock, so that when those thirty minutes elapsed, we could head out of here. Exactly thirty minutes later, I stood up. She sighed. She knew what it meant.

"Fine. Get your stuff that you need together and we'll head that way. I hope we're not making a terrible mistake."

Giving her a hug, I ran to get my stuff. I'd packed it earlier, and all I had to do was get it and we could take it out to the car and leave. She went to her and Mark's room to grab their bag. They'd traveled light. I could hardly contain my excitement at going.

Gabriel:

I was frustrated and starting to worry. The last two hours, we'd been torturing Fausto for information on places Santo might hide. While we did that, I had men out hitting every known location I knew of for him. Even the ones where the takedowns of the other guilty parties had happened.

At least that part had gone smoothly. A miracle when I thought of the feds being involved. It was no lie, they often would have the best plans and then fuck it up somehow. This time, it appeared that those plans had gone off without a hitch. All the reports coming in said they were able to apprehend their marks without trouble. Most had given up without a fight. A few had made feeble attempts to fight and others tried to run, but they didn't get far. Those would be the ones who we'd give all the information we'd collected, so they could be prosecuted.

The feds had no idea about the ones we'd personally gone after. If the people they arrested talked about them, they would have to remain unsolved mysteries when they disappeared never to be seen again. Or for a few, they might be found but would look like natural deaths or accidents. With Anderson involved, he'd steer them away from trying to dig too deeply into those, if anyone was suspicious.

Fausto had been tougher to break than I'd hoped. He'd tried to stay silent as the torture increased, but he finally had just spilled the last location. He was barely hanging on to his last breath. I was busy starting to get my men organized to hit other locations. His weak, almost maniacal laugh drew our attention.

He barely resembled a human anymore. He'd have to disappear or be set up in a massive accident, so his injuries could be hidden. One eye was barely a slit as he looked at me. I walked over to him. "What are you laughing at? I'd think for a man about to die and who has endured what you have these past couple of hours, you'd be moaning."

"I would but I'm happy because I did the last job my boss gave me."

"Oh, and what was that?"

"I stalled long enough."

"Stalled long enough for what? For him to escape?"

"No, for him to get to her."

"Her? Who?" As I asked, my heart raced. Surely, he was messing with me. He couldn't mean Gemma. No one knew where she was. She was safe with Sloan two hours away.

"Your little sweet Gemma. You didn't think he'd let you have her, did you? He's never going to stop until he has her. You've lost. She's his now and I can die happy."

"He doesn't know where she is."

"He knows. He's had long enough to get to Mahwah," he said as he laughed. His laugh was cut short by his last breath leaving his body.

Panic washed through me. The guys closest to me saw the horror on my face. My hands shook so hard, I could barely get my phone out of my pocket. I found her name and pressed the dial button. I saw Mark had out his phone too. Her number rang and rang before going to voicemail. I swore. I looked at Mark. He was shaking his head. He had a look of worry on his face too.

"It's going to voicemail, Gabe," he uttered.

"Fuck!" I screamed, as I ran for our car. I heard Mark and some of the others shouting out orders. I didn't have time to listen. As I got to the car, Beau was there ahead of me. He shoved me toward one of the passenger doors.

"I'll drive. You're in no shape to do it and neither is Mark. Get in."

I got in the front passenger seat. The back doors opened and Mark and Ben jumped in.

As Beau took off, I tried her number again. Still no answer. I began to pray. *Please God, don't let him get his hands on her. Let them be safe. Tell me Fausto was lying. There's no way he could've found where she was. No one knows of that place. We weren't followed. Please, please.*

The miles sped by in a blur. I kept calling and calling while Mark did the same. As we got no answer, the speed of the car got faster and faster, but it wasn't fast enough.

Gemma:

My car was parked outside in front of the house. It's where the guys had to leave it when they brought it from home. All we had to do was throw our bags in it and we could be off. As I closed the front door, I made sure I had engaged the alarm. I had no idea when Gabriel and I would get here again. I knew it was his hideaway and that he escaped here at least once a year. I liked it and wanted us to keep to that tradition.

Sloan was ahead of me. She was going to drive. It was dark out, but still light enough to see several feet around me. I had my bag slung over my left arm. I watched as Sloan got to the car and unlocked it with the fob. She looked back at me and smiled. I saw her smile quickly morph into a look of horror. At the same time, I felt something hard pressing against my ribs. An arm came around to tug me against a hard body. A voice I recognized, but hoped I'd never hear again, spoke.

"Don't move. Tell your friend to step away from the car and not to scream for help. If she does, no one has to get hurt. I didn't want to do it this way, Gemma, but you left me no choice."

Santo's cold voice sent shivers through me. My brain couldn't stop shouting at me, asking how he got here. He was supposed to be dead or at least in the custody of Gabriel and the others.

Sloan stepped away from the car like he ordered. She had dropped her bag on the ground. Her eyes were staring into mine. It was like she was trying to reassure me or tell me something, but I had no idea what. If Santo had found me, it was hopeless. There was no way he'd let me go. Once he took me away from here, there would be no way for Gabriel to find me.

"I did as you asked. Please, don't hurt us," Sloan begged. I heard a note of fear in her voice. Something told me that was all an act. The Sloan I'd come to know the past few days wouldn't show fear even if she felt it.

"Get your ass over here," he ordered her. She slowly began to walk toward us. Hoping that I might at least be able to set her free, I tried to distract him. I wiggled.

He shook me. "Stop it!"

"Why are you doing this, Santo? Surely, you don't want a woman who doesn't want you."

"You wanted me until that bastard showed up, telling his lies, and turning you against me. He lied to all of us, Gemma. He's not here to do what he said he is. The Rizzo family sent him to wipe all of us out, so they can take over the whole territory. They found out that the Grecos are dead. He told my men."

Those few words told me that he had met with Gabriel. Somehow, he'd gotten away. While he knew that Gabriel wasn't here for what he thought, it sounded like he had no idea who he really was. That was one small blessing.

When Sloan got as close as he wanted, he barked at her, “Stop! Turn around and put your hands behind your back.”

She did as he asked, but I could tell she didn’t want to. Once she had her back to us, he pressed what I now knew was a gun harder into my ribs.

“There, on the ground, is some rope. I want you to pick it up. Then you’re going to tie your friend’s hands behind her back. I want you to do the same to her feet. Woman, if you don’t want a bullet to your brain, I suggest you don’t fight her or yell for help. One peep out of you and you’re dead. I’ll have to punish Gemma for it,” he growled.

He gestured toward the spot on the ground where he’d dropped rope at some point. Maybe when he saw us coming out. I had no idea where he’d been hiding. He’d seemed to come out of nowhere.

He didn’t give me much room to bend down to get the rope. As soon as I had it, he pushed me forward, so I was right behind Sloan. I began to wrap the rope around her wrists. I had no idea how to tie it so she might be able to get free. As I looped it and tied the first piece into a bow, he berated me.

“That’s not how you do it! She’ll be able to get that off like it’s nothing. Undo the bow and tighten it more then make two tight knots.”

I did as he ordered. I was too afraid to oppose him. I knew he was on edge and that he’d already demonstrated before that he was insane. Once I had it tight enough to please him, he made me do the same to her ankles. After they were tied, he took a piece of cloth from his pocket. "Tie that around her mouth," he ordered.

I did it although I hated to do it. Her eyes were staring intently into mine. She shifted her eyes down to my bag then back up. My stomach flipped. I knew what she was trying to say. She knew that I'd packed one of the guns she'd been showing me earlier in my bag. Was she telling me to find a way to get to it and use it? Could I even do that? I'd never shot a gun. What if I missed or something? My terror worsened at the thought.

When he was happy with how she was secured, he jerked me away from her. I had to do something. "What're you going to do with us?"

"With her, nothing. I don't need extra baggage to drag along with us. She'll stay here. I have no idea who she is. Probably some whore one of those guards picked up. Don't worry about her. Just think, we're going to be able to start our life together, Gemma. The way it was meant to be. No one will interfere and we'll be happy. It sucks we'll have to start over, but that's alright. I've got my ways. We can do it. This time it'll be somewhere far from here."

"Where's Gabriel?"

"He's not your concern. That fucker will get what's coming to him. I'll make sure of it. No one double-crosses me and lives. I'll make him pay, but that can wait. Right now, we need to get out of here before he decides to come back."

As he was talking, he was pushing me toward another car I saw parked along the street, down from the house. At the same time, my phone began to go crazy, ringing. I could hear Sloan's doing the same. It had to be the guys. Knowing when we didn't pick up they'd come should have been a comfort, but it wasn't when it would take them two hours to get here. By then, I could be in another state.

As we reached the car, he shoved me hard into the side of it. In a flash, he had a rope wrapped around my wrists. He secured them together in front of me before opening the car door on the front passenger side. He shoved me inside. I would've cried, except he threw my bag on my lap before he slammed the car door shut.

As he rounded the car to get into the driver's seat, I was able to unzip it, although not get inside it to my gun. As he got in, I vowed to find a way to get to it. One way or the other, I wasn't going with him. I'd either kill him or he'd have to kill me. No way was I allowing this man to touch me. I knew once he stopped, he'd waste no time raping me. It was burning in his hot gaze.

I gave Sloan one last desperate look before the car shot away from the curb. She was struggling to get loose. I prayed she would. Maybe she could call the guys and let them know the direction we'd gone in. Not that it would do much good. Once we got onto a highway, we could go in any direction.

As he drove, I tried to think of ways to distract him, so I could get the gun. "Why me, Santo? Why're you so determined to be with me?"

"Because your cousin told me that I could have you. He promised that as long as I didn't take more than what was already being taken in protection from the restaurant, he'd make sure you would be mine. My mistake was in allowing it to go this long, before claiming you all the way. I should've made you honor that agreement a long time ago."

"Honor it? I didn't make it. My cousin can't just decide to give me away!"

"Of course he can. He's a male in your family. It's how it's always been done. The males ensure that any female relatives make advantageous marriages which protect the family or increase their holdings. Elijah knows this. Hell, even Emmet did too when we explained it. Your father, on the other hand, might not, so we thought it best to keep this tiny bit of information to ourselves."

Fury burned through me knowing my cousins had done this to me. They no more cared for me than they would a dog. They'd sold me to ensure their finances and security. At least my *papà* hadn't been a part of it. I could imagine the lines my cousins fed him to make him think a relationship between me and Santo would be good for me.

He was speeding through Mahwah. I thought we were heading west. I tried another question. "How did you find out where I was?"

He laughed. "Gabe thought he was so smart, whisking you away a few days ago from the hospital.

I admit, he had me running around in circles, but he underestimated how many people look to do me favors. They want to be on the right side of a powerful man like me. My people put the word out on the street that I was looking for you. Finally, right before the meeting with him today, right as we were pulling up to the abandoned factory, I got a call. One of those people had seen you. They knew what direction you'd gone in. Out of curiosity, they followed you."

"If they followed me, why did they wait three days to tell you that and where I was?" That didn't make any sense to me.

"They said they didn't know until today that I was looking for you. I was going to question them further once I was done taking care of Gabe and his men, only they brought reinforcement with them. I was lucky to escape while they were distracted. It gave me time to get to a backup car that I'd been smart enough to have hidden down from the meeting site."

That explanation sounded off to me. There had to be more to it. I wondered who the informant was. "Who told you?"

"No one you need to know. Now, be quiet. Enough questions. All you need to know is we're headed to where we'll be safe. You'll soon forget all about that man. I'll make sure of it. Once you've been with me, you'll forget he ever existed." His leer made my skin crawl and my stomach lurch. I had to act sooner rather than later.

My phone rang again for the umpteenth time. He

swore and tore it out of my purse, which somehow I'd retained ahold of. He opened his window and threw it out onto the road. There went my lifeline. As he kept going and more miles got between us and Sloan, I began to panic.

Deciding it was now or never, I took advantage of his other mistake. I reached over and grabbed the steering wheel and wrenched it as hard as I could to the right. The car began to swerve out of control. Santo swore and fought to bring it back under control. While he was busy doing that, I got my hands in my bag and searched for the gun.

I found the cold steel of the handle and brought it out of my bag just as he was bringing the car back under control. Not thinking or taking a chance I'd freeze, I pointed the gun at him and fired twice. The sound was deafening in the small confines of the car. He slumped over and the car careened off the road. I screamed, dropped the gun, and threw up my hands to protect my face as I saw a big tree approaching at an alarming speed.

I felt the tremendous impact. My head hit the dash and pain blossomed throughout my body. Immediately, I started to lose consciousness. My last thought before total blackness claimed me was this would be a hellish way to die. I killed him only to hurt myself so much that I killed myself.

Gemma: Chapter 20

When I regained consciousness, I had no idea how long I'd been out. It was still dark. The countryside around us was mostly black. Leaning back, I could feel what I knew was blood trickling down my face. I wiped it away. Glancing to my left, I saw Santo was slumped over the steering wheels and he wasn't moving.

I was afraid to touch him in case he was merely unconscious and that would wake him up, but I had to check. Tentatively, I undid my seatbelt and scooted toward him. Pain washed through my whole body. Ignoring it, I raised my bound hands. I felt for a pulse in his neck. I felt all over and there was nothing. I couldn't hear him breathing and it was too dark to see if he was.

Praying he was dead, I shoved him as hard as I could, so he fell toward the driver's window. This allowed me to get inside his coat. I fumbled around in his pocket, looking for his phone. Mine was somewhere back there in the dark. Even if I knew where he'd thrown it, I'd never find it. My only chance was to use his to call Gabriel for help.

Finally, I found it. I ripped it out of his pocket and felt until I found the buttons to make it wake up. When it did, I groaned. It was asking for a password. Why couldn't he have left it unprotected or at least requiring his fingerprint? I growled in frustration. I fought not to throw it at his head. If he was still alive, I'd brain him with it.

Fighting to calm myself, eventually, I did it enough to make my next decision. Sitting here waiting to be rescued wasn't likely to help. This road seemed to be deserted, so it could be hours before someone came along to offer help. I didn't know how badly hurt I was, so I needed to find medical help as fast as I could. On top of that, I had to find a way to contact Gabriel. He'd be losing his mind right now.

Making sure I found the gun again, I squirmed around until I could reach the door handle, then I opened my door. It would only half open since the engine compartment was crushed so badly against the tree. I didn't see flames, thank God, but I still wanted to get far away from it. Pushing and shoving, I wiggled my way out of the car. I landed on the ground when I did. I sat there for a few seconds to catch my breath then struggled to my feet. My head twirled in circles for a few moments before settling.

Deciding the best bet was to walk back the way we'd come, I set my feet on the road and started the long trudge back. I kept going by counting every step. I didn't bother looking at his phone to check the time. It would only make it worse. As I walked, I tried to picture me and Gabriel being reunited with Santo being a bad memory. It fed my determination to get back to him. I wouldn't give up. This wasn't going to beat me.

The darkness around me was scary. I heard rustling sounds and the calls of animals. Not all of them were birds. I swore at one point I heard howling in the distance. I tried to speed up but my head hurt so much, it made me sicker to my stomach. Hopefully, if anything came out of the woods to eat me, I could shoot it.

Gabriel:

My fear for Gemma and Sloan made it almost impossible for me to breathe or think. As we sped off toward Mahwah, I kept calling her number, swearing, praying, and imagining the worst. Ben and Beau tried to keep me and Mark from losing our shit, but it was close. He was as crazy as I was, trying to get Sloan to answer his calls.

"There's no way Santo knew where the women were. Fausto must've pulled that out of his ass. There has to be another reason they're not answering their phones. Maybe a cell tower is down," Ben offered as an answer. I shot him a look that could kill. He shut up.

"He's right. Besides, if Santo did find them by some crazy fluke, Sloan is there. She'd take care of his sorry ass," Beau assured us.

"Not if he found a way to shoot and kill her first," Mark growled.

My mind cleared enough to make a call. It was to one person I knew would be able to find me an answer faster than our own people. When he answered after a couple of rings, I didn't pause before starting to talk.

"Smoke, it's Gabe. I need your help. My woman and Mark's aren't answering their phones. We left them two hours from where we were doing a takedown. We think they might be in trouble. Can you get a fix on their phones?"

"If they're on, then yes. Give me their phone numbers."

I rattled them off to him along with their names. As I waited, I fought not to throw up. My anxiety over what was happening to her was building. After what felt like eternity but was more like no more than five or six minutes, he spoke to me.

"I see Sloan's is in Mahwah. It seems to be a residential area. Gemma's is further away, along Highway 287. It's on the southwest end of it. I assume this has to do with that asshole Santo you and the guys were taking down today?"

"It does. He escaped and now I'm afraid he figured out where we had Gemma hidden and has gotten to them. They're not answering their phones.

"I'll keep monitoring them and I'll let you know if they move. Both seem to be at a standstill. I'll send you the coordinates for where I see both of them."

"Thanks. I owe you."

He assured me I didn't then hung up. A few moments later, our phones dinged. Checking it, I saw both locations. The first one told me Sloan's phone was at the house. Gemma's was out in the middle of nowhere along the 287. Now we had to make a choice. Go to Sloan first or Gemma? Bringing up a map, I saw that going to either spot was roughly the same distance.

If we went to the house and they were gone and only Sloan's phone was there, then we'd lose time and allow Santo to get further away with them. I refused to believe that Sloan was dead.

I turned to look at Mark in the back seat. His face had the same haunted look I knew was on my face. "Which way do we go first?" I asked him.

"Fuck, I don't know, Gabe. My gut wants to go to where it shows Sloan's phone is, but then I think, if it's there and Gemma's isn't, at least one, if not both have been taken. Sloan's could've been left behind or forgotten, especially if there was a struggle and Santo took them. Which is the only excuse I can think of for them not to be answering us and to be separated."

He paused and took a deep breath before he continued. "If he killed Sloan and she's at the house, it's not going to save Gemma for us to go there first. However, she could be hurt at the house and need help. Jesus Christ, I don't know! I can't make the decision." He sounded tortured.

"I can't either. All those thoughts are what I'm thinking. Fuck!" I slammed my fist off the dash.

"Can I make a suggestion?" Beau asked quietly.

"Sure," I said.

"Call 911 and have them go to the house. Say you fear your wife has been hurt and she's not answering her phone. Tell them you're on your way. Ask them to call you with a report when they get there, since you're so far away. In the meantime, we head for where it's showing Gemma's phone. If I thought we could get one of our people there quickly, I'd say do that, but we can't. I agree with both of your thoughts. We don't know until we get to one of those places," he stated.

I didn't like it, because it would raise some unnecessary questions from the police that we'd have to deal with, but I'd take it.

"I say do it," Mark said.

"Okay," I responded, then picked up my phone to make the call. Just as I went to dial, Mark's phone rang. He answered it in a flash.

"Sloan, baby, are you and Gemma alright? Why weren't you answering your phone? Why is her phone showing up somewhere else?" He asked her his questions so fast they ran together.

"Mark, calm down. Am I on speaker so Gabe can hear me?" Her stressed voice came across loud and clear. He must've pushed the speakerphone button when he answered the call.

"He can. We're on our way there with Ben and Beau. We're probably an hour or less away."

"Don't come to the house. Santo took Gemma. Follow her phone. I'm alright. He surprised us outside and had her tie me up. It took me a while to get loose and call you. I'm sorry." The disgust and worry was evident in her voice. I wanted to yell and ask her what the hell they were doing outside, but now wasn't the time for that.

"Are you sure you're alright?" he asked softly.

"I am. Not even a bruise on me, which pisses me off. Go find Gemma and kill that little prick then come get me. I'll be at the house, pacing a hole in the floor. Stay safe. I love you."

"I love you too and we'll watch our backs. Stay inside and wait for us."

I could tell he was reluctant to end the call, but he did. We had work to do. Having the choice made for us, Beau checked the GPS and made sure we were on the right route to meet the signal. As the miles sped by and he kept inching the car to go faster, I prayed more. The fact the phone didn't show as moving worried the hell outta me. It could mean the phone was dropped and she was nowhere near it. Or they had stopped and she was now at the mercy of Santo. I knew he wouldn't hesitate to rape her the first chance he got.

The agony of not knowing what was happening to her and dreading it was the last one was almost more than I could bear. If he had done that to her, I would make his final days even longer and filled with even more agony than originally planned.

Smoke was good about texting to tell me the phone was still not moving. As we drew near that point, I held my breath. As we drove up practically on top of it and saw no vehicle in sight, I wanted to scream. That meant her phone was somewhere around this spot. It had been thrown out. We didn't have time to get out and hunt for it.

"Keep going. Continue southwest on this road. I'll see if Smoke can locate Santo's phone."

Why I didn't do that before, I had no idea. I quickly sent him a text.

Me: Gemma not at her phone location. See if you can find Santo's phone. His number is 732-555-2137.

After a brief wait, he answered.

Smoke: On it. Give me 5.

Waiting even five minutes seemed like forever. When he responded again, my heart leaped.

Smoke: Sending GPS to your phone. His phone is not too far ahead of you. Keep going approximately two miles.

Me: Got it. TY.

Smoke: NP, good luck.

"Smoke says it's two miles ahead of us. Keep going."

Beau sped up a tad more. Within moments, we were coming around a bend, almost on top of where the GPS said the phone was. As we rounded it, the headlights landed on a lone figure walking slowly down the road. I knew in an instant it was Gemma. Beau brought the car to a screeching halt not far in front of her. I didn't wait for him to fully stop before I was out of the car and running to her.

She tried to dart off the road. I realized in the bright light, she couldn't see who it was. "Gemma, *piccola*, it's me," I shouted.

She stumbled to a halt, turned, then began to half run toward me. I met her and picked her up to crush her against me. As I did, I heard her cry of pain. Instantly, I sat her down and tried to get a look at her.

She was a mess. She had blood running down her face from a laceration on her forehead. There were smudges of dirt all over her. Tiny pieces of glass glittered on her clothes. She was holding herself stiff.

"*Dea*, tell me where you're hurt. And where's Santo? How did you get away from him?"

I didn't wait for her answers before I whisked her up in my arms and took off rushing to the car. Ben had the backdoor open. I got in with her on my lap. He got in the front with Beau.

"I think I'm just bruised and maybe I have a concussion. You don't have to worry about Santo anymore. He's dead."

"Dead? How?"

"I made him almost run the car off the road and while he was trying to stop it from happening, I shot him. We crashed. The car is a couple of miles up that way if you want to check on him. I'm pretty sure he's dead. I couldn't find a pulse. Unfortunately, he tossed my phone and I couldn't get his to open so I could call you. He has a code to get into it," she quickly muttered as she burrowed into my chest. She was shaking. It wasn't cold out, so I knew it had to be from fright and possibly pain.

I tapped Beau on the shoulder and pointed ahead of us. He knew what I wanted. He started driving. I had to make sure the bastard was dead, then I wanted to get her checked out.

"Shh, you don't have to say more. The rest can wait. We'll just make sure he's dead then get you some medical attention," I told her.

"You have to send someone to the house! He left Sloan tied up there," she said urgently.

"She's fine. She got loose and called us. We'll go get her after we take care of you," I assured her.

She was right. We found the car a couple of miles up the road. Seeing how totaled the front was, it was a miracle she wasn't more badly hurt or had even been able to get out of the car. Ben got out to check on Santo, who was visibly slumped against the driver's window. He came back shaking his head.

"He's dead. I think the shot to the head did it or maybe the one to his heart did. Great shooting, Gemma."

She sighed in relief. Stamping down on my questions, I had Ben grab her purse and bag and make sure there was nothing else of hers in the car. He made sure to wear gloves. As much as I hated it, we'd leave Santo to be found as long as there was nothing to tie her to the car. He went as far as to wipe the dash, door, and seats with a rag to remove her prints, although I knew she wasn't in the system.

As soon as he was done, we got on the road. Beau had looked up the nearest hospital. We would take her there. It happened to be back in Mahwah. Not wanting to tie her to the accident, we came up on the drive with the lie that she'd been at the house on a ladder and had fallen through a window. It would explain the glass, as long as they didn't look too closely and see it was tempered safety glass and not the kind used in windows in a house.

As we pulled into the ER later, I turned to Mark. "Drop us off and you guys go get Sloan. Make sure she's alright then come back."

"Thanks, Gabe, we will," he said. I didn't waste time getting out of the car and hustling into the ER to get Gemma seen. Everything else could wait.

Gemma:

Three days had passed since the ordeal with Santo. Lucky for me, the wreck hadn't resulted in too serious of injuries. Besides the laceration to my head, the concussion to go along with it, various bumps, bruises, and minor cuts, I walked away relatively unscathed.

They only kept me overnight at the hospital before releasing me. Due to my concussion, Gabriel refused to make the six-hour drive back to Hampton. He said we'd go once I felt better and had a chance to mend some.

Gabriel and the guys were truly amazed when they heard the whole tale and how I had the gun in the first place. They laughed to find out I'd never fired one before and how shocked I was at how loud it was.

Sloan had apologized over and over for not being aware he had been outside. I told her it wasn't her fault. Of course, the guys were pissed at us when they found out we'd been outside in the first place because we were headed closer to Toms River. I was lucky to be hurt or I think he'd have beat my ass for that one. The way Sloan was moving the next day, she might have gotten one from Mark.

We didn't get to sit around the house and do

nothing. While I was forced to rest, he and the rest of the team finished making sure everything had been cleaned up when it came to Santo and the men they killed that day. All the others had been successfully taken into custody by the feds.

It was while they had people going through Santo's apartment that the mystery of what made the Grecos put Santo into such a high position without anyone hearing of him before was revealed. In his papers was proof and correspondence that showed Santo had blackmailed his way into that spot.

What did he have on them that would make them fear him enough to do it? And not just have him killed? Apparently, he had proof that he threatened to leak within their prison, which showed that Carlo Greco was a pedophile. Matteo had known when he found out that anything like that getting leaked would spell a death sentence for his son. No one in prison liked a pedophile, not other prisoners or guards.

Santo had threatened that if he wasn't given control and/or was killed, he had an insurance policy that would expose Carlo anyway. The Grecos hadn't been able to take that chance, so they complied and had allowed him into their organization to take the top *capo* position. They lied and said he was an old family friend's son. How Santo had known this and gotten the proof would remain a mystery. Nothing could be found to tell them that.

As things settled down and I started to feel better, Mark, Sloan, Ben, and Beau all headed back to Virginia. Gabriel promised we'd be there within the week. I was looking forward to seeing my new home. We'd have the rest of my stuff in Toms River packed up and shipped to us. I had no desire to go back. Maybe one day I'd be able to talk to my *papà*, but I never wanted to see my cousins again.

Gabriel was furious when he found out that Elijah had bargained me away to Santo and that Emmet had gone along with it. It took everything I had to keep him from going and beating the hell out of both of them. I convinced him, for now anyway, that having them lose out on the payout they used to get from the Greco family would hurt them enough. I wasn't sure if that would keep him away or not. My man had a strong retaliation drive. As for me, all I wanted was to begin my happily ever after with him.

Gabriel: Epilogue: One month Later

The past month since the day Santo escaped and kidnapped Gemma had been hectic both on the work side and on the personal side of my life. On the work side were all the things that had to be tied up and explained that dealt with the elimination of the Greco family Mafia. The feds had questions and we tried to answer as many as we could. Some things would have to remain a mystery, like what happened to several key members that those arrested swore had been in charge.

One of them, Santo Vitale, had been found dead in another part of New Jersey from two bullet wounds and a car crash. The mystery was, who had shot him? A rival? A victim? Or had it been a crime of opportunity or just random violence along a dark, deserted road? What was obvious was he'd been running from the feds who had taken down the rest of the organization.

This was on top of other business at Dark Patriots. For the most part, the team had covered for me, so I could spend as much time as possible with Gemma. She needed to heal and get settled into our home. When they couldn't handle it without me, I made sure to get in and get out as quickly as I could. I hated being away from her.

On the personal side of things, we'd been busy

too. She'd made a full recovery from the car accident. We'd left Mahwah a week after it and made the drive back to Hampton. She'd moved into my house, our house now. She refused to consider moving to a new one. She said she loved the house and after some redecorating, it would be perfect.

We'd had her things in Toms River packed and her apartment given up. She had spoken to her father twice since then. He knew why she wasn't coming back and what her cousins had done. He acted like he was torn up about it. I wasn't so sure. I'd reserve judgment. I was willing to give him a tiny bit of the benefit of doubt. As for her cousins, they got none. If it wouldn't ruin her father too, I'd make sure Mia Bella Rosa was lost to them. Who knows, it might still happen. It was her plea not to hurt or kill them that stayed my hand. It might not last forever. I was going to keep a close eye on them and any steps out of line, no matter how small, would have them feeling my full wrath.

The one personal thing that I had dreaded telling her was my biggest secret. The thing that only a few people knew about. It tied to the reason why the Rizzo family had been so willing to lie and help me take down the Grecos. It all boiled down to who I was. I didn't mean Gabriel Barberi. I meant who I really was.

The night I'd finally sat her down to tell her everything was one I would never forget. I was sick. What if she couldn't handle the real me? What if she decided she couldn't live with a man like me and she left me? I knew if that happened, I'd never recover. The guys had told me that I couldn't put it off any longer. The longer I waited, the more likely it was she'd be angry or angrier with me. Taking my last bit of courage in hand, I sat her down and told her.

"Gabriel, you're starting to scare me. Tell me what's wrong."

"I need to tell you a secret. A secret that explains why the Rizzo family helped me with the Greco situation. I need you to listen and let me tell you everything before you react or ask me any questions. Can you do that for me?"

She frowned but nodded. "I'll try my hardest. Just tell me. You're scaring me."

"Okay, so you saw how I knew Tristano and them. I obviously have a connection to the Rizzo family, a strong one. They owe me a huge debt and by helping me with the Grecos, the debt is considered partially paid. Many years ago, when I was a young man, barely eighteen, I lived a very different life than I do now or I've lived since then. I was someone I didn't like. Someone I didn't want to be.

"It was because of that life that I accidentally became aware of some very startling and dangerous news. I didn't know what to do. To ignore it was unthinkable, but to do something about it was terrifying and equally unthinkable. I wrestled with my conscience until I finally made a decision. I didn't know if it would get me killed or not, but I was going to do something about it.

"I went to the head of the Rizzo family. By rights, he should've had me killed on the spot, but he didn't. I think he was stunned that I came to him and he wanted to know why. I explained to him that there was a plot to kill him and his immediate heirs. They were to all be wiped out. He was naturally skeptical and demanded that I show him proof.

To show I wasn't trying to trick him, I offered myself as a hostage. They could hold me while the information I was to give them on where, when, and how was verified.

"He took me up on my offer and I was imprisoned. They treated me well while they waited to find out if the information I gave them was reliable. I can give you all the details later if you want. What's important is, the information I gave them was accurate. By listening to me, they were saved from death and the ones who had ordered the killing of him and his family were killed instead. Since that day, they've always sworn they're in my debt. I've never called on that debt until the Greco situation. I hope to never have to again."

I paused to see how she was taking it. She looked calm though slightly puzzled. I knew the worst part was to come.

"The people who wanted the Rizzos dead were part of another rival Italian Mafia family. Their name was Ferretti. The Ferrettis and the Rizzos had been battling each other for years. Although the current Rizzo was someone who wanted a less bloody life. Oh, they still were into illegal stuff but the bloody feuds of the past he wanted to end. No more killing entire families to stop them from getting revenge. Yeah, they might kill men but only if they had to and never involved innocent women and children in those fights. More and more families were changing the way they ran things. There were others making even bigger changes. Anyway, the Ferrettis were prevented from killing the Rizzos. However, during the fight, the head of the Ferretti family and his son, who were the ones ordering the mass murder, were killed. Their children, wives, and other males in the family who weren't directly involved were spared.

"One of the men spared was the younger brother of the Ferretti family, Ottavio. It happened that Ottavio was much less blood thirsty than his older brother and his nephew. He'd been advising them not to do what they planned. They ignored him. After they were killed, he became the head of the family. He made it clear to those who remained that the fight with the Rizzos was over. That they were not to be touched. It wasn't a well-liked idea. He knew there were some who wanted to still follow the old ways.

"The reason I knew what the plot was and how Ottavio reacted afterward is because I was there. I witnessed the planning of the murders firsthand. The dictates of Ottavio I was told about. Gabriel Pagett isn't my real name. My real name is Gabriel Ferretti. I'm Ottavio Ferretti's son and heir." This got a reaction. She gasped and her eyes widened. I hurried to tell her the rest.

"I'd been raised in the Ferretti way of life. Even with my father being a less harsh man, things were bloody. I was taught how to beat a man for information, how to torture and kill. By the time I was thirteen, my zio, my uncle, *insisted I participate in many of those things. In those I didn't, I had to watch. He said that my cousin and I would be the ones to lead the family in the future. Even if my padre disagreed, my zio was in charge. He had to do what he said, or risk himself, me, and my madre being killed."*

"Oh my God," she whimpered, then got quiet.

"It was terrible. To be in danger from not only rival families but from your own. My father knew I hated our lives but there was nothing he could do about it. He couldn't

allow me to leave. I would've been killed. After the death of my zio, even though he was the new head of the family, he couldn't run the risk of some of the others who were like-minded to my zio coming after me if he let me go, so he came up with a plan. He told everyone that during the fight with the Rizzos, I was killed along with the others.

"He knew that in order for it to be believed and for me to have any chance of a new life, I had to disappear and everyone had to believe I was dead. So, he told no one, not even my madre, that I was alive. If she knew, she'd want to see me. She might slip up. He helped me get a new identity and move to another state. All ties to him and anyone there I had to give up. The one thing I couldn't do though was hide from the Rizzos. They knew I was alive. However, since I'd saved them from slaughter, the few who know who I truly am, have been sworn to secrecy on penalty of death.

"In my new life, I took on the name Gabriel Pagett and entered the military. I didn't know what else to do. The battling mindset was set for me by that point. If I stayed in the civilian world, I might become what I hated and I didn't want that. I went to the Navy and tried out for the SEALs as soon as possible. Since then, I've tried to live my life honorably and help people. I don't kill unless I absolutely have to and it's never innocent women and children."

As I ended my tale, she sat there as if frozen. I was dying to know what she thought. Suddenly, she launched herself off the couch. I thought she was going for the door. Instead, she surprised me and tackled me in my chair. Her arms came around me and she started to cry and she kissed me over and over. After she calmed down, she and I talked more. It turned out way better than I'd ever hoped.

Another positive, other than her not holding my past against me, was she was quickly becoming best friends with Cassidy and Sloan. I loved to see her so happy and laughing. She deserved it. I was lucky that her happiness was linked to mine. She'd given me the happiest moment of my life, or at least the happiest since she agreed to be mine, when she agreed to marry me after we got home. She said she didn't want a big wedding, just us and our few friends.

In order to make it happen, we went to the justice of the peace and got married last week. Afterward, we went to dinner with my Dark Patriot brothers and their ladies. The staff at Dark Patriot threw us a party the next day. In a few weeks, we were going to have the official reception and have all our friends, including the various MCs we were friends with, attend. She'd get to meet the people she'd started to hear us talk about. She said she couldn't wait.

There were still things she was deciding on. One of those was whether she wanted to work or go to school. I was leaving that up to her. I'd support whichever option she picked. If she was happy then I'd be happy.

Today, I had to go into work for a short meeting. She'd stayed at home. She stated she had things to do. I didn't know what they were, but I didn't want her to think she had to tell me everything she did, so I didn't ask. I knew she liked exploring and finding her way around her new home. Hampton was about one and a half times the size of Toms River, plus, she'd never been to Virginia.

It was almost six o'clock before I came through the door. My meeting had run late then there was traffic to deal with. I texted her to tell her not to make dinner, that we'd go out. As I came through the door, I was greeted by the most beautiful sight. Standing in the middle of our living room was my *principessa*.

She was standing there holding a bouquet of balloons in one hand and in the other she had a piece of paper or white cardboard. It was blank. I walked toward her, smiling.

"What's all this, Gemma?"

"Stop. I want you to stay right there. I have something for you. Stay there," she cried excitedly. I stopped and waited. I was curious to see what she had for me. She came to me and handed me the strings to the balloons. They were silver and gold. On them were different words. As I read them, I started to realize they were all in different languages but they had a common theme. All of them said the same thing.

My breath caught. I couldn't believe what I was seeing. Then she flipped the piece of cardboard in her hand around to face me. On it was written a short message, which confirmed it. It read, *Congratulations, you're going to be a father*. Every one of the balloons had the word father on them.

The yell I gave was probably heard in the next county over as I let go of the balloons, allowing them to float to the ceiling. I grabbed her in my arms and hugged her as I kissed the hell out of her and swung her around in circles. She laughed until she finally begged me to stop before she threw up.

I gently sat her down on her feet. "I'm sorry, *piccola*, I didn't mean to make you sick. *Dio*, tell me, when did you find out? Isn't it too soon to know this? When is the baby due? Have you seen a doctor yet?"

She giggled then took my hand and led me to my chair. I sat down and tugged her down to sit on my lap.

"Okay, let me answer all those questions. I thought I might be a couple of days ago after I threw up when I got up. You'd gone to work already. I didn't want to get our hopes up, so I waited. This morning, I was up before you. I did it again. That's why I told you I had things to do and I didn't go with you to work. After you left, I called to see if I could get in to see a doctor. I was lucky. The clinic near here had an opening. I went to see them rather than go get one of those tests at the drugstore. They confirmed it. It's not too soon. We've been together for more than a month. They can tell as early as your first missed period. Mine have always been weird and I can have them a week or more late. I knew I was late, but that's not abnormal for me. I still have to go see an OB but based on the date of my last period and all that, we think the baby should be arriving toward the end of April or very first of May. That gives us plenty of time to shop and fix up a bedroom to be the nursery. I hope you meant what you said, Gabriel, because you're going to be a father."

"*Dio*, I meant every fucking word. Shit, this is the best news. You just keep making my life better and better. Thank you, *amore mio*. I love you. Now, I know I said we'd go out to dinner and we will, but first, I think we should call and see if the guys and their ladies can join us. I want to tell them the good news. Then, when we're done with feeding you and the *bambino*, I plan to bring you home and make love to you until neither of us can think."

"I love the sound of that, *amore mio*."

And that's exactly what I did. Who would've ever imagined when I took this assignment over two months ago that Gabriel's retaliation would turn into Gabriel's happily ever after. I surely didn't. I thought I'd never be able to have a wife and family with my past. Goes to show you how wrong you can be.

The End Until Griffin's Revelation-
Dark Patriots Book 3

Printed in Great Britain
by Amazon

59987214R00201